Amalie and the Web of Deceit

IN THE STYLE OF
VICTORIA HOLT

SABINA BOSTON

Copyright © 2022
All rights reserved.
This book may not be reproduced in whole or in part by any means without permission from the author.
Contact Sabina Boston at sabinaboston.com
Cover designed by MiblArt

Other books by Sabina Boston:
The Gift of Gisela, available on Amazon
Jillian Boone, available on Amazon
Clown of Hearts, coming in fall 2022

    Amalie and the Web of Deceit is the story of an orphan girl claimed by a royal family just before coming of age in 1865. However, it doesn't take long for events to unfold that pull Amalie into a web of deceit as the mystery of her origin begins to surface. Amalie falls in love with a handsome Captain who is betrothed to another, complicating her life. Danger follows Amalie wherever she goes when their secret love is exposed. Amalie decides to fight back against her unknown enemy and, much unlike the women of her time, she fights to regain control of her life. Amalie sets out on a journey of discovery after being separated from the man she loves as she arms herself with knowledge about her nemesis. Her adventure lands her in front of Queen Victoria, where shocking revelations are revealed, and history is revised. Will Amalie find newfound happiness with the man she loves? Follow her journey and share the exciting story of a woman driven by love.

Dedicated to Miss Victoria Holt
(Eleanor Alice Burford Hibbert)
1906 – 1993

From the author:
When I was 11 years old, I fell in love with books.
The first book I read from the school library was Kirkland Revels by Victoria Holt.
I fell in love with her writing and the genre of Victorian Suspense Romance.
I have since read everything she ever wrote, even those books penned under other names, such as Philippa Carr and Jean Plaidy.
Her writings made me want to become a writer.
Even though I don't usually write in this genre, I vowed to write a book tribute to Victoria Holt one day.
This is that book.
Amalie and the Web of Deceit is lovingly dedicated to Victoria Holt.

Chapter 1

1865

Amalie awoke from her dream thinking it was a nightmare, but when her eyes focused, she could see that it was indeed not, and forces beyond her control forever changed her life. Anger welled up inside her because she felt she had no voice, no say in her own life. But unlike the women of her time, she decided to retake control of her life and determine her fate.

(Several months earlier)

At the ancient Gilchrist Abbey, nestled in the northern mountains between the Corrington and Herzstein Territories, the sound of singing and music was a familiar occurrence daily. The high ceilings and long stone corridors helped the music echo throughout the Abbey. Father Joseph founded the Abbey in the 1300s during The Black Death when nearly half of England's population died from the plague and left many orphans needing placement. The Abbey also took in children of war or victims of poverty, and for hundreds of years, the Sisters of Gilchrist cared for and raised countless children.

Amalie was hurrying to finish her teaching session with the young children of the Abbey when Mother Superior came in with Sister Evangeline. This interruption to choir practice was unusual, and Amalie was startled.

"My dear," Mother Superior spoke softly, "Sister Evangeline will take over for you. There is someone in my office that you must meet."

"It can't wait until practice is over?" Amalie asked, puzzled.

"No, I'm afraid it can't," Mother replied firmly.

Amalie obeyed and followed Mother Superior down the long hallway to her office. Upon arrival, Amalie noticed a well-dressed woman sitting in front of the desk waiting for them. It was apparent at first glance that this was a woman of pedigree, wealth, and most undoubtedly high society. The lady was a perfectly coiffed, middle-aged woman with still beautiful features on her face. Her clothes were tailor-made and of the finest materials. As Amalie entered the room, the woman rose to greet her.

"Amalie," Mother Superior began, "This is the Duchess of House Corrington in the Corrington Territory. She has traveled all this way to meet you."

Amalie forced a slight curtsey and said, "It's a pleasure to meet you, Your Grace…but I must admit, I am at a loss. How do you know of me?"

"Oh, my sweet child, please call me Helene," the Duchess said, reaching out to embrace Amalie.

Amalie felt awkward being hugged by a total stranger and did not return the embrace.

"My goodness, you look just like your mother," Helene said, touching Amalie's cheek. "She had the same dark hair and blue eyes as you, but I think you are a bit taller than she was. She was very petite."

Amalie was stunned. "You knew my mother?"

Mother Superior put her arm around Amalie, knowing that this was a shock to the young woman. "Amalie, the Duchess has recently discovered that your mother was a distant relative of hers. She has been searching for you for quite some time now."

"I think I need to sit down," Amalie said breathlessly. Her head was spinning.

"Oh dear," said the Duchess, "I fear we've overwhelmed you with this news. Perhaps I should have been more delicate? I'm sure this must be a shock to you."

Helene's voice was sincere, and she seemed genuine, but for twenty-one years, Amalie knew nothing about her mother, and now she was face to face with someone who was a relative of hers.

Amalie sat down on the bench in front of the desk. The Duchess sat down next to her and cupped her hand. Amalie searched the Duchess' face for recognition or anything that would make sense of what she had just heard.

"How is this possible? I have been an orphan all my life. My mother died in childbirth. All these years, no one has come for me. I grew up here. I studied music, and now I teach the younger children. I am only weeks from being emancipated. Yes, this is quite a shock."

Mother Superior touched Amalie's shoulder. "We can't question God's timing. We are just thankful that a family has come for you."

"A family for me? What?" Amalie questioned.

"I have come to bring you home to Corrington House!" the Duchess said excitedly. "To take your rightful place in our family."

A cold chill ran through Amalie. "My place in your family? I don't understand. How did you discover that you are related to me? Who was my mother to you? I know nothing about my mother other than she died here giving birth to me. I don't even know her name."

"Her name was Juliet," the Duchess said sadly. "She was my third cousin and my dearest friend in childhood. I lost track of her when my father sent me to marry the Duke, but I never stopped thinking about her."

Juliet. What a beautiful name. My mother's name was Juliet.

"I'm so sorry you never knew her," the Duchess continued, "She was a beautiful soul. We were very close as children."

"This is certainly a lot to digest," Mother Superior acknowledged. "But it is a gift from God that we now have answers for you about who you are and where you came from. Try looking at it that way, dear."

"You're taking me home with you?" Amalie asked the Duchess, making sure she heard correctly.

"Yes, as soon as you can pack your things. You won't need much, though. We will provide you with everything you will possibly need. I plan to make you a Lady of Corrington House. You will have a secure place in society, and it gives me great pleasure to do this for the daughter of my dearest childhood friend."

Amalie was flabbergasted. "But I have a life here," she began when Mother Superior cut her off.

"Let's not be rude to our guest," Mother admonished. "The Duchess traveled far and has only loving intentions for you. I will take you to your room and help you pack. Will you excuse us, Duchess? I will return with her shortly."

Amalie rose and began to move in slow motion. She was in shock and utterly overwhelmed. Mother Superior took her arm and led her back to her room. Once they were inside, Mother closed the door behind her and spoke in a low voice.

"My dear Amalie, I'm so sorry. I do not have the power to stop this. It is the law that you must go if a family member claims you before you are emancipated. I have no power to keep you here. I have a thousand questions of my own, and I promise to pursue those, but you must go with her for now. You are not yet a legal adult."

"I don't understand this. A girl of fifteen can legally marry without her parents' consent, and yet I can't decide my own life at age twenty, almost twenty-one?"

"I'm sorry, dear. Those are the rules we must follow," Mother lamented.

Amalie gave in to the tears brewing in her eyes. "Oh, Mother, the children...and the sisters....I will miss you all so much. You are my family. The only one I've ever known. Why now? Why me?" and with those words, she fell into Mother Superior's arms and sobbed.

"Dry your tears, my dear. This discovery will be a good thing for you. Belonging to the Corrington House family will present you with great opportunities—more than we could ever provide you here. We will always be here for you, and the Post will keep us in touch. I will write, I promise, and I know that we will see each other again."

Amalie inhaled her tears and straightened her spine. "Yes, we will see each other again. I will hold on to that."

After packing her few belongings into a large leather bag, Amalie returned to the office, where the Duchess waited patiently.

"Your staff was kind enough to bring some tea while I waited," the Duchess said to Mother Superior as they reentered the room. She could see that Amalie had been crying and reached out to her. "Can I pour you some, dear Amalie? Please don't worry. You will be a much-cherished member of our family. They are all eagerly awaiting your arrival."

"All? How many in your family?"

"I have three sons and always wanted a daughter, but that never came to be. How fortunate I have located you after all these years, and I can now have the daughter I always wanted! It will be glorious, I promise you," Helene said, finishing her tea.

Amalie tried to force a smile, but her heart was breaking.

"The horses are rested and watered, so the coachman tells me we are ready to leave. My carriage awaits you, Lady Amalie—oh, I love the sound of that!" Helene gushed.

Amalie looked one last time upon the face of Mother Superior, the woman who raised her, nurtured her, taught her to read music, who comforted her when she was sick— the only mother she had ever known and reached deep down into her reserve of strength and smiled. "I will miss you. Until we meet again."

Mother Superior pulled her into a warm embrace. "Until we meet again. God Bess you, my child."

And without looking back, Amalie followed the Duchess down the hall to the waiting carriage. She could see the children playing out in the courtyard and had to look away before she would break down again. Amalie's entire world as she knew it was ending, and a new life into the complete unknown awaited her. It felt wrong, but there was nothing she could do or say to change it. She was powerless in a world where women have no power—and no voice of their own.

As the royal carriage made its way across the hilly landscape toward the Corrington Territory, the Duchess removed her bonnet to reveal a head of blonde curls. "This damp weather makes my hair curl up. I've given up fighting it. There's just no use!"

Helene attempted to make small talk. However, she could see that her anguished passenger was not listening. "Dearest Amalie, it will be alright, I promise you."

"Yes, ma'am," was all she could say.

"I know this has been a shock to you—imagine my surprise when I discovered that you existed. I told the Duke that I must find you at all costs. He helped me to locate you, he has more influence when it comes to things like that, and once we discovered you were at the Abbey, I immediately made haste to bring you home. I didn't want you to languish in that orphanage for one more day!"

"But I didn't languish," Amalie gently protested, "The sisters were lovely to me. I grew up surrounded by love. Of course, there was always that underlying sadness that I had no parents or family, but the sisters were my family, and the other children were my siblings. We all loved each other."

"Well, then, I shall be forever grateful to the sisters for taking such excellent care of you. However, I think you were only content there because you've never known any other way of life—a life with a real family. I want to give that to you—a life with a title and a place in society. I want to honor my friendship with Juliet if you allow me to."

Amalie couldn't help but like Helene. She seemed warm and sincere, which felt calming amid the turmoil bubbling just below the surface within her. "Please tell me about my mother. I know nothing about her at all."

Helene smiled from the memories. "We were inseparable as children. We were the same age and spent all our time together. We had some escapades as kids—we were always getting into trouble of some kind, but it was all harmless. She was the reason my childhood was so wonderful. All of my childhood memories have her in them."

"What was she like?" Amalie asked.

Helene's face softened as she remembered. "She had dark hair and blue eyes, just like you. She was shy and softspoken, but she could be quite funny too. You look so much like her. Sadly, I lost touch with her after my father sent me to marry the Duke. I was only sixteen, and my father arranged the marriage. I wrote her letters, but after a while, her letters to me stopped."

"Do you know what happened to her?" Amalie asked, thirsty for all the information she could gather about her mother.

"No, after my letters went unanswered, I wrote back home to my younger sister and asked about Juliet. Lisbeth told me that her father lost his position as stable master, and they moved away. They went to work on another estate, and I never heard from her again. I still miss her to this day. That is why I am so thrilled to have found you. For me, it's like having Juliet back in my life. I'm so happy about that."

Oddly, that was comforting to Amalie, even though she was still heartbroken over the new direction her life had suddenly taken. Helene was also the only person Amalie ever met that knew her mother, and that alone made her want to get to know Helene better.

"Do you know anything about my father?" Amalie asked.

"No, dear, I don't. I wish I had answers for you. I'm sure you must wonder about your heritage. I lost track of Juliet when we were both sixteen, so I know nothing about who she married or how she ended up at the Abbey."

Amalie spent most of her life wondering about her parents and why her father didn't claim her after her mother's death. As she matured, she wondered less about it and accepted that she might never know her origins.

"I still don't understand how you learned where I was, or who I was, for that matter," Amalie pressed on.

"Well, I never stopped trying to find Juliet. I was so unhappy for the first year of my marriage because I was homesick for my sisters—I have two of them—and missed my dearest friend. I made many inquiries at various places over the years, hoping someone might know Juliet or her father, but no one had ever heard of her. I gave up after my first child because I had something else to focus on, but I never stopped hoping to find her. Then many years later, the Duke and I were at his cousin's house in Brighton for a dinner party, and I mentioned Juliet at the dinner table. Of course, like always, no one had heard of her. However, after dinner, one of the household staff approached me and said she knew Juliet and her father. They had worked at another estate together in Fairfield, where Juliet's father died in a hunting accident. After her father passed, Juliet left, and no one knew where she went. She left during the night as if she was running away from something. She left a few personal belongings behind, and this woman still had them tucked away in the attic. She asked me if I wanted them, and of course, I said yes!"

"So, my grandfather was killed in a hunting accident? Did she give you any more information about that?" Amalie asked with heightened curiosity.

"No, dear, she didn't, but I finally remembered her father's last name because one of the items in Juliet's keepsake box was the newspaper clipping about her father's death. Their last name was Bennett. His first name was Charles. That's when I realized that you and I were related. I have several third cousins named Bennett, and I found the connection."

"Do you still have her keepsakes?" Amalie asked, trying to absorb this new information.

"Yes, there's not much there, just a small wooden box with a few things inside. The most interesting thing in the box was Juliet's journal. She wrote almost daily until she was nineteen, and then there were no entries for a long time, but then she started writing again because she was in love. Juliet had met someone and wrote about being deeply in love. She wrote that their love was forbidden, and I assume that was because he belonged to high society, and she was a commoner. Then there was a gap again in entries until the final entry where she wrote that she was going to Gilchrist Abbey to have her child. There were no entries after that."

"But that could have been any child. How do you know it was me?" Amalie asked, trying to connect the pieces of the puzzle.

"I contacted the Abbey and inquired about September births about twenty-one years ago, and Mother Superior told me that there was only one person it could be. The moment I saw you, I knew it was you. You are the image of your mother."

"I see," Amalie said, her head spinning trying to digest everything Helene was telling her. "I would like to see her journal if you wouldn't mind."

"Of course! I saved her things for you. You are the person who should have them. As I said, there's not much in the box, but whatever she left behind should belong to you."

After collecting her whirlwind thoughts, Amalie wondered about her new relatives. "How does your family feel about my pending arrival?"

"Well, the Duke wasn't so sure about it in the beginning, but once he understood how much Juliet once meant to me, he gave me his blessing. My sons were a bit confused, but they understand how difficult it is for me as the mother of only sons. The Duke insists they all follow the family tradition of service in the Duke's army, so their rearing and education are out of my hands. With you, I can guide you and teach you. I can give you a position in society and teach you how to be a proper lady—not that you're not. You know what I mean—with a title."

Amalie wondered if she should say that titles and positions in society didn't mean anything to her but decided to remain silent. It meant a lot to Helene, and she didn't want to dampen her enthusiasm.

"I didn't have a chance to pack all my things," Amalie carefully broached the subject, "I'm hoping we can send for my books and personal belongings. Some of those things mean a great deal to me."

"Of course, dear. Consider it done." Helene's smile was sincere, and Amalie felt she could trust her. Her curiosity was peaked though about the rest of the family.

"Tell me about your sons. You said they all serve in the Royal Army?"

"Oh, no, not yet. Oliver, my oldest, is the only one currently serving as a Captain in his father's army. Michael, my middle son, is in training and will be commissioned next year. Anthony, my youngest, is only ten and is still in school. He is my baby, but I must be careful not to indulge him too much. He loves music and the arts, and the Duke blames me for that. I just let him follow his passions, but I know that those things will not serve him well in the army," Helene shared.

Amalie immediately felt a kinship to Anthony—a fellow lover of music and the arts—and hoped they would become friends.

After a few hours, the carriage finally arrived at Corrington House. Amalie marveled at the grandeur of the estate and the beauty of the landscaped gardens. The Corrington Estate was built in 1729 by the Duke's great-grandfather as a gift for his new bride. The building features large columns framing the main entrance and a walk-around balcony surrounding the entire second floor. The Duke traveled to Africa to secure the red clay bricks used on the terraces around the estate. The Corrington Territory was once part of the British Empire, and the influence of that era was present in the estate's design. The original estate commissioned by King George II remains on the grounds and is now used to house the staff.

Several household staff greeted them as Helene and Amalie stepped out of the carriage. The first to greet Amalie was a tall, older gentleman who held out his hand to her.

"Welcome, Miss. I'm Gerald, and I manage the household. Don't worry about your bag. We will bring it to your room. How was your trip?"

"Just fine, thank you, Gerald. It's nice to meet you," Amalie smiled.

"We would love some tea, Margot," Helene said to the woman standing next to Gerald. "It was a long ride, and we are both parched."

"Right away, ma'am. Would you want it in the parlor or outside?" Margot asked.

"I would like it in the sunroom. I'm hoping the others will join us for tea so they can meet Amalie."

"Yes, Ma'am," Margot said with a slight curtsey.

Helene led Amalie into the sprawling estate, and the sheer size of it took Amalie's breath away. It made Amalie think of all the books she read about royalty and castles, and this estate made her imagined images a reality.

"I will take you to your room so you can freshen up for tea," Helene said as she led Amalie up the grand marble staircase to the second floor. "We have tea at four sharp. Your chambermaid will bring you down to the sunroom."

"My chambermaid?"

"Yes, dear. You will soon become accustomed to having staff that will provide you with whatever you need. I've prepared the Blue Room for you. The Duke's grandfather decorated it for his youngest daughter. She loved blue—as in sky blue." As they stepped inside the room, Helene said, "Now you see why we call it the Blue Room."

"Yes, indeed," Amalie marveled as she looked around the room. What caught her eye immediately was the high ceiling painted to look like the sky with the most beautiful shade of light blue and fluffy, white clouds. The furniture was elegant yet feminine, with gold painted trim on each piece and a pale blue lace canopy over the four-poster bed. "It's beautiful," Amalie said in awe.

A young woman standing by the window approached them and introduced herself to Amalie. "I'm Hannah. I will be your chambermaid. Welcome to Corrington House, Miss Amalie," she said with a slight curtsey.

"Thank you. Nice to meet you," Amalie replied awkwardly. *What is proper etiquette for a chambermaid?*

"I will leave you now to get settled," Helene said, turning toward the door. "I'm off to find the Duke. Is he in his study, Hannah?"

"I believe so, ma'am."

After Helene was gone, Amalie stood there, not quite sure what to do with a chambermaid. Hannah was very young. Amalie guessed she was still in her teens. Then she noticed her bag was sitting on the bench at the end of the bed.

"Gerald brought your bag up. I'll unpack it for you," Hannah said, opening the bag.

"Oh, that's not necessary, Hannah. I can do it."

"But Miss, that's my job. I'm happy to do it," Hannah said, continuing to unpack the bag.

There was a moment of awkward silence as the two women looked at each other, then Amalie said, "I'm sorry, this is all new to me. I'm not used to having people do things like this for me. After you unpack my things, I would like to be alone, if you don't mind."

"Of course," Hannah said with a warm smile. "I will leave you alone to freshen up before tea."

Hannah hung the few simple dresses Amalie owned into the wardrobe and placed her nightgown and undergarments into the drawer on the bottom.

"There's water in the pitcher on the washstand, Miss, and fresh towels. Will you be needing anything else?"

"No, thank you, Hannah," Amalie smiled.

"Just ring the bell if you need me."

"What bell?"

"You see that narrow rope with the tassel at the end that hangs down next to your bed?" Hannah pointed to the bed, "Just pull on it, and it rings in my quarters. I will come immediately."

"Oh, I see it, yes. Just let me know when it's time for tea. I don't know where the sunroom is."

"Of course," Hannah said as she left the room.

Amalie stood there and looked around the room. She felt like she was in a dream and couldn't wake up. *How do I do this? How do I live in a world that up until today only existed in my books and fairy tales?*

Hannah came to escort Amalie to the sunroom for tea at four sharp. Amalie had changed into her best dress, but it was still plain compared to how the Duchess dressed. Amalie sewed the dress from fabric that Sister Margaret gave her from the curtains that once hung in her room. It was hunter green velvet with delicate yellow flowers.

As Amalie entered the sunroom, she was surprised to see several people already gathered there. The sunroom was large and bright, with an entire wall of windows letting in the afternoon sunlight. The ever-present sunshine had faded some of the furniture that filled the room.

Helene rose from the sofa to greet Amalie. "Come, dear, I want you to meet everyone."

Helene led her to a tall and still handsome man dressed in full military regalia. His sash told Amalie that this was Helene's husband, the Duke of Corrington. "This is my husband, Oliver Corrington II, the Duke of Corrington."

Amalie curtsied and said, "A pleasure, Your Grace."

"No need to be so formal," the Duke said, holding out his hand, "We are related, after all."

Amalie went to shake his hand, but he lifted her hand and kissed it instead. "Welcome to Corrington House."

Helene then led Amalie over to the chess table, where two young men were deeply involved in their game. Helene loudly cleared her throat to draw their attention, and then they rose to greet her. "These are two of my sons—the tall one is Lord Michael, and the younger one is Lord Anthony."

Amalie curtsied to them both.

"I thought you would be younger," Lord Anthony said with child-like honesty. "I wasn't expecting a grown-up."

"Don't be rude," Helene admonished him.

"No offense taken," Amalie said quickly. "I understand you love music and the arts?"

"Yes, I love music and reading books," Anthony said enthusiastically. "I just finished Charles Dickens' Oliver Twist. Have you read it?"

"Yes, I have. It's one of my favorites," Amalie smiled. "It began as a series; did you know that?"

"Yes! My father has a large library in the east wing, and we have many of his books."

"Wonderful. I would love to see it sometime," Amalie smiled at him.

"Now, let's not get carried away with books on Amalie's first day," Helene interjected. "There is plenty of time for that."

Lord Michael reached for Amalie's hand. "You'll have to excuse my brother. He's a true bookworm. It's a pleasure to meet you. My mother has told us a lot about you. Welcome to Corrington House."

"Thank you, my Lord," Amalie said as Michael kissed her hand.

"No need for formalities. Please call me Michael."

"Alright, Michael. I hear you will be commissioned in the army next spring."

"Yes," Michael's eyes lit up, "I will be serving alongside my older brother. I hope to become a Captain like my older brother and my father before him."

Amalie marveled at how mature Michael seemed, but she guessed him to be in his teens. He shared the same facial features as his mother and was a handsome young man.

"Come dear," Helene took Amalie by the arm, "I want you to meet the rest of our clan."

The ladies went to the center of the room, where two sofas faced each other. On one of the sofas sat an older woman with grey hair doing needlepoint and oblivious to her people.

"Mother, this is Amalie, the young lady I told you about. Amalie, this is my mother, Annabelle. She lives here with us."

The woman looked up and squinted to see Amalie's face. "What young lady?"

Helene leaned in close to Amalie and whispered, "My mother has trouble remembering things."

"It's very nice to meet you, Annabelle," Amalie said with a slight curtsey.

"Do I know you? You look familiar," Annabelle said, still squinting despite the magnifying glasses on the end of her nose.

"No, ma'am, we've never met," Amalie replied.

"Mother, this is Juliet's daughter. You remember Juliet, don't you? She was my best friend in childhood. You used to braid her hair with ribbons."

"No, that doesn't ring a bell," Annabelle said and sat down to finish her needlepoint.

Helene ushered Amalie away from Annabelle and whispered, "As I said, she can't remember things anymore. After my father died, we moved mother here with us because she was not able to care for herself alone."

Then Amalie's eyes fixed on a tall man standing by the fireplace mantle, and she knew it had to be the oldest son, Oliver. He was studying her without any emotion on his face. Helene introduced them.

"Amalie, this is my oldest son, Captain Oliver Corrington III. He just arrived from military exercises in the countryside, so please excuse his attire."

Amalie could see that the sun had dusted his cheeks with color, and his dark blonde hair was wind-swept as it framed his face. "Hello, Captain Corrington."

"Miss Amalie," he said, "Welcome to Corrington House."

"Thank you," she said, unsure whether she felt a chill from him or not. She looked into his grey hazel eyes for a clue, but his face remained emotionless.

Helene then guided Amalie toward the other sofa, where a young woman looked bored and possibly agitated. "Amalie, this is Lady Davina of Herzstein, Oliver's betrothed."

"Nice to meet you, Lady Davina," Amalie said with a slight curtsey. "Congratulations on your engagement."

"Thank you," Davina said with a condescending smile. "I understand you're an orphan. How fortunate for you to land here at Corrington House."

Amalie wasn't sure of the implication but decided to be gracious in return. "I'm happy to be here, thank you."

Davina looked down her nose at Amalie and said, "I'm sure you are."

Margot wheeled in the tea cart and began to serve everyone their tea. Accompanying her was a young woman carrying a tray of biscuits and finger sandwiches, offering them to each person present along with linen napkins for the lap.

Amalie sat down next to Helene and sipped her tea. She watched others for etiquette clues. High tea was not something shared daily at the Abbey. Tea, yes, but with much less formality.

Amalie's eyes wandered back to Captain Corrington, who sat down next to his betrothed. She studied the two of them and immediately concluded that neither one was happy. It made her wonder why. Then suddenly, he spotted her watching him, and she darted her eyes away, slightly embarrassed.

"Amalie has studied music and was teaching the younger children at the Abbey," Helene announced to break the silence. "She is also an excellent piano player."

"Oh, me too!" Anthony declared. "I love to play our piano, but I badly need lessons. Could you teach me?"

Amalie perked up. "I would love to, that is, if it's alright with your parents."

Helene looked at the Duke, who wasn't happy, but she gave her blessing anyway. "Of course, it's alright. There's plenty of time for music until military school."

Anthony was delighted. "When can we begin lessons?"

"Anthony, there is plenty of time for that," Helene said, trying to diffuse his excitement. "Amalie has just arrived, and she needs some time to acclimate."

The Duke then decided to change the topic of discussion. "I read this morning that President Lincoln was assassinated in America. He was shot at the theater by someone unhappy about Lincoln freeing the enslaved people."

"He paid a great price for doing the right thing," Captain Oliver said somberly.

"Honestly, must we discuss politics at every turn?" Helene said crossly. "We are welcoming our newest family member. Let's show her some courtesy and not discuss political matters."

"Sure, let's discuss our guest—I mean the newest family member," Lady Davina said flatly. "What does one do at an Abbey for entertainment?" Davina's dark spiral curls shook as she spoke, and her thin lips seemed to be locked in a scowl.

"I read books—lots of books, and I play the piano. I teach, I mean, I taught music to the younger children. I also volunteered at the local hospital helping with the children by providing music."

"How noble of you," Davina muttered.

Amalie didn't bite. "Thank you. I believe that a life lived in service to others is a life well-lived. The sisters taught me that."

Amalie was sure she saw a small smile cross Captain Oliver's lips, but he said nothing.

"That is a lovely way to live, Amalie," Helene said sincerely. "We could all learn from you."

Annabelle's eyes fixed on Amalie. "Are you sure we've never met? I know I know you."

"I'm sorry, ma'am, but we've never met before," Amalie assured her.

"It'll come to me. I will remember," Annabelle said as she went back to her needlepoint.

"Well, I'm glad she's here," Anthony gushed, "Now I can get proper piano lessons and learn how to read music."

"You said earlier that you play the piano. How do you do that without reading music?" Amalie wondered out loud.

"By sound. I listen to the songs I like, and then I try to play them," Anthony replied.

"Goodness, that is impressive," Amalie said, smiling at him. "That requires real talent. Not everyone can do that."

"He's outstanding," Helene said proudly. "Just the other day, he played a lullaby I used to sing to him, and it sounded perfect."

Amalie smiled at Anthony. "Well, you just might be teaching me a thing or two."

The Duke was not amused by the women encouraging his youngest son with music, so he turned the discussion back to other matters he deemed more important.

"Michael will be commissioned as an officer this spring. He has excelled in his training and will make a fine Captain one day. Anthony will follow in his footsteps, just as Oliver followed in mine. It's our family tradition."

Amalie understood what he was telling her, but she never discouraged music for anyone. "I know a high-ranking officer in the Queen's army who plays the piano so well that he performed for Her Majesty. A person can succeed in his career and excel in their interests."

Now Amalie was sure she saw a smile on the Captain's face.

"How do you know a high-ranking officer in the Queen's army?" the Duke asked skeptically.

"I'm the one who taught him to play the piano," Amalie said proudly. "He still serves Her Majesty to this day. He and his wife adopted a child from our Abbey. When he marveled at how well his new son played, he asked me to teach him too."

"Well, then, it would seem we have a master teacher in our midst," Captain Oliver said, still smiling. "I look forward to hearing you play for us sometime soon."

"I'd be honored," Amalie said, sipping her tea.

"My family is coming later today to join us for dinner," Lady Davina said, returning the focus to her. "We are planning for our wedding next summer."

Amalie noticed a complete change in the Captain's expression. He was once again unemotional, which she found odd considering that Lady Davina was his future wife.

Davina went on. "My father is Duke Carl Gustav of Herzstein, and my mother is Duchess Marta of Herzstein. They will be joining us for dinner here this evening."

"Yes, I forgot to mention to you that we are having a dinner party this evening," Helene said, looking at Amalie. "Partially to welcome you, but also to begin planning the wedding with Lady Davina's parents."

Amalie just smiled, trying to hide how overwhelmed she felt. She studied Lady Davina. She appeared to be young, yet she did not possess the innocence of a young lady; instead, she seemed to be regal and tried to present herself more mature than she was.

"I look forward to it," Amalie said, hoping no one would notice she was lying. This new world she found herself in felt like a pair of shoes that didn't fit well, and she was uncomfortable.

The dinner party began at eight, but Helene came into Amalie's room carrying a dress over her arm before the guests arrived. "I think this will fit you," Helene said, holding the dress up to Amalie. "You can wear this tonight, and it might make you feel more comfortable until we can get you some new dresses."

"Of course," was all Amalie could say.

The dress was lovely and more refined than anything Amalie ever owned. She was happy to wear it so she wouldn't stand out as the only commoner in the room. The dress was dark blue silk with a high waist ribbon wrapped around it. It had a plunging neckline and exposed more than Amalie was comfortable showing.

Hannah helped Amalie tie her corset, and halfway through the lace-up, Amalie said, "No, I don't think I want to wear this. I can't breathe, and it pushes my bosom up too far."

"But Miss, you must wear it. It's just not proper for a young lady to not wear a corset in an evening dress."

Amalie relented but insisted that Hannah loosen the lacing a bit. "If I am to eat at this dinner party, I must have enough room to breathe."

Hannah helped Amalie pull her hair up into a pewter butterfly clip and decorated it with a sprig of Baby's Breath from the garden.

"You look lovely, Miss," Hannah said sincerely.

"Thank you. I wouldn't have known what to do without your help. Is there any dinner party etiquette you could bestow on me for tonight?" Amalie asked with pleading eyes.

Hannah smiled and said, "Just be yourself. Talk only when spoken to and use the silverware from the outside in, except for the soup spoon at the top. Soup is the first course. There will be several courses for the meal."

"Thank you. I feel like a fish out of water here," Amalie confessed.

When Hannah ushered Amalie into the dining room, everyone was present but not yet seated at the table. Helene came to escort her to greet the guests when suddenly, a crash of breaking glass echoed through the room. All eyes turned to Duke Carl Gustav, who had just dropped his bourbon glass, which shattered onto the tiles in front of the fireplace. Duke Carl Gustav was staring at Amalie, making her even more uncomfortable.

After a brief silence, Duke Carl Gustav spoke. "My apologies to our hosts; it just slipped out of my hand."

"Don't be the slightest bit concerned about it," Helene reassured him. "Margot is already on her way to clean it up."

Then Helene led Amalie to the center of the room and introduced her to the guests. "Everyone, this is our newest family member, Miss Amalie, but we hope to change that very soon to Lady Corrington. Amalie, please meet the Herzstein family, Duke Carl Gustav, and his lovely wife, Duchess Marta. The young lady over there with Anthony is their youngest daughter, Anneliese. You already met Lady Davina at tea."

Amalie curtsied and nodded. "Pleasure to meet you all."

"Please be seated, everyone. Dinner is ready," Helene announced.

Amalie was seated near the end of the table between Annabelle and Lord Anthony. The Dukes each sat at the head of the table with their respective families on each side. Amalie was a bit nervous sitting next to Duke Carl Gustav at her end of the table because he had not stopped staring at her since she entered the room.

Amalie remembered Hannah's advice and did not speak unless spoken to during dinner. The staff served several courses, and she just kept her head down and hoped the evening would pass by quickly. At the other end of the table, there was much discussion about the upcoming festival celebration and wedding planning. Lady Davina and her mother did most of the talking, and Amalie noticed that Oliver was once again emotionless and quiet. She wondered for a moment if he was as uncomfortable with these things as she was.

Amalie noticed Lord Anthony staring at her, so she leaned closer to him and whispered, "You're very quiet this evening."

"We're not allowed to speak at formal dinners," he whispered back.

"Got it," Amalie said with a wink.

Lord Anthony smiled at her and winked back.

"Is there something you would like to share with the table?" Lady Davina said, noticing their exchange.

Amalie's face flushed. "No, My Lady. Is there something you want to share with the table? You have my full attention."

Davina glared at her but said nothing in return.

Duke Carl Gustav finally spoke. "Miss Amalie, do you know anything about your family?"

"No, Your Grace," she said awkwardly. "I only know what I learned from Duchess Helene on our carriage ride here."

"I understand you have musical talents and play the piano quite well," he continued. "I would love to hear you play sometime."

Amalie was increasingly uncomfortable with all eyes on her and felt her anxiety level increase. "Of course, Your Grace, but not this evening. It has been a very long and eventful day. That being said, I think I will be retiring to my room; if you will all please excuse me."

Amalie stood and bowed to the table. She turned to leave when Helene said, "But dear, we haven't had our dessert yet."

"Thank you, but I am exhausted and wish to rest now." Then she turned to leave and hurried out the door. She couldn't quite remember the way back to her room, so she followed a long corridor that led to an outside terrace.

Amalie stepped outside and inhaled the cool night air deeply to calm her nerves. She sat down on a stone bench and tried to collect her whirlwind thoughts.

Back at the dinner table, Davina broke the awkward silence following Amalie's abrupt departure. "Well, that was rather rude. Her behavior is crude, but she is not highborn. One cannot expect any more from her."

Duke Oliver II spoke next. "She is a bit too impulsive with her comments. This afternoon she challenged me about Anthony taking piano lessons. I don't like women who are so free with their comments."

"I disagree, father," Captain Oliver said, "She has many qualities that I admire. Her honesty is a breath of fresh air."

"I know she has much to learn, but please give her a chance," Helene said, "She grew up in an Abbey, and we cannot expect her to know how to behave on her first day here."

"Honestly, what did she say or do that was so offensive? Is she not allowed to speak her mind?" the Captain continued his defense of her.

Lady Davina was perturbed. "You heard your father; she talked back to him this afternoon. I was there. I heard it too."

"She did not talk back to him," the Captain countered. "She told him that a person could succeed in their career and interests. She is correct about that. Why do you find that so offensive, father?"

"Enough of this!" Duke Oliver II howled, "I demand respect in my house."

"Well then, if you will excuse me also," Oliver said to his father, "I too am tired—I had military maneuvers all afternoon—and will take my leave now."

Captain Corrington stood up, bowed to the guests, and left the room the same way Amalie did.

Helene was mortified but said nothing.

"I apologize to your family, Carl Gustav," Duke Oliver said, "My family is out of sorts this evening. Perhaps adding a new family member in this setting was not wise."

"No apology needed," Carl Gustav said, which surprised everyone at the table. "I found her to be quite refreshing also. She is lovely and should be given a chance to prove herself."

"Father, honestly!" Davina said in protest.

Then Lord Anthony broke protocol and spoke, "I like her. She is very nice."

"Yes, she seems very likable," Lord Michael added. "I think my father is being a bit harsh on her first day with us."

"I am more upset that my future son-in-law left so abruptly. We still have much to plan, and he seems to be uninterested, if I may be so blunt," Duchess Marta said.

"As my son said, he had military maneuvers all afternoon," Helene said, "He must be exhausted. He should leave the planning to us anyway. Men are no good at this sort of thing."

Amalie sat in the cool night air, wondering what had happened to her life. Would she ever fit in here? Did she want to? She realized that she would be of legal age in a few short months and began daydreaming about leaving when that time came. She looked up at the stars and wondered what the sisters at the Abbey were doing at that moment. Stargazing was a favorite pastime for Amalie and Sister Margaret.

Just then, a man's voice broke the night silence. "May I join you?" It was Captain Corrington. "I'm sorry, I didn't mean to startle you. I'm surprised to see you out here."

"Truth be told, I couldn't remember how to get back to my room and ended up here, but the fresh air is doing some good," Amalie admitted.

Oliver sat down next to her. "I'm sorry about this evening," he said sincerely, "My family can be a bit much sometimes."

"It was a disaster, wasn't it?" Amalie lamented. "Please be honest with me."

"Not at all, please don't think that," he said sincerely. "May I speak frankly?"

"Of course, I prefer it."

"I was watching you this afternoon and this evening. When no one is looking, you seem nervous—and sad. Are you troubled about something?" Oliver asked sincerely.

"May I speak frankly also?" she said in earnest.

"Of course, I prefer it as well," Oliver assured her.

"I'm still overwhelmed with all of this. I don't mean to be ungrateful—I do appreciate what your mother is trying to do for me, but it just doesn't feel right. I don't think I belong here. And I'm not quite sure why I am here—now at this stage in my life. I don't think I will ever fit in here. Your father doesn't like me, and the other Duke was almost too friendly—he kept staring at me. And your betrothed indeed doesn't like me, and I'm not sure why."

"Please believe me when I say that it has nothing to do with you," Oliver assured her. "Davina doesn't like anyone. She is, by nature, a miserable person. My father wasn't sure about you coming here, he had serious reservations, but no one could talk my mother out of it. As for the Duke of Herzstein, he surprised me too. For some reason, he took to you and defended you after you were gone."

"I'm sure I must've been the topic of discussion after I left. The Duke of Herzstein defended me? To whom? Let me guess, his daughter?"

"I defended you too," he said with a smile. "I think they were rude to you, and you deserved better on your first day with us."

"Thank you," Amalie said humbly. "I appreciate that."

"Why is such a lovely young woman so sad?"

"Again, please know that I am not ungrateful to your mother, but she took me from the only home I've ever known and from the people I love….and I had no say in the matter at all. I was powerless to declare my free will. This is not the life I was planning to live, not at all. I miss my home, the sisters, and the children. I'm not sure I will ever feel like I belong here. I'm sure you can't possibly understand." Amalie was fighting tears.

"Oh, but I do understand. Completely. I feel the same way," he said with genuine warmth in his voice. "I am powerless as well, even as a Captain in the army and the firstborn of Corrington House. You see, I am duty-bound to marry Davina, and I don't think she is any happier about it than I am. It's not a love match, not at all. The Peace Treaty of 1465 between our territories requires us to marry to fulfill the decree handed down by King Henry VI almost four hundred years ago. If we do not honor it, it could cause a war between the territories. My parents groomed me to fulfill this duty since I was a boy. Can you imagine being only ten years old and being told who you are going to marry?"

Amalie felt empathy for Oliver and understood his feelings through their similar situations. "You do understand how I feel. I can't imagine marrying someone I don't love. It doesn't seem fair."

"My father always told me that life is not fair. There are many arranged marriages out of duty in royal families or for other reasons such as financial advantages, alliances, or the need for pure bloodlines," Oliver said sadly, "I have been aware of my duty since childhood."

"I'm so sorry," Amalie said, touching his hand, then immediately withdrew her hand in embarrassment. "I'm sorry, I don't know the rules here. I have a lot to learn."

"Oh please, don't ever change. No matter how much my mother grooms you to be who she wants you to be, please never lose who you are. You are a delightful person, and I would hate to see that change. Don't let them diminish your spirit."

"I will never surrender who I am, that I can promise you. I'm too headstrong for that—or so the sisters have told me on one or two occasions," Amalie said, feeling comfortable to share her thoughts with someone who is still a stranger.

"I saw you handled my father very well this afternoon. I have a feeling you're going to be just fine."

"Thank you for talking to me," Amalie said sincerely. "I feel better knowing someone understands."

"You can always talk to me. I do understand. And I will keep whatever you share with me strictly confidential—just between us."

"Thank you, and I will do the same," she replied with a warm smile. "Now, can you show me how to get back to my room?"

"Sure," he chuckled. "Follow me, Miss Amalie."

Oliver walked her back to her room, and as she opened the door, she said, "Thank you again. I do appreciate your kindness."

Oliver smiled at her. "You are so welcome. Anytime."

Amalie thought he had a beautiful smile, broad and warm. So different from the face he wore at dinner earlier. Oliver's eyes sparkled when he smiled, and it was then that he resembled his mother. When he wore his military face, he resembled his father more.

As Amalie lay in her bed that evening, she was glad to have found a friend and confidant. She no longer felt entirely alone. However, she still fantasized about leaving as soon as possible. Distant relative or not, she knew she would never feel at home in this place.

Chapter 2
The Ball

When Amalie came down for breakfast, everyone was seated at the table. "Good morning," she said, taking her seat and placing her napkin on her lap.

"Good morning, dear," Helene said, "I hope you were able to get some rest. I'm afraid yesterday may have been too much for you."

"No, not at all," Amalie lied with a smile. "And yes, I feel much better today."

"Oh, good! I was hoping to take you to the city and do some shopping. Would you like that?"

"Yes, that will be fine," Amalie said as she noticed that Lady Davina was not at the table. "Did Lady Davina leave?"

"Yes," Captain Oliver answered, "She returned to Herzstein last night with her parents."

"Amalie, I am going to plan a ball in your honor. I am hoping to have it before the month is out. It will be your introduction into society," Helene went on as she stabbed her fruit with her fork. "A formal ball with music, dancing, and all the eligible young men in Corrington Territory will be there. It will be so grand! We will stop at the dressmaker today to commission your dress."

Amalie stopped chewing her strawberry, and her eyes widened. She looked at Captain Oliver with pleading eyes.

"Mother, shouldn't we give Amalie a chance to settle in before we do something like that?" the Captain said quickly.

"It will be in three weeks. That's plenty of time," Helene dismissed his concern. "I'm so anxious to present her to Corrington society and help her take her place in it."

"I would suggest some tutoring in proper etiquette between now and then," the Duke said to his wife.

Amalie just looked down at her plate. They were discussing her as if she weren't in the room. Amalie saw Lord Anthony giving her an encouraging smile. She smiled back and then spoke to him. "We should start your piano lessons today. Would you like that?"

"Yes!" he said excitedly.

"But we're going into the city today," Helene reminded her.

"That won't take all day. I'm sure we can carve out an hour at some point today," Amalie gently insisted.

Lord Anthony was visibly excited, but the Duke cleared his throat in frustration.

Amalie changed the subject. "Helene, you mentioned a keepsake box that belonged to my mother. Would it be possible for me to have it today?"

"Yes, of course," Helene said flatly, a bit deflated over Amalie's lack of interest in the ball. "I will have Hannah bring it to your room later today."

"Thank you," Amalie said, forcing a smile as she dabbed some marmalade on her bread.

"Mother, when are you leaving for the city?" Captain Oliver asked.

"Within the hour."

"May I tag along in the carriage? I'm scheduled to meet the Lieutenant of the Armory later today. That way, we won't need two carriages."

"Of course, dear."

"How far is it to the city?" Amalie asked.

"Half an hour by carriage. Faster on horseback," the Captain answered.

"Which city are we going to? I'm sorry, I'm not at all familiar with the Corrington Territory," Amalie explained.

"Brighton is the territory's largest city and is the seat of official business. Our family has headquarters in the Corrington Building," Lord Michael said. "When I receive my commission, I will have an office there as well."

"Isn't that where my grandfather died, Helene?" Amalie remembered.

"Yes, that is where I discovered our connection—from the church records," Helene replied.

"I will anxiously await your return, Amalie," Lord Anthony said. "The grand piano is in the parlor. Perhaps I can show you the library too?"

"One thing at a time, Anthony," his mother admonished.

Amalie winked at Anthony with a smile, and the boy's face lit up. She could feel the Duke's eyes on her, but she did not look at him. Instead, she looked at the Captain and gave him a grateful nod.

Brighton was a bustling city, and Amalie was amazed at how modern it looked. The founders built the main roads with brick and stone instead of dirt roads running through the city. The sidewalks were cobblestone. Amalie admired the architecture of the tall buildings and the bright, colorful, and cheerful storefronts. There was ample room for parking the carriages or tying up the horses.

Captain Corrington went straight to his office, but before he left the ladies at the dressmaker, he leaned in and whispered to Amalie, "Just make the best of it."

The dressmaker's shop was called *The Fabric of Life* and owned by a middle-aged woman named Frieda Schleuter, who had immigrated from Prussia. The dresses in the window were beautiful, and Amalie had never seen anything like them.

Helene introduced Amalie to Frieda and told her they needed two dresses for an upcoming ball. Frieda was more than happy to get to work. After measuring Amalie and presenting several exquisite fabrics, Amalie selected her favorite pale blue color and found a dyed feather for her hair.

When Helene began to examine the fabric for her dress, Amalie asked if it would be alright if she went outside to explore the other shops. Helene had no objection.

When Amalie entered the street, she was amazed at all the different shops along that main thoroughfare, but what caught her eye was the beautiful church directly across the street. It was an old church that appeared to be hundreds of years old with stained glass windows and a beautifully crafted wooden door. The architecture drew her toward it.

The sign in front read: St. Paul's Cathedral. She walked toward the church, but she heard children playing before going inside and followed the sound. In a courtyard next to the church, several children played kickball with one of the nuns supervising. It made Amalie homesick for the Abbey. She watched the children through a wrought iron gate with nostalgic amusement. The supervising nun spotted Amalie watching them and signaled her to enter the courtyard.

"I don't mean to disturb you," Amalie apologized, "I so enjoy watching the children play. It makes me homesick for my old home. My name is Amalie Gilchrist."

"Ah," the sister said in acknowledgment, "You must be from the Gilchrist Abbey. I've been there many times. I'm Sister Monica. Most of these children live here, but a few are poor children from the area who need a hot meal every day, which we gladly provide. We school them as well."

"It's so nice to meet you. I used to teach music to the children at the Abbey. I miss that," Amalie sighed.

"Really? We certainly could use some help in that area. Our music teacher is seventy years old and very hard of hearing. Would you consider assisting her? I mean, we can't afford to hire you, but if you were willing to give your time, we would welcome the help," Sister Monica said.

"Oh, I would love to, but…." Amalie paused, thinking of needing to ask Helene for permission. "I would have to get permission from the Duchess first."

"Duchess Corrington?" Sister Monica asked.

"Yes, I am living in their household. She is a distant cousin of mine," Amalie said, still growing accustomed to that reality.

"Well, we would love to have you if they allow it," Sister Monica reiterated.

Meanwhile, Helene and Captain Oliver finished their tasks and met on the street in front of the dress shop.

"Have you seen Amalie? She went exploring, and I seem to have lost her," Helene said, looking up and down the street.

"No, but I think I might know where she is. Something tells me she found her way to St. Paul's," Oliver said instinctively.

They crossed the street, and at the corner of the church, they spotted Amalie in the courtyard with the children. Oliver watched as Sister Monica introduced Amalie to the children, and the scene made Oliver smile in admiration.

"There she is, just as I suspected," he said to his mother.

"Yes, she does seem to gravitate toward children, doesn't she? Anthony is completely smitten with her. I think it aggravates your father."

"Well, I think it's wonderful. Amalie has a child-like innocence and honesty that children recognize. People are drawn to it also. I noticed Carl Gustav was quite taken with her," Oliver said.

"Yes, he was," Helene concurred, "And that aggravated your father also for some reason."

At that moment, Amalie spotted them waiting for her and bid Sister Monica and the children farewell. She promised to return.

Amalie excitedly shared her encounter with the children on the carriage ride home and how Sister Monica invited her to assist with music for the children. Oliver noticed that it was the happiest he had seen her since she arrived.

"I would love to assist them," Amalie shared excitedly. "Perhaps one or two afternoons a week?"

"I'm not sure that's a good idea," Helene said cautiously, thinking of how her husband would react.

"Why not, mother? Every woman of standing helps with charities. You do as well," Oliver reminded her.

"I collect clothing and blankets for the needy. I don't go out and work for a charity. I'm not sure that it's proper."

"It's a church," Amalie said firmly. "How could that possibly be improper?"

"I would have no issue with it, but I'm almost certain my husband will," Helene said gently but firmly.

"He would have an issue with helping in a church—a place of worship? I can't imagine why he would," Amalie said more forcefully than she intended. "I'm not asking to serve ale at the pub."

"You see, that's just it, Amalie," Helene said, trying to be delicate. "You can be forceful when you are passionate about something, and the Duke hates it when women speak out like that."

Oliver tried to diffuse the situation. "If I agree to escort Amalie two afternoons per week to the church and back, would he object to that? She would not be unaccompanied."

"Well, that would certainly appear more proper. I think he might agree to that. But don't you have more important matters to tend to?" Helene reminded him.

"I will gladly make the time," Oliver said, looking at Amalie.

"We'll ask him this evening. Amalie, please, let me tell him. Once he gets upset, he would never agree to it," Helene said apprehensively.

"Why does my presence here bother him?" Amalie asked bluntly.

"It's not your presence. The Duke expected a meek and mild child, not a grown woman with strong opinions. Don't take it personally," Helene replied honestly.

"My father was raised by a very stern governess and never experienced motherly love," Oliver explained. "He rarely shows affection to anyone, not even his sons. His father was all military and was very strict with him. My mother is correct when she says it's not you. It's just who he is."

"Yes, all that is true," Helene said woefully. "If you want to be accepted as you are, Amalie, you must accept him as he is."

"I do believe that once he gets to know you better, he will be less critical," Oliver said to encourage Amalie.

"I can certainly accept him for who he is, but it must be mutual," Amalie declared.

Oliver smiled, but Helene had a knot in her stomach that told her that she might not mold this young woman into the vision she had for her.

While Amalie worked on the piano with Anthony, Helene and Captain Oliver spoke with the Duke about Amalie helping at the church. He was adamantly against it and said no. Helene was hesitant to challenge him, but Oliver did not hold back.

"Father, there is no harm and nothing improper about her assisting the nuns with the children. I have already said I would accompany her to and from the church. She is passionate about this, and I'm afraid we will alienate her if we deny her this. It has not escaped me that she will be of legal age very soon. If she is not happy here, she will be free to leave. Is that what you want?"

The Duke and Duchess looked at each other, and Oliver wondered about the long exchange. Suddenly, the Duke said he would approve. Their son was flabbergasted. Never in his 25 years had Oliver ever seen his father give in so quickly. However, he did not question it.

Later that afternoon, when Amalie returned to her room, she found a small wooden box on her bed. Amalie was anxious to open her mother's keepsake box. She opened it carefully, and the first thing that caught her eye was the journal. The journal was leather-bound and well worn. There were other items in the box, but not much. The first thing she examined was the faded newspaper clipping about her grandfather's death. It was dated the 25th of October, 1841. It read: The Bennington Estate reports the death of their Stablemaster Charles Bennett, who died in a hunting accident. He is preceded in death by his wife, Martha, and survived by his daughter, Juliet. Burial will be alongside his wife in Belham County.

Helene was right. There's not much information.

Amalie also found a yellow ribbon tied together with a string. *This must've had some meaning to her; otherwise, she would not have kept it.*

There was a metal hair clip and a small locket broach, but Amalie noticed the broken pin. Amalie opened the locket to find a small clip of fine dark hair and wondered whose hair it was. She carefully closed the locket to secure the hair. There was a small hand-sewn pin cushion with needles stuck in it, and there were remnants of thread still in some of them. Amalie felt a wave of sadness that these few items were all that remained from her mother's life. Still, there was joy in having these items because she had nothing that belonged to her mother until she received this box.

Amalie took the journal and sat down in the easy chair by the window for better light. She carefully opened the journal and began to read it. The first entry was dated April 20th, but no year. Juliet wrote: *This has been a wonderful birthday. I am writing in my gift from father. I asked him for a journal, and I'm so happy to have this finally. After supper, the staff presented me with a cake for my special day. Mrs. Barclay made it for me. Tomorrow I will be going riding with Helene. We went all the way down to the river last time but got into trouble for being late for supper. We will be riding to the orchard to pick some apples for the horses tomorrow. I love my horse, Star. I know she is old, but I love her just the same. They were going to slaughter her, but father asked if I could have her. She is <u>everything</u> to me.*

Several entries read similar—escapades of Juliet and Helene during their childhood. It was apparent that Juliet adored her father. She only mentioned him with love. There was little mention of Juliet's mother, so Amalie assumed she must have died before she began her journal.

Then Amalie came to the entry where Juliet wrote about Helene leaving to marry the future Duke. She wrote: *I am heartbroken to lose my best friend. Helene left this morning to marry into the Corrington Family. She was not happy to go, but her father arranged the marriage. We hugged and cried as we said goodbye. I shall miss her terribly. She was like a sister to me. I asked father if he would ever do that to me, and he said no. He wanted me to marry for love as he did with my mother. I hope to write to Helene as soon as she sends me her address. Perhaps, one day I can visit her?*

An entry just weeks later mentioned Charles becoming ill. *My father is not well today. He fainted while grooming a horse, and we summoned the physician. Father is getting older and must rest more, the physician said. He gave him a potion to drink every morning, and I made sure he drank* it. *After losing my best friend, I cannot fathom losing my father. I will care for him. I love him so.*

Another entry just days later read: *We are leaving this estate and moving to Brighton where father will work on the Bennington Estate. I think they let him go here because he could no longer do the heavy physical work, and after all my father has done for them, that is most unkind. He will have fewer duties in his new position, but I am hopeful it will be better for his health. There will be less money, so I will work in the kitchen to help with finances. I have not heard from Helene in weeks. I hope she is well. I will send her our new address once we are settled.*

The following entry, dated three weeks later, was heartbreaking. *My father died today. I am utterly shattered. They told me he went hunting and was accidentally shot by another hunter, but I am having a hard time accepting that. Father has not hunted in years. Why would he go now? And in ill health? I was working in the kitchen when they came to tell me. They brought the body back to the estate on a cart, and I did have a chance to see him and say goodbye. He was shot in the chest. It is my hope he died instantly and did not suffer. The tears will not stop. Mr. Bennington has graciously offered to pay for my father's burial next to my mother. That provides a tiny bit of comfort, but nothing will ever fill the hole in my heart. I will miss you always, father.*

Tears filled Amalie's eyes as she read about her grandfather's death and the heartbreak her mother expressed. *She must've felt so alone. I know how that feels.*

There were no entries for several weeks, but during the winter that followed her father's death, Juliet wrote again to put onto paper that she had fallen in love. *I promised my love I would not share our secret, but my heart is bursting, and I must share it here. I wish I had Helene to talk to, but we have lost track, and I have not heard from her in many months. One week after my nineteenth birthday, I met my love. I've been promoted and now work as a server for the family in the main house. I was serving a dinner party when we met. Our eyes locked, and I blushed when he kept staring at me. He was staying at the estate on business. One evening he slipped me a note during dinner and asked me to meet him in the barn at eight. I hesitated but felt compelled to go. My heart flutters every time he is near me. We began meeting there every evening, and the second time, he kissed me. I think my heart exploded. He expressed love for me, and I love him too. He is of noble birth, which means his family will never accept me. My love promises me that we will find a way to be together. I trust him completely. I daydream of being his wife. He is leaving for home tomorrow but has promised to come back very soon. He said he would send a private messenger with letters to me. He does not trust the Post to keep our secret.*

This entry intrigued Amalie and made her wonder who her father was and how her mother ended up at the Abbey.

The next to the final entry in the journal was dated several months later. It read: *We are leaving tonight. My love sent me a rendezvous location. We are to be married by the vicar in Brighton. At last, my love will be mine, and I will be his.*

The final entry simply read: *We are going to the Abbey to have our child. It's safer there. I am leaving everything behind.*

Amalie had more questions than answers after reading the journal. Why did they have to go to the Abbey to have their child? Why was it not safe anywhere else? How could she find out who her father was? If they were married by the vicar in Brighton, there should be a record of it in the church. Amalie would ask Sister Monica to help find the document at St. Paul's next week. As she clutched the leather journal to her chest, she looked down at the binding and noticed a slight gap in the pages. Amalie pushed her finger down into the gap and spread the pages. Pages were missing from the journal. It appeared that several pages were missing between the next to the last entry and the final entry. Amalie was puzzled. *Why on earth would pages be missing? Who removed them? Juliet or someone else?* The missing pages added to the mystery of Juliet's short life. Amalie was determined to find the answers.

There was an unusual silence at dinner that evening, and Amalie assumed it was because the Duke was perturbed about her volunteering at the church. She just kept her head down and ate her dinner. Captain Oliver broke the awkward silence.

"I heard you play this afternoon with Anthony. It was lovely," he said to Amalie. "What was the piece you were playing?"

"It was Beethoven's Moonlight Sonata—one of my favorite pieces," she replied.

"It was lovely. Are you teaching Anthony to play it?" Oliver asked.

"He asked me to play it. He heard it somewhere and said he loved it. Yes, I am teaching him to play it, but I don't have the sheet music. It's at the Abbey tucked in my books."

"Thank you for reminding me, dear," Helene finally spoke. "I have sent for the rest of your things. They should be here tomorrow."

"Thank you so much!" Amalie said, smiling at Helene.

"I was trying to play it from memory, but I couldn't master it. Amalie knows it by heart. I can't wait to play all of it," Anthony said eagerly.

"I love the sound of piano music waffling through this house," Michael said to Amalie. "I heard you also, and it was superb."

"Thank you," Amalie said humbly.

"I must admit," the Duke said, "It was lovely. My mother used to play the piano."

"Thank you, Sir. Please let me know if you have any other pieces you would like me to play. I would be happy to play them for you," Amalie said, surprised to receive a compliment from the Duke.

The Duke nodded, and Amalie thought she saw the hint of a smile. Perhaps he was coming around? The sisters of Gilchrist Abbey always taught Amalie that music can be a bridge for peace. Everyone can enjoy and share music no matter how contrary their differences may be.

The ball was only days away, and the estate was bustling with preparations. The dressmaker delivered the ball gowns, and Amalie was astonished at how beautiful her dress was.

She had begun her volunteer work at St. Paul's and was happy to be working with children again. Sister Monica and Sister Therese, the seventy-year-old choir teacher, welcomed Amalie with open arms. The children quickly grew to love Amalie and looked forward to her time there. On her first visit, she brought a basket full of apples for the children, and they were happy to enjoy such a rare treat.

Captain Oliver found himself looking forward to the carriage rides with Amalie. They could speak freely and share their feelings without being overheard.

"Don't be nervous about the ball. Personally, I detest them, but I always suffer through somehow," Oliver shared with her. "I know you're not looking forward to it."

"I'm very nervous about being on display in front of high society. And I think your mother wants to marry me off based on her saying that many eligible bachelors would be there. How do I put them off without being rude?"

Oliver smiled. "I will be there and if there is someone you don't want to speak to or dance with, just give me a signal, and I will save you."

"What kind of a signal?"

"Well, let's see—how about you fluff your hair or place your finger on your chin as if you are intently listening, and I will swoop in and usher you away."

"You mean like this?" Amalie said, placing her finger on her chin and batting her eyes.

Oliver laughed. "That's perfect. Those pompous gents won't know what hit them."

Amalie laughed too. She sincerely appreciated her friendship with Oliver and found him utterly charming.

"Will Davina and her parents be at the ball?" she asked.

"No, not this time. Carl Gustav is ill with a fever, and he will not allow her to travel alone. Please forgive me for saying this, but I am relieved they won't be there. Keeping up the pretense about this marriage drains me. I welcome one occasion where I won't have to pretend."

"I'm so sorry, Oliver," she said sincerely, "I can't imagine how you do it."

"We do what we must do. That has been hammered into me since I was a boy. I have accepted it," he lamented.

"I'm trying to learn from you. I am trying to accept my new life too, but I haven't had as much time as you had to grow into it," Amalie said.

"By the way, were you as surprised as I was that my father allowed you to work at the church?" Oliver asked.

"Yes! I was fully prepared to let go of the idea, but then your mother came to tell me he agreed. I was stunned. How did you convince him?" she asked.

"I'm still not sure. He said no at first, but when I told him that you would be old enough to leave in a few short months if you wanted to, there was this strange exchange of looks between my parents. Then he said yes. I swear, in all my life, I've never seen him change his mind like that without a fight."

"Hmm, that's odd. Your father doesn't like me very much, so I would think he would welcome the idea of me leaving," Amalie said, baffled.

"Yes, it was uncharacteristic of him," Oliver agreed.

"I'm just happy that it worked out this way. I love being at the church with the children. It has certainly lifted my spirits," Amalie said, smiling.

"I can see that. Those children are lucky to have you."

"Thank you," Amalie said with flushed cheeks.

The day Amalie dreaded had finally arrived. The estate was bustling with final preparations, and Amalie treated herself to a hot soak in the bathtub. There was only one washroom on the second floor, and the family had to share it. When the Duke's grandfather built the estate, it was not a priority to have a water closet or bathroom in every bedroom. When Oliver II became Duke, he ordered one of the bedrooms converted into a washroom at the request of his new wife. The hot water helped to soothe Amalie's nerves.

"Would you like more hot water?" Hannah asked.

"No, this is fine. What is that delightful fragrance you added to my bath?" Amalie asked, leaning back and relaxing in the calming water.

"Oil of lavender, Miss. It's the Duchess' favorite," Hannah replied, putting the oil bottle back on the dresser.

"It's very soothing. Thank you."

Amalie relaxed in her bath until the water got cold. She knew she couldn't put it off any longer and began to dress for the ball. Hannah laid out her dress and helped her pull her hair up into a stylish twist, securing it with a pearl-studded hairpin.

Helene knocked then burst into the room, and when she saw Amalie standing in her dress, she stopped in awe.

"You are the image of Juliet tonight. You look lovely," she said warmly.

"Thank you. And thank you for the hairpin. Hannah helped me with it. You look lovely as well. I love that color on you. The yellow matches your hair."

"Thank you, dear. It's the Duke's favorite. He never complains about the cost if he likes the dress. There are a few things I want to go over with you before we go downstairs—just a few last-minute things."

Helene explained the proper way to accept a dance request, the appropriate way to address dignitaries, and Amalie's formal introduction would occur at the center of the ballroom. "Gerald will serve as our Lord Stewart this evening and will make your formal introduction. I will be with you most of the evening and will guide you."

The ladies made their way down the main staircase to join the guests in the ballroom. As Helene and Amalie entered, Gerald greeted them.

"My, you look dashing in your suit," Amalie smiled at him.

"Thank you, Miss," then he turned to face the room and rang a bell to announce their arrival formally. "May I present to you the Duchess of Corrington and her distant cousin, Miss Amalie Bennett."

Amalie was surprised he used the surname Bennett, but she didn't question it aloud with all eyes on her. Guests filled the crowded ballroom, and the ladies had to part the crowd to enter the room. Amalie looked at the numerous strange faces as she followed Helene through the crowd. Everyone curtsied to the Duchess and then studied the newcomer behind her. Helene led Amalie over to the fireplace where the Duke and the Captain were standing. They were both wearing full military uniforms with the royal sash across the front. Amalie thought Oliver looked very handsome in his formal attire.

"You both look lovely this evening," the Captain said, looking at Amalie.

"Thank you, Captain Corrington," Amalie said, remembering to keep it formal in public after Oliver had asked her to please call him by his given name when they were alone.

Just then, a man approached them with his full attention on Amalie. "Miss, I am Jeremiah Colby, Legal Scholar and Financial Instructor, and humbly ask you for the honor of a dance. Do you have a dance card?" Jeremiah Colby appeared to be a man in his thirties with colorful red hair and a sunken, pale face.

Amalie looked puzzled because she didn't have a dance card. However, she covered quickly. "Oh dear, I must've dropped it as we walked through the crowd."

Helene realized she forgot to give Amalie a dance card and quickly said, "I will get you another one, dear. Just give me a moment, Mr. Colby," and she darted off to secure the card. In less than a minute, she returned with a dance card and handed it to Mr. Colby. "Thank you for waiting, Mr. Colby. Please sign your name, and when the music starts, you will be first in line."

"I look forward to it," he said as he signed the card and handed it to Amalie. And with a click of his heels, he was gone.

"I'm sorry," Helene said, "I forgot all about the dance card. It looks like yours will fill rather quickly."

"May I ask why you used the surname Bennet?" Amalie asked in a low voice.

"I didn't want to use Gilchrist because then everyone would know you were born in the Abbey without a family name," Helene replied.

Amalie decided that this was not the time to debate the subject but would insist on using her real name in the future. *Besides, my mother was married when I was born, and Bennett's name implies that I am illegitimate.*

"May I escort you around the room to make some introductions?" Oliver asked.

"Please," Amalie answered quickly.

The Captain held out his arm, and Amalie put her hand through it and followed him toward the guests.

"She means well," he whispered.

"I know."

Captain Oliver led Amalie through the crowd and introduced her to many guests. There were Lords and Ladies and scores of wealthy Brighton business owners. Amalie smiled and was as gracious as possible despite hating every minute of it. Several more men signed her dance card, which caused Amalie to ask, "How many do I have to dance with before I can say no?"

Oliver looked over his shoulder and took the dance card. He signed several fake names until the card was complete. When Amalie realized what he was doing, she smiled warmly.

Helene appeared and took Amalie by the hand. "I will formally introduce you as the new Lady of Corrington House so that the music can begin. Helene led her to the ballroom center to present her to the guests. They stood under an enormous crystal chandelier.

As Gerald rang a bell to get everyone's attention, Amalie and Helene stood at the center of the room on a small platform placed there just for the announcement. When the room quieted down, Helene spoke.

"The Duke and I welcome you to Corrington House for this grand special occasion. I have recently discovered a distant cousin in my family, and after months of searching, I found her. I would like to present to you the newest Lady of Corrington House, Miss Amalie Bennett." There was polite but ongoing applause.

Duchess Helene stepped down and stood next to her son, Captain Oliver, behind Amalie.

Captain Oliver was distracted when some movement caught his eye. He looked up to see the chandelier moving as it swayed a bit back and forth. His eyes followed the heavy rope that held the chandelier, which the staff used to lower it to be cleaned and to light the candles. He saw the rope sagging and immediately recognized the danger and sprang forward to rush Amalie off the platform as the chandelier came crashing down violently in the spot where Amalie had stood. The loud crash of hundreds of glass prisms crashing startled everyone in the room, and there were audible gasps and screams.

Captain Oliver still had Amalie firmly in his arms when he felt her knees buckle, and she began to wobble. He guided her over to the window seat and gently sat her down. He opened the window to give her some air. The incident left Amalie severely shaken, and her hands were trembling.

Gerald began escorting the guests out of the ballroom while the Duke and Duchess ran to Amalie.

"Is she alright?" Helene asked her son. "That was too close."

Amalie stared straight ahead. Her breathing was quick.

"What could have caused that chandelier to fall like that?" the Duke demanded. "I will have someone's head for this."

"Father, I saw it happen. The chandelier moved before it fell as if someone was loosening the rope. The rope station is behind the draperies, and there is no way to know who was doing it, but I fear it was intentional," Oliver said.

"My God, who would want to hurt Amalie?" Helene said, but then as if she recalled something, looked at her husband and said, "We need to investigate this."

"I assure you that I will," he replied, then walked off to speak with his household staff.

"Amalie, are you alright, dear?" Helene asked.

Amalie nodded but said nothing. Helene could see that her hands were shaking. "Oliver, please take Amalie to the parlor. I will have Margot bring her some tea."

"No, I just want to go to my room," Amalie said.

"I'll take her upstairs," Oliver said as he helped Amalie to her feet.

Oliver held on to Amalie's arm in case her knees buckled again as he escorted her to her room. As they entered her room, he sat her down on the bed when Hannah ran in.

"Hannah, please stay with Amalie for the night. The accident has deeply upset her."

"Of course, Sir. Shall I fetch some brandy to calm her nerves?" Hannah offered.

"That would be good," he replied as Hannah left to get the brandy. "Are you sure you're alright? I hate leaving you like this."

"Yes. Thank you for saving me. It just hit me how close I came to...."

"Don't think about that. We will get to the bottom of what happened. I promise you."

Amalie nodded. "Your mother must be crushed that the ball is ruined."

"My mother's only concern was for your well-being. My father as well. Seeing how close you came to extreme danger made him very angry. Trust me. He will find out what happened—as will I."

"Thank you. I will be fine. You don't need to stay," Amalie said, but her trembling voice gave her away.

"But I want to stay," he said without thinking. "I'm very concerned for you." Their eyes met, and she felt some comfort from his sincerity.

Just then, Hannah returned with a tumbler of brandy. "Here, drink this, Miss. It will help calm you."

"Now that you are in good hands, I will leave you," Oliver said. "Please get some rest. Hannah will take good care of you."

Amalie lifted the tumbler and took a long sip of the brandy. It felt warm going through her body.

Oliver rushed back downstairs and joined his parents, who were still in the ballroom questioning staff members.

"How is she?" Helene asked.

"Very shaken. Who would want to hurt Amalie? This was no accident," Oliver replied.

"You are correct, son," the Duke said, "I've questioned the staff, and no one saw anything. However, Gerald determined that the rope was not worn or frayed and said someone cut it."

"There were so many people in the room, and no one saw anything?" Oliver said, shaking his head. "This is very troubling. I fear we need to add security for Amalie. Someone did this deliberately, and I cannot fathom why."

"Yes, I agree," said the Duke. "Someone wants to hurt her, or worse, kill her."

"I will head up her security detail. I am the logical choice. The staff is not equipped to protect her, and junior ranking officers are not allowed to carry weapons outside of active duty," Oliver said, volunteering to protect Amalie.

The Duke agreed. "Yes, I will put you in charge. In the meantime, we must keep our eyes and ears open. We may have a traitor in our household, and we need to be on keen alert at all times."

As household staff swept the shattered crystals and melted candle wax from the floor, Helene was pacing and wrapped her arms around herself. She was anxious, realizing that someone deliberately tried to hurt Amalie.

"Mother, are you alright? You seem shaken as well. Perhaps a brandy to calm you?" Oliver suggested.

"No, I'm fine," she lied. "I am fearful for Amalie, that's all. That sweet child must be wondering what kind of hell she's landed in. We must find who did this, or I won't have a moment of peace."

"Amalie was worried you would be upset about how the ball turned out," Oliver shared.

"Oh, heavens no, that isn't important right now. Knowing that someone wants to hurt her is all-consuming right now," Helene replied.

After resting for a while and being unable to sleep, Amalie climbed out of bed. She was having a delayed reaction to what happened at the ball. She was restless and needed some fresh air. Amalie slipped on her robe and stepped out onto the large balcony wrapped around the second floor. She breathed in the cool night air and sat down on the stone bench to clear her head. Her hands began to shake every time she realized how close she came to disaster.

"May I join you?" It was a familiar voice.

"Yes, of course. What are you doing up so late, Oliver?"

"I couldn't sleep. I was concerned about you. Are you alright? That was too close for comfort." Oliver said as he sat down beside her. He thought she looked beautiful with her hair down falling loose around her face.

Amalie couldn't hold back her tears. "Why would someone want to hurt me? I have no enemies. I've harmed no one. I heard you say it was deliberate. How could that be?"

Her tears moved Oliver to be unexpectedly emotional. "Please don't cry. It hurts me to see you so distressed. My father assigned me to your security detail. Please believe me when I say I would lay down my life to protect you."

"That is very reassuring, but the problem is—why do I need to be protected? Who wants to hurt me? And why? I have no clue why this happened tonight," Amalie sobbed.

Oliver reached into his robe pocket, pulled out his handkerchief, and handed it to Amalie.

"Thank you," she said, blotting her tears. "You always seem to be rescuing me one way or another."

"My parents are very concerned about you. My father has vowed to find out who did this, and my mother seemed very shaken as well. Nothing like this has ever happened in our family. If there is a traitor in our midst, my father will find him."

"But there were so many people in the ballroom. How would you ever know who did it? It could have been anyone," Amalie sniffled.

"I would have a hard time believing it was one of our staff. Each of them has been with us for years, and we trust them. I have to think it was someone from outside, and I'm not sure how to protect you from an unknown enemy."

"I miss the Abbey so much right now. I always felt safe there, and Mother Superior was always comforting. I would give anything to go back there, at least for a visit. It was my home, and I miss my home."

Oliver understood her pain and tried to comfort her. "I know you don't think of this as home yet, but I sincerely hope that you will soon. We all care deeply about you and want you to feel safe here too."

"Please forgive me if I sound ungrateful. I truly am not," Amalie said, "I'm just a bit homesick for the Abbey—if that makes any sense for someone to miss an orphanage."

"Oh, I know that, Amalie. Your entire life has been turned upside down since you left the Abbey. I wish I could ease your pain and calm your fears. Just know that I am here for you. You are not alone," Oliver said sincerely.

Amalie looked into his eyes filled with warmth and affection, which moved her deeply. She felt the same way about him—he was her only friend, and she was becoming drawn to him in ways she couldn't resist. Their eyes locked together for several moments when Oliver gave in to his impulse and leaned in to kiss her, but at the last moment, before he touched her lips, he pulled back.

"Forgive me," he said, looking away. "I apologize."

"There is no need to apologize," Amalie said honestly, "I should also apologize to you because I wanted you to kiss me. However, I am fully aware that we cannot allow that to happen. You are betrothed to another."

"Yes, though she will never have my heart," Oliver said, looking into Amalie's eyes.

"The heart can be a strong master," Amalie said, repeating something she read in one of her favorite books.

"Yes, I'm beginning to understand that," he said softly. Then he stood to leave before he could no longer fight his desire. "I am always here if you need me. I bid you goodnight."

"Goodnight, my friend. Sleep well," she said sincerely. Amalie watched him walk back to his room, feeling conflicted. She felt such a connection to Oliver and was drawn to him in ways she didn't understand, yet she knew it could never be.

Chapter 3
History Lesson

Amalie was on edge for several days after her near-death experience. She forced herself to focus on happier things, like her work at St. Paul's and teaching Anthony to play the piano. The Duke seemed kinder, and Helene hovered like a mother hen.

One afternoon, a letter arrived for Amalie from the Abbey. Sister Evangeline wrote the letter to report that Mother Superior was gravely ill. She suggested that Amalie might want to visit before it's too late. Amalie shared the letter with the Duke and Duchess, along with Captain Oliver, privately in the parlor.

"I would like to see her before she passes," Amalie said sadly, "She is very dear to me."

"Is it wise to travel while we still have not found who sabotaged the chandelier?" the Duke said out of concern.

"I would feel horrible if she died before I had a chance to visit her," Amalie continued.

"I completely understand, dear," Helene said, "However, we need to make sure it would be safe for you."

"That is why I asked you to meet me in here away from staff who might overhear us," Amalie said. "No one needs to know but the four of us."

"I would accompany her for protection," Oliver said. "I will take an extra coachman with us for extra eyes during the journey. I will also carry an extra pistol."

"Well, I think it would be alright," the Duke said reluctantly. "I don't want to deny Amalie the chance to say goodbye."

"Thank you from the bottom of my heart," Amalie said to the Duke. "When could we leave?"

"Tomorrow morning before dawn would be my preference," Oliver said. "We would be at the Abbey before midday."

"I will be ready," Amalie assured him. "Thank you."

In the dark hours just before dawn, when the sun was just a glow on the horizon, Amalie and Oliver departed on the journey to the Abbey. Oliver insisted on using their best-closed carriage as it had more metal in the frame and would be sturdier if attacked.

Amalie was somber during the ride, and Oliver tried to reassure her. "Please know that you are safe with me," he said, breaking the silence.

"I have every confidence in you," she assured him. "I'm sad to think that she might die before I get there. That would break my heart."

"About the other night...." he began nervously, but Amalie cut him off.

"Please, we need never mention it again. I understand your position all too well. It was just a sweet moment of caring between close friends. Nothing more, right?" Amalie said, trying to sound convincing.

"I think we both know it was more than that, and I want to promise you that I will control myself better in the future. I care too much for you to begin something I cannot finish," Oliver explained.

"I understand."

"Do you? I mean, do you truly know how much you have taken my mind hostage? From the day you arrived, I have not been myself. Thoughts of you fill my mind, day and night, and I have always had enough discipline to control myself, but with you—I seem to be struggling," he confessed.

Amalie listened intently. She also struggled with her feelings for him and had to acknowledge that there was something unspoken between them that she did not understand.

"I have similar feelings too, and I promise you in return that I will not do anything to entice you in any way. I've never had a male friend, and I thought it was just friendship, but when that chandelier crashed, I wanted only to seek comfort in your arms. Perhaps it is my fault that you are struggling."

"No, not at all," he said quickly. "You've done nothing other than being honest and sincere, not to mention beautiful, and I've never met anyone like you. You are perfect the way you are. It is I who should have more self-control. My military training taught me to always be in control of my emotions, but I'm finding that very difficult with you."

"I would say I'm sorry, but it flatters me that you feel the same way I do."

"You see," he smiled warmly, "That honesty is utterly refreshing. My father would disagree, but I cherish it."

"Perhaps a change of topic might be in order?"

"Yes, please," Oliver replied reluctantly.

"I read my mother's journal, and it left me with more questions than answers. She wrote about my father but never mentioned him by name, other than he was of noble birth. She wrote that they would be married by the vicar in Brighton, but she didn't write anything after that other than going to the Abbey to have their child—me—because it was safer there. There were no entries after that," Amalie said, shuffling the braided cords that tied the dark red cape Annabelle gave her.

"That sounds very mysterious. I wonder why it wasn't safe for them. Do you think his family somehow threatened them if they disapproved of the marriage?" Oliver guessed.

"Would his family do that to his wife and child?" Amalie asked in disbelief.

"I wish I could say no, but royalty over the years has done some horrific things in the name of family honor. Nothing would surprise me," Oliver said, shaking his head.

"I was going to ask Sister Monica to help me find their marriage record. If they were married by the vicar, there should be a record of it, right?"

"Yes, but there are two churches in Brighton that house records. St. Paul's is one, and the other is The Holy Trinity, located on the other side of town. One of those should have the record," Oliver said.

"When we return from our trip, I will visit both churches. I am determined to find out who my father was."

Oliver couldn't help but smile. He loved her determination as much as her honesty. "I would be happy to help you in any way I can."

"There's more mystery in the journal. Pages are missing. Near the end, there is a slight gap, and it looks like several pages were intricately cut out. There are no rough edges like someone ripped them out—someone did it deliberately with a knife."

"Hmm, that is mysterious. I would assume there was something in the journal that someone never wanted to be shared. But why not destroy the entire journal. Why leave some information but remove only one section?" Oliver wondered.

"I thought of that, and that is why I think my mother removed those pages herself perhaps to keep their secret, but either way, those missing pages hold the key to the puzzle, and I have no clue where they could be."

"Perhaps the woman who gave the box to my mother might know? Or someone at the Bennington Estate where your mother lived and worked?" Oliver suggested. "If you like, we could travel there and inquire about your mother."

"You would do that for me?"

"You should know by now that I would do anything for you," Oliver said sincerely.

Amalie felt compelled to change the subject and reached into the bag she packed for the trip and pulled out two apples. "Breakfast?"

"Yes, and thank you for saving me from myself."

The carriage arrived at the Abbey by midday, and Ivan, the groundskeeper, greeted them. "Miss Amalie, how nice to see you again," he said, setting his rake aside. "They have been expecting you."

"Is Mother Superior still....?"

"Yes, but she is not long for this earth. She's had some kind of apoplexy and is not able to speak. She fades in and out," Ivan said, wiping his hands on his apron.

"Please take me to her," Amalie said eagerly.

Oliver and Amalie followed Ivan down the long, familiar hallways to Mother Superior's room. In the hallway, they ran into Sister Evangeline.

"Oh, praise the Lord, you have come!" Sister Evangeline bellowed, "Mother asks for you every day. Please know she is very confused and has difficulty speaking, but I can clarify what she wants to say. Several of us believe she is only holding on until you got here. She was inconsolable after you left."

"Sister, this is Captain Corrington. He has graciously escorted me so that I could come and see her," Amalie said.

"Sister," Oliver nodded to her, "Pleased to meet you."

"Thank you for bringing our Amalie back to us, Captain Corrington. This will mean the world to Mother. Shall we go in?"

"I will leave you and go tend to the horses," Oliver said. "Take all the time you need, and I will be waiting when you are done."

"Thank you," Amalie said and took a deep breath to prepare for a painful reunion.

Amalie followed Sister Evangeline into the room and went straight to Mother Superior's bedside. She was taken back at how pale Mother looked as she lay sleeping, her mouth contorted with a droop on one side. Sister

Evangeline lovingly took the cloth from the nightstand and dabbed away the drool.

Amalie sat down on the side of the bed and reached for Mother's hand. "I'm here," she said softly. "I've come to see you. Can you hear me?"

Mother opened her eyes and focused on her visitor. When she recognized Amalie, she squeezed her hand. She tried to speak but could only utter faint sounds.

"It's alright. You don't need to speak if it's difficult," Amalie said, gently stroking Mother's hand.

Mother seemed to have a burst of strength and pushed herself to speak. "I'm sorry," she stammered, barely audible. "Forgive me."

"Shh," Amalie soothed her. "There is nothing to forgive."

Mother shook her head. "No....I knew—no right—birthright...."

Amalie looked at Sister Evangeline for help to encipher what Mother was saying.

"She's confused. She doesn't make sense most of the time, but I dare say, seeing you has made her more animated than she's been since she fell ill," Sister Evangeline marveled.

Mother shook her head again to disagree with what was just said. "Amalie....society....father...."

"Mother, are you saying father, as in my father?" Amalie asked gently.

Mother nodded, closed her eyes, and took a deep breath before she could speak again. "He....protect you....society...."

Amalie could not make sense of the words. "Do you know who my father was? I'm not sure what you're saying."

Suddenly, Mother Superior's eyes rolled back, and she fell asleep. Sister Evangeline checked to see if she was still breathing.

"She's faded out again, but she's still with us. We need to let her rest now. Can I make you some tea while she rests? After some rest, you can come and see her again before you have to leave."

"That would be wonderful, thank you," Amalie said as they left the room.

Amalie went to the meeting room while Sister Evangeline went for tea. Within minutes, Oliver joined her.

"How did it go?" he asked as he sat down at the table to join her. "I met the sister in the hallway, and she pointed me to this room."

"Mother is confused. I couldn't make sense of what she was trying to tell me. It breaks my heart to see her like this."

"I'm sorry. I know this must be painful," Oliver sympathized.

"When I go back in, I'm just going to tell her how much I love her. I want her to know that before she passes. That is the reason I came, and to say goodbye. I am disturbed, however, that she mentioned my father. It didn't make sense, but I think she knows who my father is."

"Really? What did she say?" Oliver asked.

"Just gibberish, really, but she seemed to want me to know something about him. Perhaps she has regrets for not telling me who he is? But why would she keep that a secret and then let me leave with your mother if she knew who my father was? As I said, it didn't make sense."

"Perhaps she was talking about the Holy Father? She is a nun," Oliver offered up.

"You know, that could be it," Amalie said in a moment of realization. "She was trying to tell me that the Holy Father was protecting me. That makes more sense than anything else."

Just then, Sister Evangeline brought in a tray of tea and biscuits and began to pour the tea. "I'm so glad you were able to come before she passes," the sister said as she offered them biscuits. "The physician said yesterday that he is surprised she's hung on this long."

"Could you make any sense out of what she was trying to tell me?" Amalie asked, sipping the hot tea.

"No, I'm sorry. Mother has often mentioned you since she fell ill, but we can't quite understand what it means. She does seem very anxious to tell us, but her speech is challenging to understand, as you just saw."

"Do you think she might be referring to the Holy Father?" Oliver asked.

"Very well could be, but there is no way to know for sure," the sister replied, "She hasn't made sense since she fell ill. If you will excuse me, I am going back to check on Mother. I will come for you after the physician leaves. He arrived just after we left the room."

Amalie turned to Oliver, "Please come with me when it's time to see her again. I just want to know if you hear more than I can."

"Of course, I'd be happy to."

After half an hour, Sister Evangeline returned and said Mother was awake but that the physician was still there. Her breathing had changed, and he felt the end was near. He summoned the priest to administer the last rites.

Amalie's heart sank as they rushed back to Mother Superior's room. As they entered, the physician had just finished his examination. He shook his head as a silent signal that there was nothing more he could do.

Amalie rushed to Mother's side and touched her hand. "I'm here, Mother," she said, her voice breaking.

Mother Superior's eyes met Amalie's, and in a surprising moment of clarity, Mother said, "Gift," and opened her hand to reveal her rosary. "You….gift."

"She wants you to have her rosary," Sister Evangeline said. "She said that yesterday too."

Tears filled Amalie's eyes as she took the rosary from the only mother she had ever known. "I will treasure it always, just as I have treasured you. I love you dearly. I pray for your peace as you leave us. You always told me not to fear death, that it is only painful for those left behind. Now I know what you meant. I will miss you always."

The Abbey priest, Father Sebastian, came in and administered the last rites. Mother Superior squeezed Amalie's hand, and Amalie reached up and touched her cheek. "Go in peace, beautiful angel," she whispered through her tears.

Mother Superior's face suddenly relaxed and had an angelic glow. She took one last deep breath, and she was gone.

Amalie began to sob at the bedside. She lifted Mother's hand and kissed it one last time.

"Praise God for her peace," Sister Evangeline said, wiping away her tears.

"I'm so glad I was here to say goodbye," Amalie sobbed. "She was present when I entered the world and was there with me ever since. I feel blessed to have been here when she left this world. It will never be the same without her."

Oliver's heart was breaking for Amalie. He never fully understood the bond between Amalie and Mother Superior, but now he did. They loved each other like mother and daughter.

Amalie slowly rose from the bed and clutched the rosary to her heart. "I will cherish this last gift from her."

Oliver took her arm and led her out of the room. "We should head back now. It will be near midnight when we get home."

Amalie couldn't speak. She nodded in agreement.

Amalie sat in silence, still clutching the rosary, as the carriage headed home. Losing Mother Superior broke her heart. Oliver decided not to try and make small talk and just let her have quiet time. After what seemed like hours, Amalie finally spoke.

"Thank you for bringing me to say goodbye. It meant the world to me to be there in her final moments."

"I was glad to do it. I can see how much she meant to you."

"Yes, she meant….." and suddenly Amalie broke down and cried. She covered her face with her hands and sobbed.

Oliver couldn't stand it and climbed over to the other side of the carriage to sit next to Amalie. He put his arm around her and let her cry on his shoulder. He wanted to comfort her, but the right words failed him, so he let her cry in his arms. He reached into his jacket pocket, pulled out his handkerchief, and handed it to her.

Amalie took the handkerchief and blew her nose. "Once again, you come to my rescue. I'm sorry, I just can't stop crying."

"You've suffered a great loss. Lean on me; it's alright," Oliver said softly.

Amalie cried until she had no tears left. Then she sat in silence, still in his arms, and realized that she found comfort there. She didn't want to move. "When you're with me, I feel less alone. I have come to depend on you, and I fear it might be too much," she confessed, "But I can't help myself. You comfort me the way no one ever has before. And you put my mind at ease when I am over-worrying about everything. Just talking to you makes me feel better."

Oliver pulled her closer. "I feel the same way, Amalie. You bring me comfort when life weighs me down. You have moved my heart in ways that I never thought possible."

Amalie looked up at him, and his loving eyes melted her heart. "Me too," she sighed, "I am feeling things I don't understand, but I do know that when you're not with me, I count the minutes until I see you again. I know it's wrong to feel this way, but I cannot control it. It controls me."

Oliver looked deep into her eyes and lost himself in them. He leaned forward, and his lips gently touched hers. She wrapped her arms around him and welcomed his kiss. Then he pressed his lips over hers and kissed her with all the pent-up passion he had withheld every time he was near her.

When their lips parted, Amalie stayed in his arms with her eyes still closed. "Let me feel this moment. My first kiss, and I am so happy it was with you."

"I promise you, my sweet Amalie, it will not be the last kiss I give you," and with that, he pressed his lips over hers and kissed her again. She kissed him passionately as she wrapped her arm around his neck, holding him captive in her arms. Suddenly, she began to feel stirrings in her body and felt heated.

Oliver realized that if he didn't pull back that very moment, he would not be able to stop, so he gently pulled himself away. Amalie had the same realization and sat straight up, catching her breath.

"Forgive me for taking advantage of your vulnerability just now," he said softly, "I cannot resist you, but somehow, I must learn to."

"This is so unfair to you and me that you must marry someone you don't love for some old peace treaty," Amalie protested. "What would happen if you didn't marry her?"

"It would be seen as an insult to the Herzstein Territory and could cause war between the two nations," Oliver replied, trying to compose himself.

"What? In earnest?"

"Yes."

"Forgive me, but that's absurd. A war over an arranged marriage? In these modern times we live in," Amalie said, straightening her jacket, composing herself.

"Amalie, do you know anything about the Peace Treaty? Or how it came to be?"

"No, I studied history but never learned about these territories because they no longer belong to the United Kingdom," she replied.

"Well, let us take our minds off things, and I will tell you why my life is not my own. Then you might understand how serious this could be."

As Amalie opened the wrapped food that the sisters packed for their journey, Oliver explained how it all began. Four hundred years ago, King Henry VI ruled over the United Kingdom, including the two territories known as Corrington and Herzstein. Before being overtaken by the British, Corrington belonged to the Austrian Empire, and Herzstein belonged to Prussia. King Henry VI was not a great ruler. He hated governing and often refused to do it. However, when war broke out between the two territories, King Henry decided that he no longer wanted the territories in his kingdom because the long-lasting war reflected poorly on his leadership.

"What caused the war?" Amalie asked, handing Oliver some food.

Oliver recounted the tale of Ronan and Maria. Ronan was from Corrington and Maria was from Herzstein. Ronan was royalty, and Maria was a commoner. Their love was forbidden. Rather than live without each other, they jumped to their deaths together off the cliffs north of Brighton. Each territory blamed the other for their deaths, and a war broke out which lasted almost two years. Countless lives were lost, and villages burned.

"Oh, how sad," Amalie said, biting into her bread and cheese.

Oliver continued. King Henry was disgusted and angry about the never-ending war, so he decided to rid himself of the ruling responsibility by Decree. The king hated "the dueling Dukes," so he surrendered both territories and forced them into self-rule by Royal Decree. Part II of the Decree stated that a Peace Treaty was in effect, and both sides must abide by the Decree. To maintain unity between the nations, every hundred years, the firstborn of each house must marry to uphold the peaceful union and honor Ronan and Maria. Every hundred years, there shall be a festival to honor Ronan & Maria called the Festival of Lovers and name the next couple to be married. If the firstborn is not the proper sex, the Duke will choose the nearest relative or the second born. Part III of the Decree created *The Society*, an ultra-secret group created solely to enforce the Peace Treaty and eliminate any person who would violate the Royal Decree.

"So, you see, it could be disastrous if I refused to marry Davina," Oliver lamented.

Amalie thought for a moment and then asked, "But if King Henry VI surrendered the territories and forced them into self-rule, how could he still enforce his Decree? He relinquished his domain over them."

"It's written into our laws. It has been this way for four hundred years. We have lived in peace all this time, and there has been no conflict between our nations. It is my duty as firstborn to honor the treaty."

Amalie studied the anguish in Oliver's face and realized how tormented he was. "I'm so sorry. I will stop questioning the treaty, even though I find it quite barbaric. I understand your duty, and I respect your dedication to it. You are an honorable man, Captain Oliver."

"I doubt that," he said, looking deep into her eyes. "If I were truly honorable, I would resist kissing you, and I would stop myself from feeling what I'm feeling for you."

Amalie felt ashamed of herself. "I am equally to blame, and for that, I apologize. I just realized how difficult I am making this for you. I have not discouraged you, and from now on, I will do just that—now that I understand the dire consequences you would face."

"I wish I could argue against that, but in good conscience, I cannot. We must not allow our feelings to carry us away."

"Agreed," Amalie said sadly. Then she reached into her pocket and pulled out Mother Superior's rosary. "I will pray for you, Oliver. I will pray for both of us to find new strength."

"Thank you," he said woefully. "May I ask you a personal question?"

"Of course."

"You grew up in an Abbey. Why did you not become a nun?"

"I never had the calling. Yes, I have faith, but I never felt called to that life. Besides, I love children and hope to have them someday," Amalie shared freely.

"Yes, of course. I've seen you around children. You will make a wonderful mother one day."

"Thank you," she said, looking away to keep from revealing her feelings. She closed her eyes and leaned her head back as if to rest, but her inner turmoil made that impossible.

Amalie processed everything she learned about the Peace Treaty and how Oliver could be in danger if he defied it. Then it hit her.

"Wait—did you say the King created *The Society* to enforce it?" she asked quickly.

"Yes, why?"

"Something Mother Superior said to me. I'm sure I heard her say the word society when she mentioned the word father. She said it twice. Could it be possible that my father was in danger from *The Society* for marrying my mother? He was nobility, and she was a commoner. Could they somehow have violated the treaty?"

Oliver thought for a moment. "That would explain why it was not safe for them to have their child at home. You may be on to something."

A cold chill ran through Amalie. "I think I may be in danger too. The chandelier was no accident."

Oliver's mind was racing. "Amalie, that means that someone out there knows who you are and who your father is. But why target you? How could you possibly be a threat to the peace treaty? I will discuss this with my father, and we will convene our security council to see if we can't find some answers."

"Oh, Oliver, I'm frightened. That is why Mother Superior was so adamant about telling me. She knew something but could no longer convey it to me. Now, that secret has died with her."

Oliver took her hand in his. "I won't let anything happen to you. We will figure this out."

Amalie looked into his eyes. "Do you realize that we are like Ronan and Maria? We are forbidden too."

"That makes me sad, but yes, you are my Maria, and I am your Ronan."

"That makes me sad too," Amalie said, pulling her hand away.

Oliver and Amalie were silent on the remainder of the journey home. Their hearts were heavy trying to imagine how they could suppress their feelings for each other. Their minds were also in turmoil considering the information they learned at the Abbey.

Oliver could not fathom how he would ever remove Amalie from his heart, and he was more concerned than ever for her safety.

Amalie felt utterly conflicted, knowing that she would have to find a way to distance herself from Oliver while knowing in her heart that all she wanted was to be near him. Her life could be in danger, and the only person she trusted was Oliver. Added to that was her guilt that she was the reason for his torment.

Chapter 4

Julian

Amalie kept to herself following the death of Mother Superior and needed the time to sort out her feelings. She also wanted to give Oliver room to do the same. She also needed to grieve the loss of someone she loved.

After the trip, Oliver spoke to his father and brought him up to date on what they learned. The Duke convened his security council and held a secret meeting at the Corrington Building. Oliver was astonished that no one on the council had any idea who made up *The Society,* let alone who they could contact for information. Their understanding of that group was that the monarchy was still in control. Still, when Oliver argued that the territories had been under self-rule for 400 years, someone should know who was responsible for enforcing the peace treaty. His father agreed. The Duke appointed his most trusted council member to investigate the matter. Oliver also pleaded for more security for Amalie and a thorough investigation into the chandelier incident. The Duke appointed two council members to investigate who might have committed the crime and increase security around the estate. All household staff would be subject to additional scrutiny until they found the perpetrator.

After the meeting concluded, Oliver and his father remained in the conference room to talk privately.

"I'm very concerned about Amalie," Oliver told his father. "If *The Society* is somehow involved, they will not stop until their target is dead. I learned that in Military School from General Osborne. I was thinking of contacting him to see if he had any idea who heads up that group."

"I will inquire. It should come from my official office. Your mother and I are concerned also. In many generations, we have never had anything like that happen.

To think that we may have a member of *The Society* in our home leaves us all vulnerable, not just Amalie. Why on earth would someone think that this young woman is a threat to the peace treaty? Then again, we do not know if it was *The Society* and not some insane person with a grudge against our family. As for Amalie's father, if she could find any record of the marriage, that will give us a place to start looking."

"I will take her to both churches to begin the search, although perhaps you should assign someone else to her security," Oliver said reluctantly.

"Why, son?"

Oliver hesitated but told his father the truth. "I have feelings for her, and I'm finding it difficult to fight them."

"I see," said the Duke. "Does she know this?"

"No," Oliver lied to protect Amalie.

"Well, that places you in a complicated situation. There is no future for the two of you, and you must accept that."

"Yes, I am trying. I understand fully what my duty is," Oliver assured his father.

"Then there should be no further conflict. Be professional in your duty as Captain and nothing more. Right now, you are the only one I trust with her safety. You must let this go; do you understand?" the Duke said forcefully.

"Yes, sir."

The following day, Oliver escorted Amalie to St. Paul's for her work with the children. On the way, he asked her to search for the marriage record. "It's the only way we will ever know the truth and if *The Society* is after you."

"Yes, I planned to ask Sister Monica for help today," Amalie said. "But if they were married by the vicar, wouldn't that be the other church since St. Paul's has a priest?"

"It's possible, but we need to check both churches anyway to be sure."

"I will see what I can find out," Amalie said, stepping out of the carriage without looking back at him.

"I will pick you up after I finish things at my office," Oliver said, watching her walk into the church. He could see she was trying to avoid close contact, and he hated this new distance between them.

Amalie finished her session with the children and then asked Sister Monica about the records. She explained why she needed them. "Being born at the Abbey, I know nothing of my parents other than what I learned from my mother's journal, which we found recently. I only know my mother's name, which was Juliet Bennett, but she never mentioned my father by name."

"I would be happy to help you find the record," Sister Monica said sincerely. "I will need a date or at least the year to narrow down the search."

"It would be twenty-one or twenty-two years ago. I have no exact date."

"Let's go down to the archives, and I will pull the ledgers from those years. You may take all the time you need to search through them," Sister Monica said, leading the way down the hall.

Sister Monica led Amalie into a room in the rectory where the ledgers were stored. She searched for 1844 and 1845 and pulled the heavy, leather-bound registers from the shelf.

Amalie sat down at the table while Sister Monica lit the lantern. "If the marriage took place in our parish, the record would be in here," the sister said, placing both ledgers on the table in front of Amalie. "Take all the time you need."

Amalie began to comb through the columns to find her mother's name. She lost track of time when Oliver appeared in the doorway.

"Have you found anything?" he asked as he sat down next to her. "The sister told me you were in here."

Amalie tried to hide how happy she was to see him. "No, not yet. I am almost through 1844."

"Can I help?" he offered.

"Please! You can begin to search 1845."

Oliver opened the ledger and began to search the columns for Juliet Bennett. After two hours, Amalie and Oliver had finished both books with no success.

"They must've been married at The Holy Trinity," Amalie concluded. "There's nothing here. I found one surname Bennett, but it was Alfonse at fifty years of age."

"We will go to the other church on Thursday after you finish with the children," Oliver said, placing the ledgers back on the shelf.

Amalie and Oliver left the church when Sister Monica ran after them on the sidewalk, calling out. "I'm so glad I caught you before you left. I spoke to the Priest about your search, and he reminded me that several years ago, during your time frame, some marriages were performed by the Vicar of Brighton in the courthouse after the Holy Trinity burned down. It took months to rebuild the church, so you may want to check the courthouse records also."

"Thank you, Sister Monica," Amalie smiled at her. "You have been most helpful."

After Sister Monica left, Amalie turned to Oliver. "Is the courthouse far?"

"Two blocks from here, right next to the Corrington Building. And yes, we can go there now," Oliver said, seeing how eager she was.

They walked down the street toward the courthouse when Amalie said, "It has occurred to me that if we don't find the record, that perhaps they never married. What will happen if I find that out?"

"What do you mean?" Oliver asked.

"It will mean that I am illegitimate and could bring shame to your family," Amalie said, unable to look at him.

"That will never happen. It would be our secret, and my mother would never let anyone find out," he assured her.

"Her journal said they would be married, but she never wrote that they were married. If only I could find those missing pages, it would fill in all the blanks."

Just then, a young man in top hat and suit approached them and stopped to chat. Amalie recognized him from the ball but could not remember his name.

"Captain Corrington, Miss Amalie," he said, tipping his hat to reveal his curly blonde hair. "I hope you remember me from the ball. I'm Julian Cartwright, and I signed your dance card. However, I never had the pleasure."

"Oh yes, I remember you now. It's nice to see you again," Amalie said politely.

"How fortunate to run into you here," he went on, "I was going to travel to the estate and ask the Duke for permission to call on you, but here you are. Would you do me the honor of escorting me to the Harvest Ball on Friday evening?"

"I'm very flattered, sir, but may I ask, what is the Harvest Ball?" Amalie asked, surprised.

"Oh, that's right, you are not from here. It's an annual ball held at the Winston Estate to celebrate the harvest. It's a grand tradition, and I would be honored if you would go with me."

Julian's request put Amalie on the spot, but then she thought she should go with this handsome young man and maybe forget who she would rather have on her arm at the ball. "I would be happy to accompany you to the ball."

"My family will also be attending," Oliver interjected. "We can bring Amalie with us."

"Splendid!" Julian said, tipping his hat to Amalie. "I look forward to Friday evening and the pleasure of your company."

After Julian left them, Oliver and Amalie kept walking in silence until Amalie broke the silence and asked, "Do you know Julian at all? Is he noble like you?"

"I don't know him well. His family is very wealthy, but I don't know what he does professionally. His mother is a friend of my mother's. You should ask her about the family." Oliver knew he wasn't hiding his displeasure about the date.

Amalie wondered if she should broach the subject with Oliver but decided not to say anything. What was there left to say? They both had to move on and let go of what was between them.

When they arrived at the courthouse, Oliver inquired about the records of marriages after the church burned down. A clerk sent them to room D.

Once there, another clerk gave them a ledger that covered all the marriages during the eleven months it took to rebuild the church. Oliver and Amalie combed each line looking for Juliet Bennett but found nothing.

"I'm getting very discouraged," Amalie sighed. "And if we don't find anything at the Holy Trinity next week, then I will know that my parents were not married."

"No, all that does is prove they didn't get married here. They ran away together. Maybe they ended up getting married somewhere else. Don't give up. Not yet. I won't stop looking until I find that information. I need to know if *The Society* was involved with your father—and now possibly you."

"I won't give up, but I'm beginning to think that this marriage was the best-kept secret of the century. Someone didn't want the information made public. I know it's in the missing pages of the journal," Amalie said, disappointed.

"Let's go home and put this to rest for today," Oliver said, handing the ledger back to the clerk.

At dinner that evening, Oliver broached the subject of Julian. He told his family that they met Julian on the street, and he asked if Amalie would go to the Harvest Ball with him and that Amalie accepted.

The Duke looked at his son but immediately looked away. He was the only one at the table who knew how much that must have upset Oliver.

"Wonderful!" Helene gushed. "He is from a wonderful family. I have known his mother for years. He is handsome, don't you think, Amalie?"

"Yes, he is. I met him here at the ball but never got to dance with him that night."

"His family made their millions in trade and shipping. I think his father owns a line of ships from here to London. They transport everything from cotton to whiskey. Julian works for his father, but I'm not sure what he does exactly. He has an office somewhere in town. I'm so happy you will be at the ball with him. He would make a nice suitor, don't you think?" Helene hinted.

Amalie just smiled. "I've just met him. Suitor is a bit premature."

"Of course, dear, but he certainly would be a good catch. He has his own house near town complete with staff. Many of Brighton's ladies would love to be mistress of that house," Helene pushed on.

Oliver began to squirm in his seat, and his father changed the subject. "I wonder if I could impose on you, Amalie, and have you play the piano for us after dinner?"

"Of course, I would love to. Any particular piece?"

"How about the Beethoven piece?" Anthony said excitedly. "We played that at my last lesson. I love that one."

"You mean Moonlight Sonata? Of course, I would love to play it for all of you. One of the sisters at the Abbey is from Vienna, and she secured the sheet music for me."

The usually quiet Michael finally joined the conversation. "I am truly enjoying hearing piano music throughout the house. I stop what I am doing and listen when you give Anthony lessons."

"Thank you," Amalie smiled. "I'm glad you enjoy it."

"I do, but I don't enjoy his plinking," Michael teased.

"Hey!" Anthony mock protested.

"Alright, boys, enough nitpicking," said the Duke.

"Well, if Anthony keeps practicing, very soon you won't be able to tell which one of us is playing. He is a quick study," Amalie said with a wink to Anthony.

"If you all will excuse me, I will retire early tonight," Oliver said, rising from the table. "I have early maneuvers at dawn."

"Of course, son," Helene said. "Sleep well."

Amalie watched Oliver leave the room, and she knew precisely why he left early. Then she saw the Duke looking at her, and he knew it too. He also realized that Amalie knew how Oliver felt about her.

Amalie tried to lighten the table talk. "Is there anything special I need to wear on Friday? I've never been to a Harvest Ball before."

"Tomorrow, first thing, we will find you a dress to wear. I want you to look ravishing on the arm of the most eligible bachelor in Brighton!" Helene said excitedly.

"The Duke and Duchess of Herzstein will be there also, along with Lady Davina," the Duke said. "It will be the perfect opportunity for Oliver and Davina to make a joint appearance before their official engagement."

"Yes, that will be wonderful," Amalie said, hoping to lay any suspicions the Duke had to rest.

After dinner, Amalie played the piano for the family. Oliver heard the music from his room and opened his door to listen to the beautiful music echoing through the halls. He was on his third tumbler of whiskey and still wasn't numb enough to calm his heart.

The ballroom at the Winston Estate was grand and decorated in a fall harvest theme. The caterer filled the food service tables along the wall with food representing the harvest—a colorful cornucopia of various vegetables and wild game from the hunt. Grapevines lined the walls, and towers of cornstalks stood in each corner of the room.

The Master of Ceremony formally announced the Corrington Family entering the ballroom. Julian immediately approached Amalie to greet her.

"There you are," Julian said, kissing her hand. "You look beautiful this evening. That shade of blue brings out your eyes."

"Thank you," Amalie said with a blush on her cheeks.

"Let me take you to meet some of the guests," Julian said, holding out his arm to her. "Your Graces, I will take good care of her this evening."

Amalie linked her arm in his, and he led her off to mingle in the crowd. Helene smiled brightly at the sight of the young couple together. Oliver had to look away.

Just then, the Duke and Duchess of Herzstein and Lady Davina greeted the Corringtons.

"There you are, my Captain," Davina said, holding out her hand to him. Oliver kissed her hand.

"Nice to see you are feeling better," Helene said to Carl Gustav. "I'm sorry you had to miss our ball, but then again, you were lucky to miss that horrible incident."

"Yes," said Carl Gustav, "I heard about that. Have you found the responsible person?"

"No," Duke Oliver replied, "But our security council is investigating. I assure you that I will get to the bottom of it."

"Why don't you young people go mingle and dance," Marta said to her daughter. "Make your first official appearance a memorable one."

"Come, darling," Davina said to Oliver, "Let's make this official. I will be the envy of every woman here tonight with the Captain by my side."

Oliver took her arm, and they headed toward the dance floor. Davina was talking, but Oliver wasn't listening. He was searching the crowd for Amalie. Then he spotted her dancing with Julian. Amalie was smiling and looked radiant in his arms. Oliver's insides were churning.

"How did that girl ever get someone like Julian Cartwright to dance with her," Davina said with a scowl.

"She is his date for the evening," Oliver responded.

"Goodness, I wonder what his family thinks of that."

"They are lucky to have her," Oliver said firmly.

"Oh, that's right, you are her defender," Davina snapped.

"Look, let's just get through this evening and play our roles for everyone, alright?" Oliver growled.

"Certainly, darling," Davina said, flashing a broad, fake smile in case anyone was watching.

On the other side of the ballroom, Amalie and Julian took a break from dancing to have a drink. They were at the refreshment table when Julian introduced her to his family.

"Mother, Father, this is Miss Amalie Bennett, the young lady I met at the Corrington Ball. Amalie, these are my parents, Harriett and Ambrose Cartwright."

"How lovely to meet you," Harriett said in a squeaky voice.

"Son, you didn't tell me she was beautiful," Ambrose said with a wink.

"It's a pleasure to meet you both," Amalie said, sipping her champagne. "Ooh, this is good. I've never had champagne before. It's delightful."

"I understand you're a distant cousin of the Duchess?" Harriet asked.

"Yes, she recently discovered our family connection through some church records," Amalie said and immediately realized that Helene told her she found the connection in church records. However, after searching through hundreds of records, Amalie wondered how that was possible since the ledgers only included the bride and groom's name, along with their witnesses. There is no mention of relatives.

"How fortunate for you, dear," Harriett said.

"I would say they are the lucky ones," Ambrose stated with his eyes fixed on Amalie.

"I would say I'm the lucky one," Julian said, putting his arm around Amalie. "I feel fortunate to have met this beautiful creature and that she is my date for the evening."

"Who are your parents, dear?" Harriett asked. "I know several Bennetts from the area."

"My parents are deceased," Amalie half lied. She was growing uncomfortable with Julian's family's assessment of her.

"Such a shame," Harriett said condescendingly.

Just then, Helene came over to them and joined the conversation. "I see you've met my newest family member," she said to the Cartwrights. "We are thrilled to have her with us."

"Yes, Your Grace, we heard about that horrible incident at your ball," Ambrose said. "So glad no one was hurt. My son told us all about it."

"Yes, a very ill-timed accident," Helene admitted, "But we have taken corrective measures to make sure nothing like that ever happens again."

"When will Captain Oliver announce his formal engagement to Lady Davina?" Harriett asked.

"We are planning to make it official at the Lover's Festival this spring, as required by law," Helene answered.

"How perfect," Harriett babbled, "Lovers announcing their engagement at the Lover's Festival. I, too, look forward to planning such an affair for my Julian."

"Mother, honestly, you are embarrassing me," Julian joked, but he was dead serious.

"He's twenty-seven and not married—a handsome man like him. Any woman here would be lucky to have him." Harriett driveled on.

"Amalie, may I have another dance?" Julian said, trying to free them both from interrogation.

"Yes, please," Amalie replied as she set her glass on the table.

When they reached the dance floor, Julian apologized for his mother. "She wants grandchildren and gets a bit overbearing."

"I understand. No need to apologize," Amalie assured him.

"I am having a wonderful time with you. I'm not very good at dancing, but you make it easy," Julian said as they twirled around the dance floor.

Amalie laughed. "I have no idea what I'm doing. I never formally learned to dance. I just follow your lead. You are a better dancer than you think."

"You are most kind," he said smiling.

Oliver was dancing with Davina, but his eyes were on Amalie. At one point, during the waltz, they nearly bumped into Julian and Amalie. Amalie forced a smile, but it hurt her to see him with Davina.

After pleasantries and goodbyes, the ball concluded late in the evening. The Corringtons were silent during the ride home until the Duke spoke. "I think Julian Cartwright is quite taken with you, Amalie. He has already asked my permission to court you officially."

"He did? What did you say?" Amalie asked, surprised.

"I said, of course. He's a fine young man from a good family," the Duke replied.

Amalie nodded in acknowledgment and forced a smile.

"This is so exciting," Helene gushed. "Amalie, you now have an official suitor. We will invite his family for tea very soon."

Oliver clenched his jaw at the thought of Amalie with another man but remained silent.

Amalie was crawling out of her skin. Again, her life was not her own, and others made decisions for her without asking what her feelings were. She took a deep breath to steady herself and determined that she would have to find a way to make her wishes known, but she had no clue how to go about it in this world she was now living in where women remained silent and obedient—two things Amalie knew she would never be.

The following Tuesday, Oliver and Amalie visited The Holy Trinity Church to search the marriage records. They spent hours combing through the ledgers looking for Juliet Bennett to no avail. There were a few Bennetts, but no Juliet and no one of similar age. While they were in the study with the ledgers, Amalie shared her concern with Oliver.

"Your mother told me she found our family connection through church records," she began nervously, not wanting to imply that Helene lied. "Now that I've seen the ledgers, I have to wonder how that was possible. None of the entries include other family members."

Oliver thought for a moment and then replied, "Well, she did say it went back generations. Perhaps the older records did have other family names listed."

"Yes, perhaps. Do you think your mother would take offense if I asked her about it?"

"I don't think so, but it would depend on how you approach the subject," Oliver answered honestly, knowing Amalie well enough to know that she is rarely subtle.

Amalie felt the need to explain herself. "It's just that people keep asking me about that connection, like Harriett Cartwright at the ball, and I have no answers. I never questioned it that day your mother came to claim me. I assumed she had presented the information to Mother Superior."

"I see....the Cartwrights. You want to make a good impression on your suitor's family," Oliver said, unable to hide his jealousy.

"That's not the real reason," Amalie countered quickly, "I want to know for my own sake, but it is embarrassing when I cannot answer those questions."

"I understand. Well then, you should ask those questions, and perhaps my mother can put your mind at ease," he said, sounding harsher than intended.

"Are you angry with me?" Amalie asked but then wished she hadn't said it.

"No," his tone softened, "I could never be angry with you. I am angry at the situation. I won't lie, it was painful for me to see you with Julian, but I have no right to be jealous."

"And I found it painful to see you with Davina," she admitted. "But I have accepted that this is how it must be."

"I don't know if I will ever accept it, but that is the burden I will carry for the rest of my life."

"I'm beginning to understand how Ronan and Maria felt," Amalie sighed.

"Yes," Oliver concurred, "It's the same for me."

The following day, Julian came for tea. He came alone after asking his parents for a chance to get to know Amalie better without family pressures. Harriett thought that was an excellent idea.

Helene escorted them into the parlor, and Margot brought them tea. After Margot served the tea, Amalie found herself alone with her new suitor. It felt strange for her, but she would try to make the best of it.

"I had the most wonderful time with you at the ball," Julian said, loosening his collar. Amalie thought he looked nervous.

"Yes, I can't remember ever dancing so much, and I discovered how wonderful champagne tastes."

Amalie could see that Julian was searching for conversation, so she decided to put him at ease. "Please, just relax. This is all new to me too. I have never had a suitor before. You can just be yourself with me."

Julian exhaled and smiled. "Thank you. Was it that obvious that I am nervous?"

"Just a little," Amalie smiled. "But it's awkward for me too. I like being honest with people so let's just chat without any pretense, alright?"

"You are so refreshing," he said, relaxing his shoulders. "I felt comfortable with you right from the start. I am usually very socially awkward, which is why I have not yet married, much to my mother's disappointment."

"Well, you can be yourself with me. A person shouldn't marry to please their parents. They should marry when they fall in love and for no other reason," Amalie said, for reasons of her own.

"How very modern of you," he said sincerely. "I don't think I've ever met anyone like you."

"I like being honest, and I'm discovering that in certain circles, people do not appreciate when a woman speaks her mind. But I must be myself. I have great difficulty with pretense."

"Yes, as do I. I have had many disagreements with my parents because I am not yet married. It has caused me much unhappiness. I feel pressured to do something I don't want to do. My mother constantly reminds me that in our social standing, it is almost scandalous not to be married at my age," Julian shared.

"What is the reason you have not married? Have you not met the right person, or you just don't want to be married?" Amalie asked with unbound curiosity.

"May I speak frankly? You are a very modern woman, and I think you would understand," Julian said delicately.

"Yes, please, I prefer frankness and honesty," Amalie said, remembering a similar conversation she had with Oliver.

"I would like to be with someone special, but I am not attracted to women," Julian confessed.

Amalie was innocently unaware of what he was trying to say. "Is that because most women in your social circle are snobby and pretentious?"

"No, it is because they are women."

Finally, Amalie understood. "I see. Let me say up front that I do not judge people. I have heard of men loving each other and women too, for that matter, and I feel strongly that each person should decide for themselves what is right for them. Each person should determine their happiness."

Julian got choked up, and tears filled his eyes. "You don't know what a relief it is to talk to someone who understands. I feel the weight of the world lifted from my shoulders. It is such a blessing to talk with someone who has an open heart. I would love for us to be friends, but that is all I could ever give you—honest friendship."

"I must confess, that is all I want. I would be honored to be your friend," she said sincerely.

Julian smiled. "And I am honored to be your friend. You are a treasure."

"I promise you that our conversation will never leave this room," Amalie assured him. "No one will ever know unless you want them to know."

"Thank you, from the deepest part of my heart."

"I assume your parents don't know?" Amalie said, pouring them more tea.

"No, I don't think I could ever tell them. They would never understand, and it would ruin their social standing," Julian said woefully.

"How sad for you. Please don't let that stop you from finding your true happiness."

"I think I have already found it," he said cautiously. "My business partner and I feel the same way about each other. It is so challenging to love someone in secret."

"I know all about that," Amalie said without hesitation.

"You are in love, Miss Amalie?"

"Yes, but he can never be mine. Loving someone from afar and knowing you cannot be together is the hardest thing I have ever experienced, and it robs me of my sleep every night," Amalie confessed.

"My heavens, you do know precisely what I'm going through," Julian said, and then, he had an epiphany. "I have the most glorious idea."

"Please, share it with me."

"Let us both carry out this charade for a while longer. We both could benefit if your family and mine think we are a couple. My parents won't pressure me to find someone, and the Duchess will stop trying to find you a husband if she thinks you are with me."

Amalie thought for a moment and then smiled. "That is brilliant! It will take the pressure off both of us. And since we are good friends, we can make it believable; however, we won't be able to fool them for too long. They will begin to wonder why we don't get engaged."

"True, but it will buy us both some time, and right now, that is all we have—time to sort things out."

"Yes, my friend. I'm in complete agreement," Amalie smiled at him.

"You don't know how happy this makes me," Julian said enthusiastically. "Miss Amalie, meeting you has been a Godsend to me. It will not be difficult to show the world how fond I am of you. I wonder if you know what a gift you have given me."

"I feel the same way," she said warmly.

There was a knock on the door, and Helene entered the room. "How are things going?"

Julian rose to greet her. "My time with Miss Amalie was most special, Your Grace. She is a true gem. I look forward to spending more time with her."

"I'm so happy to hear that," Helene beamed. "You are welcome anytime."

"Thank you, but now I must bid you farewell. I have business in town," Julian said, taking Amalie's hand and kissing it. "Until next time, my sweet."

After Julian left the room, Helene sat down next to Amalie. "I'm so happy for you! You seem to have raptured him."

"He is extraordinary," Amalie replied honestly. "And very likable."

"I see special things coming for you," Helene carried on.

"Helene, while I have you here, there is something I want to ask you."

"Certainly. Would it have anything to do with wedding planning?"

"Heavens, no, it's way too early to even think about that. I want to talk about how we are related to each other."

Helene's tone changed. "I've already told you—you are a distant cousin of mine."

"Yes, but since the chandelier incident and added security, Captain Oliver and I have been searching for the marriage record of my parents. I'm sure you read the journal where she wrote of their impending marriage by the vicar in Brighton, but we have scoured the records at both churches and found nothing. I noticed that most of the marriage records do not include the names of relatives, and I wondered how you made the connection."

Amalie could see Helene became uneasy.

"I'm only asking because as my relationship with Julian progresses, his family will be asking me these questions, which Harriett already has. I would like to be able to answer the questions for his family, so they won't doubt that I am worthy of their son," Amalie lied. "How did you find the connection?"

"I'm fairly certain that I read that in the church records, but perhaps I was confused and read it somewhere else. Let's not dwell on that right now. When the time comes, I'm sure I will be able to calm any fears they may have about you," Helene said, pivoting.

"I would like to know for myself too."

"Perhaps I read it in one of Juliet's letters," Helene grasped at straws.

"There was no mention of that in her journal. She referred to you as her friend, not her cousin."

Helene became rattled. "Must we dwell on this now? The important thing is that I found you, and we all feel you belong here with us."

"Please don't be upset. I'm sure you can imagine how important it is to me to be certain that I'm not illegitimate," Amalie said, trying to calm Helene down. "Julian's family is high in society, and I don't want to bring any scandal to his name."

"Even if that were the case, no one needs to know. Our good family name will be enough to marry you into Julian's family. Now, stop worrying about it and just enjoy all this good fortune that has come your way."

"Yes, ma'am," was all Amalie had left to say.

Amalie had a restless night following her talk with Helene. Helene was hiding something from her, but why would she lie about being related? Each day in the Corrington House brought more mystery to Amalie's life. Someone wanted to harm her, and she had no clue why. There was a mystery surrounding her parents and who her father was. She was in love with Oliver, and he loved her, but they could never be together. Amalie wasn't sure she could stand by and watch him marry another woman. As she tried desperately to sleep, she was more tormented than ever.

The only bright spot in her day was her new friendship with Julian. He would bring her a reprieve from the pressure to marry, and she would do the same for him. She understood his pain of loving someone forbidden, and she looked forward to having him as an ally and a confidant—since Oliver was beyond her reach.

Chapter 5
Ronan and Maria

After tossing and turning for half the night, Amalie got up to go down to the kitchen and make herself some Chamomile tea. Mother Superior always brought her Chamomile tea whenever she couldn't sleep at the Abbey. It didn't always bring sleep, but it soothed her, and her mind needed comfort. She slipped into her satin robe and bed slippers and made her way down the long stone hallway to the kitchen.

As Amalie passed the parlor on her way to the kitchen, she caught a glimpse of someone sitting in the dark alone. There was enough light from the lantern she was carrying to see Oliver sitting there. Amalie was surprised to see him. She was going to walk by, but she couldn't bring herself to keep going. She tiptoed into the parlor and saw that he was drinking. He looked up and saw her standing there.

"What are you doing up?" he asked her.

"I couldn't sleep."

"There's a lot of that going around. Do you want some whiskey? Trust me; it will help," he offered.

Amalie thought he looked tired. His face was showing an unshaven shadow, which made him look rugged.

"I took a sip of whiskey once and shuddered for two minutes. How can you drink that?" Amalie asked, sitting down next to him.

"It makes me numb, and I need that right now," he said, swirling the whiskey in his glass.

"Okay, pour me some. I was going for tea, but this might work better," Amalie said as she put the lantern on the table.

Oliver poured her a tumbler of whiskey and handed it to her. "Only the first sip is tough. After the second or third, it will get smoother."

Amalie gulped the whiskey and shuddered. She made a face that made Oliver smile. "Sip it, don't gulp."

"It burns going down. This is horrible," Amalie said, her brow curled and lips puckered.

"It will help you sleep, Amalie. If you are anything like me right now, my tortured mind keeps me from sleeping. This will help."

"Yes, I am just like you. So many thoughts run through my mind when I try to sleep, and nothing makes sense anymore," Amalie shared freely.

"I understand you had a visitor today," Oliver said, taking a long sip of his whiskey.

"Please, Oliver, don't ask me about Julian. Why torture yourself?"

"Because the mere thought of you with him is what is torturing me. My mother thinks he will propose," he said, looking at Amalie for a reaction.

"Goodness, we just had tea. I barely know him," Amalie said, sipping her whiskey. "I did ask your mother today about the family connection, and now she is having trouble remembering where she read that information. She was very nervous. It was unsettling."

"That's odd. I distinctly remember when mother first told us about you that she said she found it in church records."

"Oliver, forgive me for saying this, but I think she is hiding something from me. She knew my mother. Do you think she knows who my father is?" Amalie asked, uninhibited by the alcohol.

"No. After the chandelier incident, she would have come forward with that information. She knows how important it is to find out who tried to hurt you. She wouldn't keep that from my father," Oliver rationalized.

"Why was she looking through church records?"

"For the family Bible. We have a very old family Bible in the library that goes back to my great-great-grandparents. There was one death record missing, and she was trying to find it."

"Can you show it to me?"

"Now?"

"Yes, please. I need to know," Amalie begged him.

"Alright. I can't say no to you," Oliver said, finishing his drink.

Amalie gulped the last of her whiskey and tried hard not to make a face but could not prevent it. Again, Oliver had to smile.

Oliver led her down the long hallway to the library. He lit another lantern, and they walked over to the stand that held the large, leather-bound Bible and opened it to the family section. They both studied the entries and the dates.

"This is beautiful handwriting," Amalie observed.

"Annabelle did that. The writing before that was done by my great-grandmother Ellen. Hers is hard to read because she wrote in the old-fashioned script. This book goes back to 1748."

Amalie studied every entry, and the name Bennett never appeared. "There is no mention of any Bennett," Amalie noted sadly. "And I don't see any record missing. All your family and their offspring are listed, as well as who they married. No one married a Bennett."

Oliver studied the book again to make sure he didn't miss anything. "That's odd. You are right."

"Why would your mother lie about this? I just don't understand," Amalie said, feeling the effects of the whiskey.

"I don't understand either. I'm just as baffled as you are. I promise you; I will find out."

"I think I better go to bed. The floor is moving a little," Amalie said, trying to steady herself.

"You're not used to drinking 80-proof whiskey. I will walk you to your room."

"Thank you, Ronan," she said, steadying herself.

"You just called me Ronan."

"I did? A slip of the tongue."

"Come on," he said, taking her arm to guide her out of the room. "You will sleep better tonight."

As they walked down the corridor to the bedrooms, they heard voices coming from the master bedroom. The voices were getting louder. Oliver and Amalie both stopped to listen.

"What did you expect when you brought her here?" the Duke raged. "I warned you, but you didn't listen."

"You are the Duke of Corrington!" Helene cried. "Yet, you are powerless with this. My God, it's been twenty-one years."

"Now she's asking questions. Did you seriously think that she wouldn't at some point? The Cartwrights will too. You and Harriett with your matchmaking!"

Oliver was shocked. He had never heard his parents argue before.

It hurt Amalie that the argument was about her. She pursed her lips to keep from crying.

"Bringing her here has created nothing but chaos, and now we may have someone in our household from *The Society*. Even if you marry her off to Julian, do you think that will stop them? You're more naïve than she is!" the Duke raged on.

With that, Amalie burst into tears and ran down to her room. She closed the door behind her and leaned up against it crying. Oliver wanted to go after her but felt he needed to hear more.

"Now Oliver has feelings for her, and I think there is something between them. If *The Society* gets wind of that, they will undoubtedly act against her. You've put a target on her back!" the Duke yelled at his wife.

"I meant well," Helene sobbed. "I didn't want her to emancipate and go into the world with no family and no means. I wanted to do that for Juliet."

"But she is not our family, and just how long do you think it will be before she figures that out?"

Oliver couldn't take one more minute and opened the door. He burst into the room to confront them.

The Duke and Duchess were stunned when he walked in on them. They were standing at the end of their bed in their nightclothes.

"What are you doing here?" Helene gasped.

"I couldn't sleep and heard you arguing. Is there something you want to tell me about Amalie? I just heard you say that she is not related to us."

The Duke and Duchess looked at each other.

"I want the truth! Why did you lie to her and our family?" Oliver demanded.

The Duke closed the door for privacy and said to his son, "It was the only way your mother could legally claim her. Yes, it was a lie, but your mother had good intentions."

"So that makes this deception acceptable?" Oliver growled. "She's a smart woman. She's pretty much figured it out on her own. She deserves to know the truth."

"Son, I know you have feelings for her," the Duke began, "But you must not lead with your emotions. I warned you about this."

"I love her. I love her with every fiber of my being, and I am in agony that I cannot honor those feelings. You were wrong to deceive her regardless of my feelings for her."

"You love her?" Helene said calmly. "You love Amalie?"

"Yes."

Helene looked at her husband. "You knew this and didn't tell me?"

"There was no need to tell you. Oliver knows what his duty is and that nothing can come of it. I thought it was just an infatuation, but I now realize it's more than that."

"I can see why you love her, Oliver," Helene said softly. "She is wonderful. I'm so sorry you are suffering over this."

"If you had just left things the way they were, none of this would be happening right now," the Duke said in frustration. "If she finds out the truth, she is free to leave, and that would put her in a dangerous position. If indeed *The Society* is after her, we cannot protect her if she leaves us."

"Why would they be after her? What do you know that I don't?" Oliver asked angrily.

"You know as much as I do," the Duke insisted. "You know the issues we discussed at the council meeting. Until we find out who her father is or discover who controls *The Society*, we won't know for certain who is trying to harm her. All we know is that someone is targeting her."

"So, you see, Oliver," Helene said, "We must keep her here. Her life could depend on it."

Oliver shook his head. He knew they were right, but he also knew that Amalie would not stop until she knew the truth. "I refuse to lie to her. She already knows there is no family connection, but she was too kind to accuse you of deception. You must tell her the truth and that she will be in danger if she leaves. She is reasonable. She will understand."

"I will take it under advisement," the Duke said. "Now, let us all get some badly needed sleep."

"There is a problem," Oliver said before he left the room. "Amalie heard you arguing. She was with me in the hallway. She heard you say she is the cause for all the turmoil. She was in tears. There will be more questions tomorrow. I hope you will be truthful with her. She deserves nothing less."

"Why were you together in the hallway in the middle of the night?" the Duke asked.

"Don't worry. It was not a secret rendezvous. Amalie found me in the parlor when we both couldn't sleep. She asked me to show her the family Bible, and I took her to the library and showed it to her. As I said, she already knows."

Oliver left the room and headed for Amalie's room. He listened at the door, and the room was silent, so he continued to his bedroom.

When Oliver came down to breakfast, he was surprised to see Amalie was not there. He assumed she was sleeping late from the whiskey and lack of sleep. As he sat down, he could feel the tension at the table between his parents.

"Amalie must be sleeping late," he said to break the silence.

"No," Annabelle said, "She was out walking early this morning. I was sitting in the garden when she headed to the woods. She stopped to chat with me. Nice young lady."

"What time was that?" Oliver asked.

"Half-past six. I like sitting in the garden to watch the sunrise. I was surprised to see her there. She sat with me for a few minutes. Then she said she wanted to walk in the woods and clear her head. I think she had a headache."

"What did you chat about, mother?" Helene asked.

"She told me I have lovely handwriting. She saw it in the family Bible. She asked me about our Bennett relatives, and I told her she was mistaken. We don't have any Bennett relatives."

Oliver looked at both of his parents, then turned to his grandmother, "Did she say where she was going?"

"Just to walk in the woods. Why all these questions?" Annabelle asked, annoyed.

Just then, a member of the Duke's security team came into the room and asked to speak to the Duke. The Duke nodded and signaled him to approach.

"Sir, I know you told me always to follow Miss Amalie, and I did, but this morning she left very early, so

Gilbert was on watch. He followed her to the garden, where she was with Miss Annabelle. When he looked again, Miss Amalie was gone, so he asked Miss Annabelle where Amalie went, and she pointed to the woods. Both of us combed the woods, and we could not find her. We went as far as town and walked the streets but did not see her. I'm afraid we lost her."

Oliver jumped to his feet. "This is unacceptable! How could you lose her?"

"You can't miss her," Annabelle said. "She was wearing that red velvet cloak I gave her, and she was carrying a bag. If she got lost in the woods, you should be able to spot that red cloak easy enough."

The Duke rose to his feet. "I want every person on detail to be out looking for her! I want every part of that area covered with men. Now!"

"Yes, sir," the man said, quivering, "Right away."

Oliver and his father followed the security officer to aid in the search. They understood the danger Amalie could face.

"Mother, it's crucial. Did Amalie say anything else? It could help us find her," Helene said with fear rising in her throat.

"I don't think so. I did wonder why she was carrying that old leather bag of hers just to go for a walk."

Helene shot up from the table and ran up the stairs to Amalie's room. She searched her wardrobe and found only the new dresses still hanging there. Amalie took her old clothes. Then she searched the room for Juliet's box. She found the box on the dresser, but the contents were gone. Amalie had taken them with no intention of ever coming back. Helene sat down on the bed and cried.

Amalie isn't lost. She ran away. This is all my fault. Oh, Amalie, please come home.

The search filled the entire day, and there was no trace of Amalie. Oliver knew in his heart that she had left and had no intention of coming back. He was worried and angry at the same time. He felt he had failed her and vowed not to stop until he found her.

That evening Oliver met with his parents in the parlor to plan a strategy.

"Her things are gone. She left with no intention of coming back," Helene sighed. "How can she manage? She has no money."

"I suspect she will return to the Abbey. We should go there at once," Oliver said, his mind spinning. "She does have some money. I gave her some to buy fruit and treats for the children at St. Paul's. That is more than enough to get her back to the Abbey. I pray that is where she is because if not, I wouldn't know where to begin to search."

"Have a carriage made ready," the Duke said. "We will leave at once."

"But you will arrive in the middle of the night," Helene said. "Shouldn't you wait until morning?"

"No," Oliver said adamantly, "If she is not there and is on the streets somewhere, time is of the essence. She could be in danger."

The Duke agreed. "She is at great risk. *The Society* may be after her, and the bad elements of the street could harm her as well. Pickpockets, thieves, and rapists are alive and well in the dark shadows of the night."

Oliver was heartsick. At that moment, nothing else mattered but finding Amalie, and he vowed that he would. He went to the stables and ordered a carriage be made ready for their trip to the Abbey. Every minute that passed was another minute that Amalie was in danger, and Oliver knew that time was a factor in finding her safely.

At midnight, they arrived at the Abbey. The large wrought iron gate was locked, but there was a bell, and Oliver rang it furiously. After several minutes, Sister Evangeline came out to the gate.

"She's not here, Captain," she said to Oliver, "But she was here. Before she left, she asked me to give you this."

Sister Evangeline reached through the gate and handed Oliver an envelope with a wax seal. "She knew you would come here first and left that for you. And before you ask, no, I don't know where she's gone."

Oliver took the envelope. "Please, she could be in danger. If she is here, please tell me."

"She left hours ago. We gave her some supplies to carry her over."

"Thank you," Oliver said with his heart in his throat.

"I am the Duke of Corrington," the Duke declared through the gate. "I have information that Amalie could be in danger. If you know where she is, you might help us save her life."

"I do not know where she is, Your Grace. I would not lie to you. We all care about Amalie too."

"Yes, of course, I meant no offense," the Duke apologized.

Sister Evangeline turned to walk back to the building with her heart pounding in her chest. After she closed the door behind her, she turned to Amalie and said, "I will have to go to confession tomorrow. I just lied to a Duke."

Amalie reached out and hugged her friend. "I'm sorry to put you in that position, but you understand why I can't go back there."

"Yes, I do. And we will help you in any way we can. You are safe here for now."

"I need one more favor," Amalie said, pulling another letter from her pocket. "Please take this to the Post. It's a letter to Julian Cartwright. He is a friend that I trust."

"I will mail it tomorrow," Sister Evangeline assured her.

Oliver clutched the letter in his hand on the trip home. His father grew impatient and asked him to open it.

"I need a moment. I fear that this is goodbye, and I don't know if I can bear that," Oliver said woefully.

"Son, your duty….."

"To hell with duty and honor!" Oliver raged. "Being honorable has cost me the only woman I will ever love. But you wouldn't understand that, would you?"

"I understand more than you think. You have not slept for two nights and are not yourself. You don't have to read the letter if you don't want to, but it may hold clues that will help us find her."

Oliver lit the small lantern mounted on the inside of the carriage. Then he slowly broke the wax seal and began to read.

My dearest Ronan,

It is with a heavy heart that I write this to you. Upon learning that I am not truly part of your family and that your mother lied to me after she upended my whole life, I cannot continue in your household. Your father never wanted me there and blamed me for recent events. It is excruciating to live somewhere where you are not wanted.

But that is not the main reason. The main reason is that I love you beyond measure, and I cannot remain there and watch you marry someone else. It has been so painful to be near you and not hold you. It breaks my heart each time I see the anguish in your face when you tell me you must honor your duty. Since I met you, I have never known such love—and I have never known such heartache. I cannot remain there and torture us both any further. I know you understand. You have chosen to do the honorable thing, and I have decided to make it easier for you.

Please do not try and find me. I had some money saved here at the Abbey, and it is enough to get me started on a new life. I will be leaving here shortly, assuming a new name. Please let me go. It is for the best.
You will be forever in my heart.
I will always be your Maria.

PS—I left my sheet music in a folder for Anthony. I want him to have it now that he can read music.

Oliver broke down. Her letter shattered his heart. The letter fell out of his hands as he cried openly. The Duke picked up the letter and read it. Words failed him to comfort his son. He carefully folded up the letter and handed it back to Oliver.

After a long silence, the Duke finally spoke. "She is a very honorable young woman to make such a sacrifice for you. But it pains me greatly that she thinks we didn't want her with us because we did."

"Perhaps you could have shown that to her," Oliver said, composing himself.

"Your mother will be heartbroken that she is gone, but I truly think it might be for the best. Still, I worry about the danger she might be in."

"I will never rest until I find her," Oliver said, fully aware of the implications of what he was saying. "I must follow my heart. And Amalie is my heart."

"What will you do if you find her? Bring her back here where she still cannot be with you and possibly in danger?"

"I will find a way—even if I must surrender my position as future Duke to Michael. I will never have any joy in my life without Amalie," Oliver lamented.

"You will heal in time. You've trained your whole life to assume my role. You would throw all that away for a woman?"

"Yes," Oliver said without hesitation. "My God, father, have you never been in love? Do you have any idea what I feel right now?"

"I have grown to love your mother."

"But have you ever been so hopelessly in love with her that you couldn't live without her?"

The Duke didn't answer.

"I knew it. You don't have a clue what I am feeling right now. Your mother raised you without love, and your whole life centered around your title and the military. Mother raised me with love and nurtured me. I thank God for that. However, right now, I wish my heart was hard as stone, like yours, so that I wouldn't be feeling this pain."

The words his son spoke to him stung deeply, but he couldn't relate to ever feeling such emotions. They rode home the rest of the way in silence. The Duke was confident Oliver would rest and have more clarity. Oliver was making plans in his head to venture out and find his love. He silently vowed not to stop until he found her, no matter how long it took or how far he had to travel.

The following day at the Corrington House, Helene was distressed to hear about the letter and that Amalie left believing they did not want her there. The three of them spoke privately in the parlor.

"I am riddled with guilt for deceiving her," Helene said tearfully, "But I hope she knows I did it out of love for Juliet. I meant no malice of any kind."

"She is fond of you, mother, so much so that when she realized you lied to her, she didn't want to confront you or upset you," Oliver said, trying to soothe his mother.

"Where will she go? What will she do? She has no means. Oh dear, what about Julian? He will be crushed. Harriett will hate me for this," Helene said in a slight panic.

"Julian and his family are not important right now," Oliver quipped. "All I care about is finding Amalie."

"But you said she doesn't want to be found. How on earth will you ever find her?" Helene asked her son.

"Oliver, are you seriously still thinking about finding her?" the Duke asked in exasperation. "You would risk everything for this woman, even a war?"

"Please be serious, father. Our nations have lived in peace for four hundred years. Do you honestly think they would launch a war over who I love? Yes, I am dead serious about finding her. I plan to leave later today. She can't be far yet, and I know her well enough to know where she might go."

"If you are serious about this, you have my blessing," Helene said to her son. "I want Amalie back too."

"Good Lord, woman, are you out of your mind?" the Duke shouted. "How can you encourage this? He is talking about abdicating his position!"

The Duke's outburst did not faze Helene. "Oliver must decide his path for himself."

"Thank you, mother," Oliver forced a slight smile.

"This is madness," the Duke said and sat down in defeat.

"I will report back any information or progress I make in my search," Oliver said to his mother. "I may be gone for a while. Please make my excuses to the Herzsteins."

"What will I tell them?" Helene asked.

"I don't care. Tell them the truth. Davina and I have talked about our union numerous times, and she isn't any happier about it than I am. She is in love with a printer, and she informed me that she plans to keep him as a lover after our marriage."

"Is this true?" the Duke scowled.

"Yes, and I agreed to it so we wouldn't have to consummate our marriage."

"Goodness, this is shocking," Helene declared. "Do her parents know?"

"I think so. Davina told me her mother was the one who suggested it to get her to agree to the marriage."

Helene shook her head. "You think you know people."

"So, you see," Oliver said, "They have no right to be outraged."

"Her father will not take it so lightly," the Duke said.

"I will leave you two Dukes to sort that out. As for me, I will find Amalie, and when I do, I will bring her back here to be with me. I will not return until I find her," Oliver said forcefully.

"I will keep you and Amalie in my prayers, son," Helene said, "Go find her. Find your love."

Later that afternoon, Oliver left on his horse and set out to find Amalie. The seasons were changing, and the days were getting colder. The trees were changing colors as nature prepared for the coming winter. Oliver dressed in his full military uniform covered by a heavy wool coat as he rode, which helped to keep the chill from his legs. He was armed, had plenty of funds, and had an unbreakable resolve to find the woman who ran away with his heart.

Chapter 6

Halston Harbor

Days later, a visitor arrived at the Abbey to see Amalie. One of the sisters brought him to the study after approving his entry. When Amalie saw him, she greeted him with a smile and a hug.

"Julian, thank you for coming," she said warmly. "I'm so glad to see you."

"Of course, I would come. When my dear friend writes to me and says she needs my help, I will come. I must say, your letter was shocking. I understand about affairs of the heart, Amalie, and I am here to assist you in any way I can," Julian said sincerely.

"Thank you. As I explained in the letter, I need you to transport me to the shipyard at Halston Harbor. I want to buy passage to London," Amalie said as they sat down on the sofa.

"Is it money you need? I'll give you whatever you need," Julian offered earnestly.

"No, I have some money. You see, I suspect Oliver is out there somewhere looking for me, and he is looking for a single woman traveling alone. He will never be looking for a couple traveling together."

"Ah, I see. I would be happy to do that for you, although I must say, I'm so sorry to see you leave. I was looking forward to our charade playing out, but I understand your situation. How dreadful that someone wants to hurt you. I do have a pistol, and I know how to shoot it," Julian said.

"Did you come in a carriage?" Amalie asked.

"Yes, as you requested. I also burned your letter after I read it, as you asked."

"What did you tell your parents?" Amalie asked.

"I told them I was going out of town on business. I take a lot of business trips, so they never thought twice about it."

"I very much appreciate this, Julian. You're a lifesaver. Literally."

"When shall we leave?" he asked.

"We can leave this evening after supper. If we travel by night, fewer eyes will see us," Amalie replied.

"You have planned this well, but I must ask you, as your friend, are you sure you don't want him to find you? You love each other. Surely, there is a way to work this out."

"I love it that you are such a romantic at heart, but no, there is nothing I can do. Oliver is duty-bound to marry Lady Davina. Nothing can change that, and I can't stand by and watch him marry someone else. It would tear me apart. No, there is no way to work this out."

"I understand completely, my friend. My love is a married man, and he was married when we became business partners. One day I took a huge risk and told him how I felt. Luckily, he felt the same way. We manage to find our special time together, but when he goes home at night to his wife, it eats me up inside. Believe me when I tell you that I know how you feel," Julian empathized.

"Maybe someday life won't be so restrictive," Amalie sighed, "And people can just love who they want, and others will be more accepting."

"Maybe, my friend, but until that day comes, we have to accept the way things are."

Oliver rented a room at the hotel in Brighton. He wandered through town, talking to locals asking if anyone had seen Amalie. He stopped at St. Paul's and asked the children if they had seen her. They told him they hadn't seen her and they missed her visits. He inquired at Carriage Depots, asking if a young woman may have purchased passage somewhere. No one saw or heard anything, but it was early in his search, and he did not let this discourage him. Eventually, he knew someone would have seen her and point him in the right direction.

Meanwhile, Helene went to Brighton to visit the Apothecary to buy something to help her sleep. Her friend, Boris, knew her well and always had whatever she needed. She purchased the sleep aid, and as she was leaving the store, she almost bumped into Harriett Cartwright.

"Fancy meeting you here," Harriett chirped.

Helene dreaded the questions she suspected were coming. "Yes, always nice to see you, Harriett."

"I was hoping we could all have tea this week, but Julian was called away suddenly on a business trip, so it will have to wait until he comes back."

"Oh? He is out of town?" Helene asked, her interest piqued. "How long will he be gone?"

"He didn't say, which is odd, but I know nothing about business matters, so I don't question. Isn't it wonderful that our darlings have hit it off so well?"

Helene realized Harriett knew nothing about Amalie leaving and relaxed a bit. "Yes, it is wonderful. Julian is a fine young man."

"And Amalie is just exquisite! He is quite taken with her. I would have preferred a better-known family name, but after hounding him for so long to find someone, I am happy he chose her."

"Well, I must be off," Helene said quickly. "I have other stops to make before I head home."

"We will have our tea once Julian returns. Goodbye for now," Harriett said as she entered the Apothecary.

Helene's mind was racing. Was it just a coincidence that Julian was gone at the same time as Amalie? She doubted it. Helene hurried down to the hotel where she knew Oliver was staying and hoped she could catch him before he moved on. Helene was heading toward the front desk when she spotted Oliver in the dining room having a meal. She rushed to his table.

"Mother, what are you doing here?" Oliver said, rising to greet her. "Please join me."

"Oliver, I just ran into Harriett Cartwright. She told me something that concerns me," Helene said, settling herself at the table.

"What is it? Is there a shortage of tea or something?" Oliver said sarcastically.

"No. Harriett told me that Julian was suddenly called away on business and is out of town."

That got Oliver's attention. "Oh?"

"Don't you think it's a very odd coincidence?"

"Yes, I do, but...." Oliver was trying to process what it could mean. "Are you suggesting that Amalie and Julian are together?"

"I know it seems farfetched, but that is the first thought I had."

"I can't even fathom that she would run away with him," Oliver said, but somewhere deep inside, he knew this wasn't a coincidence. "Did Harriett say where he went on business?"

"No, and I didn't think to ask. I'm sorry, I was a bit rattled when she told me," Helene apologized.

"I'm glad you caught me before I left Brighton. I was going to leave this afternoon for the north country to begin searching there, but I think I will stop at Julian's office and make an inquiry before I go."

"Any luck so far?" Helene asked, knowing the answer.

"No, but I have been asking about a young woman traveling alone. Perhaps I need to expand my search with this new information."

"I wish you success, my son. I will be praying for you."

Oliver left the hotel and went to the Cartwright Shipping Office to inquire about Julian. Edmond, Julian's business partner, greeted him.

"I was hoping to speak with Julian Cartwright," Oliver said, shaking Edmond's hand. "I wish to finish my conversation with him about shipping items for our family."

"I'm sorry, but Julian is out of town on business. Is there something I can help you with?" Edmond asked.

"Oh," Oliver feigned surprise. "That was rather sudden, wasn't it? I just spoke to him at our home a few days ago when he called on Amalie. He didn't mention it."

"I beg your pardon, sir, I didn't realize who you were. Yes, it was quite sudden and surprised me too. I didn't realize we had holdings in Halston Harbor, but I assume he went there to seek a new shipping contract. He should be back next week. May I make an appointment for you?" Edmond offered.

"No, thank you, it's not urgent. It can wait until Julian returns. Thank you for your assistance."

Oliver raced out of the building and hurried to the hotel to grab his bag. He checked out and rushed to the livery to get his horse. Oliver suspected that Julian had taken Amalie to Halston Harbor and knew he had to hurry before Amalie left on a ship.

Then he might never find her. His insides were churning with the thoughts of them leaving together, but he had to focus on the task at hand and hoped he would get there before she was gone. He knew Amalie didn't love Julian, but he also knew that she believed there was no hope for him and Amalie being together, so he feared she might settle for Julian.

Amalie and Julian arrived in Halston Harbor, a town known for fishing and shipping. It was dawn, and the city was coming to life in the daylight.

"Let's find a place to eat until the offices open. I will stay with you until you have a ticket in your hand and are safely on board," Julian said to a sleepy Amalie.

"Thank you. Some food sounds good," Amalie said, forcing her eyes to open.

They left the carriage at the Livery Stable in town and walked down the main street looking for a café. They found a small café called Eleanor's and went in for breakfast. After their meal, Julian planned to escort Amalie to the ticket office at the harbor docks.

Oliver rode as fast as his horse could carry him, stopping only to water the horse and eat a bite of jerky. He arrived in Halston Harbor just before noon and prayed he was there in time. Oliver found the Livery Stable and presented his horse to the attendant. As he was about to leave the livery, he spotted Julian about to climb into his carriage.

Oliver ran toward him and shouted, "Wait! Stop!"

Julian turned and waited to greet him. "You're too late. She's gone."

"Please, Julian, tell me where she's gone," Oliver pleaded.

"Why do you torture her like this? She is heartbroken and wants to leave all this behind. Being with you puts her in danger, and if you truly loved her, you would let her go," Julian said on behalf of his friend.

"She told you about us?" Oliver asked, surprised.

"Yes, she was always honest with me. That is why she is a cherished friend."

"I need to find her. I told my father I was willing to give up my position as future Duke to be with Amalie. I cannot live without her, please, tell me where she's gone," Oliver begged.

Julian could see the desperation in Oliver's eyes and knew exactly how that felt. "I think you're too late, but she bought passage on the *Hyacinth* to London. They were boarding the ship when I left her."

"Thank you!" Oliver said as he ran out of the livery toward the docks.

Julian stood there for a moment wishing Edmond would one day do the same for him, but he held out little hope of that ever happening. He hoped Oliver would reach Amalie in time.

When Oliver arrived at the dock, the ship was still in the harbor, and dozens of people lined the pier waiting. He searched the crowd for Amalie but didn't see her. He went up to the dockworker for information.

"Is this the *Hyacinth* to London? I thought it had boarded already," Oliver asked him.

"Yes, sir, we loaded the passengers, but there was a problem with the helm, and departure has been delayed for repairs. It will be hours before she sails. You still have time to buy a ticket."

"No, I'm looking for someone," he said as he reached into his pocket for a gold coin. "This is yours if you can tell me if you've seen her."

Oliver described Amalie and what she was possibly wearing. The dock attendant nodded. "Yes, she was here. You can't miss that red cape. When the Captain delayed the departure, she was waiting over there," he said, pointing to a sandy spot near the water's edge, "But I don't see her there now."

Oliver handed the man the coin and turned to walk in the beach direction when a woman stepped forward and called out to Oliver.

"Sir, I saw her too, and I alerted the constable when I saw a man forcing her to go with him. He grabbed her arm, and she called out for help. She managed to free herself from him and ran off down toward the other dock with the man chasing her."

"When was this?" Oliver said, his heart pounding.

"Just moments ago. The constable went after them too," the woman said, pointing in the direction.

"Thank you!" Oliver said, nearly paralyzed with fear. Amalie was in danger, and he knew every second was critical. Oliver ran along the water's edge, hoping he would get to her in time. He saw the next dock but couldn't see past it because a boat shed blocked his view. Oliver then saw the constable lying about fifty meters away on the empty pier when he rounded the boat shed. Oliver ran to him and saw he was bleeding from the abdomen. It appeared to be a stab wound. The constable uttered faintly, "She's in the water. He's got her."

That's when Oliver saw them. Amalie was struggling in the water with a man. He threw off his jacket and jumped off the pier into the frigid water, swimming as fast as he could in their direction.

Amalie did not know how to swim and when the man threw himself at her and knocked them both into the water, she knew she would die. The man was trying to hold her under the water, and she fought as hard as she could against him but could feel her strength waning with each passing second. Her lungs felt like they would burst, and Amalie could feel the life slowly leaving her body. Then a calm swept over her, and she stopped struggling. That is when the man let go. She felt herself falling into the depths, and everything went black.

Suddenly she felt arms around her and instinctively began to fight again, but she could feel sand under her feet and knew she could touch the bottom. All of a sudden, her head was above water, and she gasped to breathe. She fought hard and hit the man with whatever strength she had left, and then she heard, "Amalie, it's me, Oliver!"

She opened her eyes and saw his face through a blur. "Oliver?" she whispered, and everything went dark again.

When she woke up, she was lying in a bed in an unfamiliar room. The light in the room was dim, and she tried to focus to see where she was when Oliver leaned over her and said, "Thank God, you're awake. You had me so worried."

"Where am I?" she asked in a weak voice.

"In the home of the widow Crosby. She offered her home to me when I carried you out of the water," Oliver said as he sat down beside her. "The physician was here, and he said you had water in your lungs. He turned you over and pushed on your back several times, and you coughed up most of it. You've been asleep for the longest time. I was afraid I lost you."

"Oliver....the man....he tried to kill me. He stabbed the constable and pushed me in the water," Amalie recalled.

"I know, and that man will never hurt you again. I killed him with my bare hands. He's dead."

"You killed him?"

"Yes. I broke his neck as we fought in the water. Then I dove down for you. Thank God I found you in time," he said, touching her hand.

"The constable?"

"He survived."

"Oh, thank goodness," Amalie sighed. Then she remembered her bag at the dock.

"Oliver, my bag! I left it at the dock to take a walk. A woman with a small child said she would watch it for me. We have to get it back."

"Don't worry about your bag. That woman brought it here after she saw what happened. It's right over there. I gave her a small reward for her honesty," Oliver said.

"Thank you. Once again, you come to my rescue," Amalie said, trying to sit up. "But I must ask—why did you come for me? I asked you not to. I cannot bear any more heartbreak."

"I came because after I got your letter, I realized what I already knew—that I can't live without you. I don't care about being Duke. I don't care about the peace treaty. I don't care about anything—but you. I love you, and I will find a way for us to be together."

"But how? Your father will never allow this," Amalie said, trying not to make eye contact with Oliver. She didn't want to weaken her stance by looking into his loving eyes.

"It's not his choice to make. It's mine. I have my mother's blessing. She wanted me to find you and bring you home."

"I don't know if I could ever go back there, Oliver. Too much has happened, and I will never be safe there," she said, still avoiding his gaze.

"My sweet Amalie, you're not safe anywhere until we can find out who is behind *The Society*. A man just tried to kill you even after all the precautions you took coming here with Julian."

"How do you know that?" she asked, looking at him.

"Sheer luck and seeing Julian at the livery as he was leaving. He told me where to find you."

Amalie had to smile. "Julian is a hopeless romantic. I think he's rooting for us."

"For a moment, I thought you had run away with him, and it broke my heart, but then I realized that your love for me runs deeper than that. I trusted that and set out to find you."

Just then, Mrs. Crosby came into the room. "Welcome back, dear," she said, lighting the lantern on the dresser, "You gave us all quite a scare. How are you feeling?"

"Sore but thankful to be alive."

"You've had quite the ordeal. I undressed you and put my late husband's nightshirt on you. It's way too big, but I didn't have anything else. I dried your clothes by the fire in the living room. I folded them and put them on the chair over there. Can I bring you some tea and something to eat? You must be starving," Mrs. Crosby said as she headed for the door.

"That would be lovely, thank you," Amalie said.

"I'll bring a tray for your husband too. Just give me a few minutes. I have stew on the fire."

When Mrs. Crosby left the room, Amalie turned to Oliver and said, "My husband?"

"She assumed that, and I didn't correct her. I was afraid she wouldn't let me stay in the room with you. She has no idea who I am, and I do not plan to tell her," Oliver confessed.

Amalie smiled at him. "Your secret is safe with me."

"Mrs. Crosby has been so accommodating, and I will certainly reward her for her kindness. She told me she lives on a widow's pension, but it isn't much, as you can see by her humble home."

"Her husband must've been a huge man," Amalie said, looking down at the nightshirt that was falling off her shoulders, trying to slide it back into place. "Were you in the room when she undressed me?"

"No, my darling, I was in the living room changing out of my wet clothing," he said with a warm smile. "And yes, her husband was a huge man. She gave me his old shirt and trousers to put on, and I had to rope the pants to keep them up."

"Oliver," Amalie began stammering a bit, "I don't know if I can go back with you. I will bring scandal to your family, and if you give up your title, it will bring shame to your family and possibly cause a war. I can't be the reason for that. I just can't."

Oliver took her hand in his. "Please don't worry about all that. I've discussed it with my parents, who know how I feel. I told my father I would abdicate my title to Michael if necessary because I cannot marry any other woman but you. Davina doesn't want this marriage any more than I do. There won't be a war over this. I am certain of it. Not after four hundred years of peace. My father is trying to uncover *The Society* and expose them. His council members are working on it."

"But why would *The Society* be after me? How am I a threat to the peace treaty?" Amalie asked, exasperated.

"Because I am the future Duke, and somehow, they discovered our relationship. My father thinks we have a spy in our household. There can be no other explanation."

"This is frightening. I thought I died today—under the water," Amalie said with a shudder. "It was terrifying."

Oliver put his arms around her and held her. "You are safe with me. I won't let anything happen to you."

Just then, Mrs. Crosby pushed the door open and carried in a large tray. "Don't mind me, you lovebirds. Your husband had a terrible scare today. He was frantic he would lose you. I'm sure he must be quite relieved that you are alright."

Mrs. Crosby set the tray on the table next to the bed. "Here is some stew for both of you and some tea. I cut you both a slice of figgy pudding for dessert. Enjoy your supper."

"Thank you so very much," Oliver said, standing up to take the food. "You have been most kind."

"Oh, I love having folks to fuss over. With Stewart gone, I am all alone. My only son is in the Queen's Army, and I only see him every few months. I'm happy to do it."

As Mrs. Crosby was leaving the room, she remembered to tell Oliver where she kept the firewood. "It's going to be cold tonight, and I don't want your wife to catch a cough after what she's been through."

After supper, Oliver built a fire in the fire pit. The small room began to warm immediately.

"I take it we are both sleeping here tonight?" Amalie asked, trying to hide how nervous she was.

"Well, she thinks we're married, so I would say yes, but don't be concerned, my love. I slept in that chair last night, and I can do it again tonight," he assured her.

"Are we going back to Corrington House tomorrow?" Amalie asked anxiously.

"Yes, I still feel it's the safest place for you until we figure all this out."

Oliver blew out the lantern, and the only light in the room came from the fire. He leaned over the bed and kissed Amalie on the forehead. "Goodnight, sleep well."

He went to the old easy chair in the corner and made himself comfortable. Amalie watched him with loving eyes. With Oliver, she felt safe.

Hours later, Amalie awoke from a nightmare and sat straight up in bed. Her breathing was heavy, and her hands were trembling. Oliver rushed to her bedside.

"Shh, it's just a dream," he said, putting his arm around her. "I'm here. You are safe."

"Oh, Oliver, I was under the water, and I could feel the life leaving my body. It was so real," Amalie said, quivering.

"You've been through something traumatic, my love. I'm just so thankful I found you when I did—I shudder to think what would have happened if I hadn't."

"Stay with me until I stop shaking, please."

"I'm not going anywhere," he whispered.

Oliver sat beside her on the bed and held her in his protective arms. Amalie put her head on his shoulder and snuggled into his loving embrace. After a few minutes, she looked up at him and said, "I love you."

"I love you too," he said, looking into her eyes. Then he leaned forward and placed his lips on hers. She welcomed his kiss. Their lips melted together with fulfilled longing. Oliver was almost at the point of no return when he leaned back and stopped himself. "I don't want to take advantage of you," he said softly.

Amalie nodded but was sorry that he stopped. "I'm fine now," she said stoically, "You can go back to your chair."

Oliver got up and headed back to the chair but stopped to put another log on the fire. While he stood there to make sure it took flame, Amalie got up out of bed and went to him.

"I lied. I don't want you to go back to your chair. I want you with me—beside me—holding me—loving me. I almost died today. I want to live my life and stop denying myself the love that I desire with you," she uttered breathlessly.

Oliver looked at her standing there before him with her nightshirt sliding off her shoulder and thought she was the most beautiful woman he had ever seen. He cupped her cheek in his hand. "You are so beautiful," he whispered.

"When I am with you, I want to be near you. And when I'm near you, I want to touch you, to feel you and have you wrap your arms around me. When you kiss me, things happen to my body that I've never felt before. You make me tingle inside. I want you to touch me the way men touch the women they love."

Oliver covered her mouth with his and pulled her close to his body. Amalie wrapped her arms around him. He parted her lips with his tongue and tasted her. She loved the sensation that it caused in her body.

Amalie pulled back and dropped the nightshirt from her body. She stood naked before him, filled with heat and desire. "Please touch me, Oliver."

Oliver felt his knees weaken, but he was as aroused as he had ever been. He cupped her breast in his hand and ran his other hand down her body. Amalie started to undress him.

"I want to see you too," she whispered.

When his clothes were in a heap on the floor, they stood looking at each other and touching each other's bodies.

"Oh, God," he breathed heavily. "I love your touch."

Amalie explored his body with her hands. When she touched his manhood, Oliver moaned with pleasure. He felt like he would explode if he didn't lay with her, so he picked her up in his arms and carried her to the bed. Oliver laid down beside her and kissed her again. She wrapped her arms around him and pulled him close. He climbed on top of her and whispered, "I will try to be gentle; I know this is your first time."

"I don't need gentle—I need you! I can't get you close enough—please put out this fire in my belly," she breathed heavily.

Oliver couldn't wait for one more second and penetrated her. She let out a slight gasp but then pulled him even closer. He was burning with desire for her.

Amalie could feel him inside her body, and the sensations were like warm waves moving through her. She held him close, and her body began to automatically move in rhythm with his. The hot tingling in her loins was making her moan and breathe heavily. The thrusting became quicker, and Amalie could feel herself building to an explosive climax. The moment she felt Oliver pulsing deep inside her, her body began throbbing with sensations that were so intense it made Amalie cry out with pleasure. Their lovemaking took her breath away.

Within moments, they were in complete ecstasy and unable to move. When they both relaxed, he held her in his arms so they could catch their breath. Amalie couldn't believe the sensations she was feeling. Oliver was in such euphoria that he couldn't speak.

Finally, Oliver whispered, "I have never felt such love," he said, kissing her forehead.

"I have no words for what just happened, but I have never been so happy in my life. So, this is love."

"Yes, my darling Amalie, this is love. Men have been willing to die for this kind of love—for centuries—to be with the woman they love."

"Oliver, if this night is all we ever have, I will die happy in my old age knowing that you loved me, and I loved you in this way. This night is precious to me, and I want this feeling to last forever."

"I promise you, my love, I will do everything in my power to make this last forever," Oliver professed.

"I love you, Oliver."

"And I love you with all my heart and soul."

Within moments, they were asleep in each other's arms.

Oliver and Amalie got up to greet the day when the morning sun came streaking through the window. Amalie tidied the bed while Oliver gathered up their things. When they were dressed and ready to leave the room, Amalie took his hand and said, "I'm ready to face whatever comes."

Chapter 7

Web of Deceit

Oliver sent a messenger ahead to let his parents know he had found Amalie and that they were coming home. He also stated that his position had not changed. Oliver commissioned a carriage to take them home. Oliver tied his horse to the back of the carriage for the ride to Corrington House.

During the long ride back, Oliver firmly held Amalie's hand as they relished in the love they shared the night before. Amalie was filled with dread to return to Corrington House but wanted to be with Oliver no matter the price she might have to pay. Oliver would take a stand for the woman he loved and had no qualms about surrendering his title to Michael, who always wanted it more than Oliver ever did.

When they arrived at the estate later that afternoon, Gerald greeted them at the door. "Welcome back, Captain and Miss Amalie. They are all waiting for you in the parlor."

"They? Who?" Oliver asked.

"Your parents and the Herzsteins," he answered. "Lady Davina is there, as well as Miss Annabelle."

Oliver looked at Amalie. "Looks like we're about to have a family meeting. Are you ready?"

"As ready as I'll ever be," she sighed.

The families were engaged in earnest conversation as Oliver and Amalie arrived hand in hand. The room fell silent as they entered.

The Dukes were seated in the chairs framing the fireplace, while Helene, Anabelle, and Duchess Marta were sitting on the red velvet sofa, directly across from the green velvet sofa. Helene refurbished both sofas a few years back and couldn't decide on red or green velvet, so she decided on one of each. Lady Davina got up from the green sofa to make room for Oliver and Amalie and moved to a chair near the window.

Helene rushed to Amalie. "Oh, I'm so relieved you're alright! I'm so sorry you had to go through that awful ordeal. Are you sure you do not need a physician?"

"I'm fine," Amalie replied, more reserved than she intended, "Thanks to Oliver. If he hadn't found me when he did, I would be dead."

"Come sit down," Duke Oliver said, "We were just discussing our current situation."

"I'm sure you were," Oliver said as he led Amalie to the green velvet sofa. "As I stated in my letter to you, my position has not changed."

"So, you're going to launch us all into a war over a woman? Have you lost your mind?" Duke Oliver barked from his chair in front of the fireplace.

"Father, we've had this discussion, and I won't debate it again with you. I love Amalie, and I don't want to marry Davina. And no, I have not lost my mind. No one wants a war after four hundred years of peace, and I think you know that," Oliver said firmly.

"Let me interject here," Duke Carl Gustav said, clearing his throat. "Lady Davina has informed me that she does not wish to marry Captain Corrington. She is in love with a printer named Parker. Certainly, we can all come to some kind of arrangement that we can all live with."

"Such as?" Oliver asked.

"I want it known that none of this sits well with me," Duchess Marta said, "and I do not approve of what these two men are discussing."

Helene sat back down next to Annabelle on the red velvet sofa, looking down at the floor, appearing very uncomfortable. "I am not in favor either."

Lady Davina stood up and looked at Oliver. "They want us to get married and keep our consorts on the side. I already told my mother that I intended to do just that, but they shouldn't expect you and Amalie to do the same. I can play out the charade, but something tells me you couldn't. Not after observing you at the Harvest Ball."

"I would never even consider such a thing," Oliver said, shaking his head. "That is your solution? You want us to live a lie? You want Amalie to be my secret consort like some concubine? Truly, you insult her and me with the suggestion."

"It's certainly better than what you are thinking of doing, and that is to surrender your title. I won't have it! You should be thankful that I am offering this solution," Duke Oliver bellowed at his son.

Amalie wanted to speak but decided to wait until everyone else had their say. She was also distracted by Annabelle, who was staring at her over her needlepoint. Every time Amalie looked at her, she was staring in her direction.

"There's still the issue of Amalie's safety," Oliver went on, "someone nearly killed her at Halston Harbor. They seem determined as ever to harm her, and that is my main concern right now, not how the people will react to my situation. What have you learned from your council about *The Society*? What are you doing to keep her safe?"

Duke Carl Gustav spoke. "We have been unable to learn anything about them. It has been extremely frustrating as Duke to learn that I have no control over this matter. Neither does your father. We seem powerless to stop them."

"That is simply unacceptable," Oliver said firmly. "Someone controls them. Someone issued a command to harm Amalie, and both of you are telling me you cannot control them?"

"We don't even know who to seek out," Carl Gustav admitted, "We don't know who the leader is. No one does."

"That is utterly terrifying," Oliver said, looking at Amalie. "I killed that man with my bare hands. Now I wish I would have spared him to learn who sent him to harm Amalie."

"Chances are he wouldn't have divulged any information. They are sworn to secrecy and are willing to die to uphold it." Carl Gustav said.

"How do you know this?" Oliver asked quickly.

Duke Carl Gustav seemed unable to answer and searched for the words. "I'm assuming that based on the ultra-secrecy of the group."

"Nothing like what happened at our ball has ever happened in this family," Duke Oliver said, "And to think someone in our household may have done that. All of these troubles began when she arrived here, and it seems to follow her wherever she goes."

That was the moment Amalie had enough. "I think it's my turn to speak now," she said forcefully and rose from the green sofa. "You are discussing me as if I am not in this room, and I most certainly am going to add my voice to this discussion!"

Then she turned to Duke Oliver and spoke directly to him. "I would like to remind you that it was not my choice to come here. That decision was made for me by others. To be honest, I didn't want to come. I was happy where I was. Two attempts have been made on my life since I arrived here. Are you implying that I caused this? I have no clue why someone would want to hurt me. I am a threat to no one. Yet, I can't stop what is happening because I am a commoner with no voice or power. But *you* are the Duke of Corrington, you hold all the power, and you stand before me and tell me that you are powerless to stop this?"

Amalie had a surge of adrenaline and began to pace as she spoke. "You two Dukes think that your grand solution to this marriage is to allow Oliver and Davina to have consorts on the side? I'm amazed you would even suggest that for your children, but since you never asked me my feelings on the subject, the answer is **NO**! Unequivocally no. I would never allow myself to be anyone's mistress. How dare you suggest it."

Duke Oliver was angry now. "I have never liked your strong opinions, and I will not tolerate being spoken to in that manner in my house!"

"You disrespect me by suggesting I become Oliver's concubine, and you are angry that I spoke up for myself? I'm sorry, sir, but if you want respect, perhaps you should try respecting others first," Amalie seethed.

Oliver sat in admiration of his love. She spoke to his father the way he often wished he could have.

"Please," Helene pleaded, "This is not helping the situation. Please let us all calm down."

"She is right," Duke Carl Gustav said, risking the wrath of the other Duke. "We did not consider her wishes, and that was our shortcoming. Davina has made her own choice of how she wants to handle this, and Amalie should be free to make her own choice as well."

Amalie walked over to Duke Carl Gustav and stood before him. "Thank you, Your Grace. I am most appreciative of your support and understanding for how I feel."

Suddenly, Annabelle stood up and pointed toward Amalie and Carl Gustav. "Yes! I do remember you! You two were married right here in this room all those years ago. I knew I recognized you."

Helene rushed to her mother. "Mother, you are confused. Amalie was never married here," she said nervously, "You are mistaken. Please sit down."

"No! I will not sit down. They were married right there where they are standing. My late husband, the Vicar of Eddleston, married them. Her name was Juliet then."

"What?" Amalie said, stunned. "What are you saying?"

"She is confused," Helene repeated, trying to make her mother sit down.

"No, let her speak," Amalie insisted. "I want to hear what she has to say. Please, Miss Annabelle, tell me what you remember."

"Helene summoned us here, my husband and me, to perform the marriage ceremony for her dear friend Juliet and her fiancé Carl Gustav. He was not a Duke then. The vicar in Brighton couldn't marry them because the church burned down, and he was in the hospital recovering from burns. There was some urgency, and I'm not sure why, but my husband agreed to do it. They stood right there, and I witnessed the marriage. So did you, Helene."

Amalie stood in stunned silence. Then she looked at Helene, who hung her head in shame, and she then looked at Carl Gustav, who had tears in his eyes.

"What is happening?" Amalie cried, "I don't understand."

Oliver rushed to Amalie's side and put his arm around her to support her.

"What is the meaning of this?" Duke Oliver demanded. "What is she saying? Where was I when this happened? Helene, for God's sake, tell me the truth."

Helene couldn't speak, but Duke Carl Gustav stepped forward and spoke. "It's true. It's all true. Amalie, your mother Juliet was the love of my life. We were married right here in this room twenty-two years ago. Our marriage was forbidden, so we ran away together. I was prepared to do what Oliver plans to do—surrender my future title for the woman I loved. It was a joyous union until the day she died. I lost her when she gave birth to you. Yes, Amalie, I am your father."

There were audible gasps in the room. Amalie tried to absorb what she was hearing but couldn't comprehend the shocking news.

"You were on a hunting trip," Annabelle said to Duke Oliver. "You weren't here. I remember it all now."

"Helene, is this true?" Amalie pleaded.

"Yes, it's all true. I'm so sorry, dear, that you had to find out this way. I only had the best intentions for you. You must believe me. I loved your mother dearly, and when she came to me with Carl Gustav and asked me to help them get married, I couldn't say no. I summoned my mother and father to come and perform the ceremony. There was some danger, and your mother was worried for her safety. My father was happy to marry them. They left for the north country the very next morning. That was the last time I saw her. She died ten months later."

"After her death," Carl Gustav continued, "I returned to my family's home to assume my title. Without Juliet, there was no reason to surrender my title."

"No reason?" Amalie said as tears filled her eyes. "You had a daughter. How could you leave me there at the Abbey?"

Carl Gustav's face softened as he spoke to Amalie. "I didn't want to leave you there, but *The Society* had tried to kill your mother. That is why we fled to the Abbey to have our child. It was safer there. I couldn't risk bringing you home and putting you in danger. Please, dear daughter, forgive me for abandoning you. It has been the deepest heartache of my life—losing Juliet and then losing you too. That is why I dropped my glass the day you arrived when we came for dinner. When you walked into the room, I saw my Juliet before me. You are the image of her."

Amalie's mind was racing, trying to absorb the shocking truth. Then she turned to Helene. "You cut out the pages of her journal, didn't you? It was you."

"Yes. I'm so sorry. I couldn't let you read those pages. Juliet wrote about the marriage and who performed the ceremony. She mentioned her new husband by name. I had to remove them," Helene confessed.

"So, you are my sister?" Davina said in disbelief.

"Yes," Carl Gustav answered. "She is your half-sister."

"I am utterly mortified," said Duchess Marta. "How could you deceive me in this way? This revelation will bring nothing but scandal to our good name."

Amalie stood frozen in time while everyone around her began to argue. Loud voices echoed all around her, but she couldn't hear them. She had just learned the truth about who she was, and the shock ran deep. Her knees felt weak, and she sat down on the chair next to the fireplace. She felt as if she couldn't breathe. The room was growing louder and louder, and too many voices were flooding her brain—until she suddenly felt a surge of strength move up her spine and stood up and shouted, "**STOP! STOP!**"

The room grew silent.

"I can't believe what I have just learned here. I have much to say, and I hope to find the words. First, thank you, Annabelle, for remembering. It saddens me to say that I had to learn the truth from you instead of Helene or my father, but I do thank you for telling me."

Then Amalie turned to Helene. "From the day I met you, you have been lying to me. You brought me here under false pretenses and took me away from everything I knew. Even when someone tried to kill me right here in your house, you stayed silent and said nothing. You say you loved my mother, yet you have done nothing but deceive her daughter. What kind of love is that? I had a right to know the truth about my life, and you kept it from me. How could I ever trust you again?"

"Please, dear," Helene pleaded through her tears, "I truly meant well. I felt it was safe because twenty-one years had gone by, and I was certain whoever was trying to hurt Juliet had forgotten about you after all these years. I was wrong, and I'm so sorry. Then Oliver fell in love with you, and it complicated things."

Amalie turned to Duke Carl Gustav, and a surge of anger swept through her. "You say you are my father...but what kind of father denies his daughter? All those years, I grew up thinking no one wanted me—that I belonged to no one—and all that time, you knew where I was, and you never came. Not once. You never came to see me. You went on with your life as if my mother and I never existed. That is not a father. That is a coward."

"Watch how you speak to the Duke!" Duke Oliver howled.

"Silence!" Duke Carl Gustav shouted back at him. "She is right. I was a coward. She deserved better than I gave her, and I will take that regret to my grave."

"You do realize," Davina said to Amalie, "That you are firstborn of the Duke of Herzstein. It is you who should marry Oliver, not me."

"The people will never accept that," Duchess Marta said quickly. "They will not recognize the marriage because Juliet was a commoner, and they were not married in the church. Amalie's birth will be considered illegitimate."

"Again, you speak of me as if I'm not here!" Amalie cried. "I and I alone decide who I will marry. I want no part of this—I want no part of this web of deceit you have spun all around me. I want no part of a family who spins lies and deception at every turn without ever considering the effect it has on anyone else. No! I do not want to be a part of any of this!"

Amalie turned to leave the room, and Oliver grabbed her hand. "My darling, I had no part in this. I did not know any of this. I swear to you, I heard it just as you did. You must believe me."

Tears flooded Amalie's eyes. "I don't believe you. I don't believe anything anymore. You didn't want to marry Davina, and you used me to achieve that. You stole my heart....last night....oh, God, I want to be free of all of you!"

Amalie ran from the room, and Oliver was about to go after her, but Helene stopped him. "Son, she's had a terrible shock. She needs time. Just let her have some time to accept this."

Oliver looked at his mother with angry eyes. "If I lose her over this, I will never forgive you. Ever."

Amalie ran to her room and locked the door behind her. Her mind was in turmoil, and her heart shattered. She paced in her room like a caged animal, trying to grasp what had just happened. Then she realized that she had to get out of there—for good this time. She needed to get as far away from this pain as she possibly could.

After they arrived, Gerald left her bag in the room, and she grabbed it. She dried her tears, put on the red cape Annabelle gave her and left through the secret hallway that Anthony showed her one afternoon after his piano lesson. It led into a tunnel that went underground to the barn and horse stables. It was built by the Duke's grandfather as an escape route if the estate was ever under attack.

After two more hours of discussion, the Herzstein family decided to leave without reaching any solution. Carl Gustav wanted to acknowledge Amalie as his daughter publicly. He wanted to test the waters to see the public reaction. However, the Duchess, Lady Davina, and Oliver were vehemently against the idea for different reasons. Duke Oliver was still seething with anger at Helene for her betrayal, and Helene could not get him to forgive her.

Annabelle had a rare day of clarity and spoke first after the Herzsteins left. "Why on earth did you keep the truth from that dear girl? When you were growing up, Helene, I told you that when you weave a web of deceit, you end up getting caught in it yourself. I wish you had listened to me."

"I wish she had too, grandmother," Oliver said sadly. "I still can't believe Carl Gustav is Amalie's father—and that you knew that all along. Honestly, how could you?"

"I spoke to Carl Gustav after Amalie got here," Helene said, sniffling her nose. "We both felt it was safer for her to do it this way. That was—until the chandelier came crashing down. He was very angry with me for bringing her here."

"That is something the Duke of Herzstein and I agree on," Duke Oliver said, somewhat calmer.

"I am still finding it hard to accept that you and the other Duke are powerless to stop *The Society*. How is it possible that the two ruling authorities in these territories have no power against them? And if not you, then who does?" Oliver said, pacing by the fireplace.

"We are going to have to find that out," Duke Oliver said.

"I'm astonished that you have not done that yet," Oliver said, trying to suppress his anger. "The look on her face still haunts me—she is devastated, but she is also angry, rightfully so."

"Are you going to marry her, Oliver?" Annabelle asked.

"If she'll still have me, yes, most definitely. I am done with charades," Oliver said firmly.

"I never liked that Davina," Annabelle giggled. "Amalie has a pure heart, and I like that about her."

"Her mother was just like that," Helene sighed. "I always wanted to be more like Juliet when we were children."

"Did you see the look on Carl Gustav's face when he spoke to Amalie?" Annabelle asked. "I've never seen him emotional like that."

"He truly loved Juliet," Helene said, wiping her nose. "Amalie looks just like her. I'm sure he sees Juliet in her."

"He was willing to give up everything to be with Juliet," Oliver said. "He's the only one who understands how I feel about Amalie."

"I will never understand how you could be willing to give up everything for this woman," Duke Oliver said, "But I will no longer stand in your way. I cannot force you to assume your duty."

"Thank you, father," Oliver said, surprised by his father's change of heart.

Just then, Hannah came into the parlor, followed by one of the security officers. "Your Graces, I went to check on Amalie since she was so upset earlier, but the door is locked. When she didn't answer, this officer used his master key to open her room. She is not there, and I do not know where she is. The officer posted outside her door said she never left her room. I thought I should alert you."

Oliver felt a shock wave flow through him. "No, oh dear God, not again."

"But how could she leave without anyone seeing her?" Helene cried out.

"The escape tunnel," Annabelle said calmly. "Don't you remember telling me about it?"

"Yes," the Duke said, "It runs from the Blue Room to the stables. How on earth did she ever find it?"

"Anthony," Helene concluded, "I've admonished him several times for playing in it. He must have shown it to her."

Oliver ran out the back door of the estate toward the barn. Once there, he searched for one of the stable hands.

"Evening, sir," said Barton, the Stable Master. "What can I do for you?"

"Was Miss Amalie here?" Oliver asked, out of breath.

"Yes, but she left already. I didn't realize you were going too," Barton replied.

"By horseback or carriage?"

"Carriage. Miss Amalie said there was an emergency at the Abbey, and she needed to leave right away. Barney drove her. Did we do something wrong, sir?"

"How long ago did she leave?" Oliver pressed urgently.

"Almost three hours now. She should be at the Abbey before dark. Is there a problem, sir?"

"No, just saddle my horse. I need to leave right away."

"Yes, sir, but wouldn't you rather take a carriage? It will be dark soon."

"No, just get my horse!" Oliver bellowed.

"Yes, sir," Barton said and scrambled to prepare Oliver's horse.

Oliver rode as fast as possible in the direction of the Abbey. Of course, she would go there, they helped her last time, and they will assist her again. His heart was pounding, and his mind raced as he made his way down the long road to the Abbey. He was distraught, thinking Amalie believed he was part of his family's deception. Nothing mattered but finding her and proving to her that he would never deceive her in that way.

Amalie paid Barney one of her gold coins to change course and take her to Halston Harbor. She still had a ticket for passage to London and decided to get on the ship, and no one would find her this time.

When Oliver arrived at the Abbey hours later, he frantically rang the bell at the locked gate. Once again, Sister Evangeline came out to greet him.

"Your Grace, what on earth are you doing here at this hour?" she asked him.

"Is she here? I know you helped her last time, and I am not angry about that, but please, this is different. She is in danger, and I must find her."

"No, she's not here, honestly. I haven't seen her since Mr. Cartwright took her to Halston Harbor. We assumed she was in London this whole time. Are you saying she wasn't?" Sister Evangeline replied with concern.

Then it hit him. Amalie used the Abbey as a decoy. She deliberately sent him in the wrong direction to buy herself some time.

"No, someone tried to kill her at Halston Harbor, and I got to her just in time. Now she is traveling alone again, and I fear for her safety. Please, if you know where she is, tell me."

"No, Your Grace, I would tell you if I knew. I don't want anything to happen to Amalie. I will pray for her safety," Sister Evangeline said sincerely.

"May I swap out horses so I can continue my journey with a fresh horse?"

"Of course, the stable is around the back. Just tell Stanley that you have my permission. God speed, Your Grace."

It took another hour, precious time in Oliver's mind, to secure a fresh horse. Stanley needed to verify with Sister Evangeline that he indeed had permission, and then he took his time saddling one of the horses for the journey.

"She's an old girl, this one," Stanley said as he secured the reins, "But she's a steady horse. We don't have the caliber of horses you must use, Your Grace, but this is our best one. Just let her rest when she wants to, or she'll stop in a full gallop and throw you over her head."

"Thank you," Oliver said hurriedly. "I will remember that. I will return her to you as soon as I can."

Oliver rode off into the night toward Halston Harbor in a desperate search for the woman he loved. He hoped and prayed that he would get to Amalie in time before *The Society* found her.

Stanley was right about the horse. She traveled at her own speed and stopped several times to rest or graze. Still, once he let her rest, she was always willing to resume her gallop. His journey to Halston Harbor took him through the night. The twilight of dawn was beginning to appear in the sky as he arrived on the outskirts of Halston Harbor. He dropped the horse at the livery, which he was familiar with from his last trip there. He hurried to the docks and hoped he wasn't too late.

When he arrived, he sought out the Harbor Master and inquired about the ship to London.

"That would be the *Hyacinth,* and she's leaving from pier seventeen, but I think you are too late. She's pushing off as we speak," the Harbor Master said, pointing toward the pier.

Oliver ran to pier seventeen and hurried down toward the ship. The *Hyacinth* had pushed away from the dock and slowly headed out to sea. Oliver ran and followed the ship's length, searching for a glimpse of Amalie. Several people were on the deck waving as the ship departed, and his eyes searched desperately for a familiar face. Then he saw it— the red cape. He knew it was her.

"AMALIE!" he shouted, "AMALIE! IT'S OLIVER!"

The woman turned around, and it was indeed Amalie. She looked down at Oliver running to keep up with the ship, and she called out to him. "OLIVER!" as loud as she could.

"I LOVE YOU!" he shouted, "I DIDN'T KNOW!"

Amalie realized what her heart already knew—that Oliver was not part of his family's deception. She doubted him in her shock and confusion, but seeing him on the pier chasing the ship made her realize she was wrong. "I LOVE YOU TOO!" she shouted back.

"WAIT FOR ME IN LONDON!" he shouted as the ship moved further and further away from the pier. "I WILL COME FOR YOU! WAIT FOR ME!"

"YES! I WILL WAIT FOR YOU!" Amalie shouted and waved. She blew him a kiss and waved goodbye.

Oliver blew her a kiss and stopped running as he had come to the end of the pier and could go no further. The ship was almost out of sight now, but he waved, hoping she could still see him. His heart was pounding, and he was overjoyed that Amalie said she would wait for him. Oliver intended to immediately go to the ticket office and buy passage on the next ship to London when he passed the familiar boat shed. Oliver stopped for a moment as he remembered what happened the last time he was there when suddenly he was violently hit over the head, and everything went black.

Chapter 8

Lara

Amalie arrived in London in good spirits despite the endless rain during the crossing. She disembarked and headed toward town. She found a quaint place called *The Restful Inn* right across the street from the docks on the corner. Amalie went inside to rent a room to wait there until Oliver arrived. She was pleased to see that the inn also had a dining room. Mrs. McCoy, the owner, checked her in.

"How many nights will you be staying, Miss Bennett?" Mrs. McCoy asked, writing the name Amalie gave her in the guestbook.

"One, possibly two when my, uh, husband arrives. When does the next ship arrive from Halston Harbor?"

"The ship arrives the same time every day. Weren't you on the *Hyacinth?* I thought I saw you walk up with others from the ship," Mrs. McCoy said.

"Yes, but he missed the ship. I expect him tomorrow," Amalie said quickly.

"Well, he should arrive the same time you did. Supper service begins at six in the dining room. Meals cost extra, but our food is tasty and reasonable."

"Thank you, Mrs. McCoy. I'm looking forward to it. I was a bit queasy during the crossing, but by then, it should be fine," Amalie said.

"First time on a ship?" Mrs. McCoy asked.

Amalie nodded.

"Yeah, that gets everyone—that first time rocking over those waves. Drink some peppermint tea; that will help. We serve it in the dining room."

"Thank you," Amalie said, taking her room key from Mrs. McCoy.

Amalie found her room on the second floor and was happy to see that she had a view of the harbor from her window. She was excited that she could see the *Hyacinth* at the dock. *I'll be able to see when Oliver arrives tomorrow!*

The following day, Amalie headed to the dock mid-afternoon to wait for the ship to arrive. The *Hyacinth* was right on time, and as passengers began to disembark, she grew excited to see Oliver. However, after everyone left the ship, he was not there. She approached the Harbor Master to inquire.

"Is that everyone?" she asked.

"Yes, ma'am. That's everyone for today," he replied.

Amalie's disappointment ran deep. *What could have kept him? Something must have happened. I'm sure he will be here tomorrow.*

Oliver not arriving as promised weighed heavily on her as she walked back to the inn, but she was sure there was a reasonable explanation for his delay. He would explain it all to her tomorrow.

Amalie waited again the following day, and again, he did not arrive. And once again, she approached the Harbor Master to ensure everyone had disembarked, and he assured her that everyone was off the ship.

Amalie slowly walked back to the inn with a heavy heart. As she entered, Mrs. McCoy greeted her.

"I was expecting to see your husband today. He wasn't on the ship?" Mrs. McCoy asked.

"No, and I am getting worried. I fear something may have happened to keep him from coming. He's a Captain in the army and….."

"Oh, don't you worry your pretty little head about it," Mrs. McCoy tried to cheer her up. "I'm sure he'll be along soon."

"Yes, I'm sure too. Maybe tomorrow," Amalie said, trying to convince herself.

"You could write to him, but by the time that letter gets to him, he will most likely be here already. Try again tomorrow, deary."

Day after day, the same scenario played out. Amalie waited at the dock, she watched the passengers disembark, and Oliver was not on board. She began to question whether she was a fool for believing he would come for her, but she tried to shake those thoughts from her head as soon as they crept in. She was sure she heard him correctly at the dock in Halston Harbor. He said he loved her and that he would come for her. She tried to hold on to that, but it was more challenging to do with each passing day. She decided to try one more day, and then if he did not come, she would leave for the north country by train.

She waited in her usual place and watched the passengers disembark the following day. Oliver was not among them. Amalie turned to the Harbor Master, and before she could ask the familiar question, he said, "Sorry Miss, that's everyone."

"And the next ship from Halston Harbor?" she asked, already knowing the answer.

"Just like today and every day, ma'am."

"Oh, well, thank you and goodbye. I won't be here tomorrow," Amalie said sadly.

"No? Well, I will miss seeing you," he said, tipping his cap to her.

Her resolve was wearing thin. Was she being duped again? Could she still trust him after everything that happened? Anger began to well up deep within as she turned to walk away from the dock for the last time.

Amalie reminded herself that she now had other matters to consider. The nausea she felt since the ship crossing was not from the ship rocking and had everything to do with the life she suspected was growing in her belly. Her body was changing, and she was so queasy every morning that she could not eat.

When Amalie returned to the inn, she stopped at the desk to purchase a train ticket to the north country. Mrs.

McCoy brokered the tickets to her many guests who journeyed through her inn on their way up north.

"Have you given up, deary?" Mrs. McCoy asked her.

Amalie was in no mood for conversation, so she simply said, "Yes," and headed to the dining room for her first meal of the day.

Amalie found a small table by the window in the crowded dining room. She ordered the special and some tea. She sat staring at her train ticket with a heavy heart. *Why didn't he come?*

Just then, Amalie felt a tap on her shoulder. It was Mrs. McCoy standing at her table with an impeccably dressed attractive woman with a large, feathered hat with blonde hair flowing from under it.

"Deary, would you mind sharing your table with the Countess of Attenbury? We're full up, and she has traveled far."

"Of course, please sit down," Amalie said, tucking the train ticket into her pocket.

"Thank you so much," the Countess said, removing her hat. "I always stop here on my way home from visiting my family, but I have never seen it this full."

"A ship just came in," Amalie explained.

"Ah, that must be it. I would have been so disappointed if I couldn't eat here today. Thank you for sharing your table," the Countess said, pulling off her gloves.

"You're welcome."

The server brought Amalie's food and tea, and the Countess looked at the plate and asked the server, "Ooh, that looks delicious. What is it?"

"Roasted pheasant, ma'am, with salt potatoes and carrots," he said, then added, "But be careful, you may find some buckshot."

"Sounds wonderful. I'll have that." Then the Countess looked at Amalie and said, "By the way, my name is Lara," and held out her hand to shake.

"Maria Bennett," Amalie answered and shook her hand, then continued to eat.

"Are you traveling through, or do you live here?" Lara asked, trying to make conversation.

"I'm leaving on the London and Northwestern Railway tomorrow for the north country. I hope to secure a teaching position there," Amalie answered, taking a bite of her dinner.

"Are you traveling alone?"

"I'm sorry, Lara, but I'm not very good company right now," Amalie said, unable to hide her unhappiness.

"Oh, dear, you do look sad. I hope it's nothing serious," Lara said sincerely.

"I….I just lost my love. I'm heartbroken and am not sure where my life is going now that I'm alone," Amalie said, surprising herself at how much she shared with a total stranger.

"Oh, I'm so sorry," Lara said warmly, "You're too young to be a widow! You have my sincerest condolences."

Amalie realized that Lara thought she was mourning a loss and decided not to correct her. After all, she would never see this woman again after today. "Thank you."

The server brought Lara's food, and they ate in silence for a few minutes until Lara felt compelled to converse with her tablemate. "So, you're a teacher? What do you teach?"

"I'm a music teacher. I teach piano."

"Really? That's marvelous! When I married the Earl, my father gave me a grand piano, but I never learned to play it."

Amalie couldn't help but like Lara. She was warm and friendly, but most importantly, she seemed genuine. "I always say the saddest thing in the world is a piano no one plays," Amalie said, sipping her tea.

"That is so true. Wait, did you say you hope to secure a teaching position?"

"Yes, why?"

"I just had the most brilliant idea!" Lara gushed. "I will hire you to teach me to play the piano. You can work for me. I will offer you room and board as well until I've mastered the piano. I must warn you, though, it could take a while."

Amalie was hesitant, and Lara recognized that. "I know you don't know me at all, but I assure you, I am a respectable lady. I am the Countess of Attenbury. Mrs. McCoy has known me for years. I have been stopping here every few months on my trips back to visit my family. The inn is the halfway point, and I always stop here to eat. I promise you; I pose no threat to you."

"I'm sure you are a proper lady, but ….." Amalie stopped short of telling her about the recent danger she faced.

"Mrs. McCoy," Lara called out. "Could you come here for a moment?"

Mrs. McCoy came to the table. "Is your food not satisfactory?"

"Oh, heavens yes, as always. I need you to vouch for me with this young woman. I want to hire her as a music teacher, and she is hesitating because she doesn't know me."

"Oh, you don't need to worry about the Countess. She's good people. I've been serving her for years now. You needn't worry about working for her," Mrs. McCoy assured her.

"Thank you, Mrs. McCoy," Lara said. "You see, I'm good people, as she said."

After Mrs. McCoy left the table, Amalie's mind was racing with the offer. "Where is your estate?"

"West of here about another two hours by carriage. The estate itself is quite secluded, which sometimes drives me crazy it's so quiet, but we are only minutes from the nearest town."

"It sounds lovely," Amalie said, trying to decide quickly.

"Oh, it is. A bit too large for only two people, but it is gorgeously decorated by yours truly. And you would be great company for me. Please say you'll accept my offer and leave with me when we finish our meal."

Amalie found it difficult to refuse. It would solve her immediate problems—room and board, a safe location, and income. She was also confident that *The Society* would never find her there. "Yes, I think I will accept your offer of employment."

"Splendid! I'm so happy I met you here today!" Lara said, gently clapping her hands together.

"Yes," Amalie smiled. "Me too."

Amalie finished her meal and went up to her room to pack. When she stopped at the front desk to settle her account, she was surprised to learn that the Countess had paid it in full. She joined Lara in front of the inn, and they boarded the carriage to the Attenbury Estate.

"Thank you for paying my account. It was very kind of you but not necessary," Amalie said graciously.

"I was happy to do it. Just consider it an employment bonus for agreeing to work for me when you hardly know me," Lara said, smiling.

Amalie noticed that Lara was still young and close to her in age. She wondered how young she was when she married. "How long have you lived at the Attenbury Estate?" Amalie asked.

"Six years now," Lara replied, but the cheerfulness vanished. "I was married at sixteen. My father arranged it. The Earl had massive gambling debts and needed an influx of money, so he sought a wife with a large dowry. My father was willing to pay for his daughter to be a Countess. I still haven't forgiven my father, but I don't need to bore you with my tale of woe."

Once again, Amalie learned that wealth, title, and royalty often come at a price and that many affluent families were not necessarily happy ones. "I'm sorry you had to marry so young. I wish we women had a say in our destinies, but I'm learning that we often don't."

"Yes," Lara sighed, "It's a man's world, for sure, but we women do assume our power—we just have to do it in subtle ways." A wry smile formed on her lips.

Amalie liked Lara immediately. She knew they would become good friends.

The following day at the harbor in London, the *Hyacinth* docked, and a weary Captain disembarked. He searched the dock for any sign of Amalie, but she was not there. He suspected she wouldn't be, after waiting for over nine days without seeing him there. Still, he approached the Harbor Master to inquire if she had been there.

"Have you seen a beautiful young woman with dark hair and eyes of blue, most likely wearing a red cape?" Oliver asked.

"Oh, yes, sir, she was here every day waiting for someone. Yesterday she told me she wouldn't be coming back. Poor thing, she was so sad. She was staying at the inn right over there. Mrs. McCoy might know where she's gone."

"Thank you!" Oliver said, shaking his hand. He was encouraged that he only missed her by one day.

"Are you alright, sir? You look like you've been in battle," the man asked as he noticed the bruises on Oliver's face.

"Yes, just a fall from my horse," Oliver lied. He wouldn't tell him that *The Society* captured him, beat him, and held him for several days.

Oliver made his way to the inn and rang the bell at the front desk. A man appeared from the back room and greeted him.

"You be needing a room, sir?" the man asked.

"I would like to speak to Mrs. McCoy."

"I'm her husband, Walter. We own this place. My wife is out getting supplies. How can I help you?"

"I'm looking for a young woman who stayed here until yesterday. Her name is Amalie. I'm hoping you can tell me where she's gone. I was to meet her here, but I was delayed," Oliver said anxiously.

"Well, let's have a look at the ledger," Walter said, putting his eyeglasses on his nose. "The only woman who paid her account yesterday is Maria Bennett. It shows that she purchased a ticket on the train to the north country."

"Yes, that's her," Oliver said quickly. "Does it say specifically where in the north country?"

"No, sir. That train makes many stops on that route. Hard to say which one is her destination."

"Thank you for your help," Oliver said, his heart in his throat. How would he ever find her once she disappears in the vast north country? "Please, I want to purchase the same ticket she has."

Walter issued him a ticket, and Oliver hurried to the train depot to board the train into the unknown, but he vowed to find her—no matter how long it took or how far he had to travel.

Amalie and Lara arrived at the Attenbury Estate just in time for afternoon tea. Lara guided Amalie to the plush guest room, which included a bathtub, a rarity in older estates. Then the ladies went down to the sitting room to join the Earl for tea.

"Darling, I want you to meet my new piano teacher, Maria Bennett," Lara said to the man seated in a throne-like chair. Amalie could see he was older than Lara and seemed close in age to her father, Duke Carl Gustav. "Maria, this is the Earl of Attenbury."

The Earl rose, and Amalie curtsied to him. He looked down his nose at her and said flatly to his wife, "I see you're still bringing home stray kittens."

Lara was unfazed. "Now darling, mind your manners. Maria will be living here while she teaches me to play my piano."

"Well, perhaps that is a good thing," the Earl said, sitting back down on his throne. "If you have something to occupy your time instead of hounding me incessantly, then I will have more time for my other interests."

"Of course, dear," Lara placated him.

Amalie immediately could sense there was no love between them at all. "I'm happy to be here," she said, accepting the tea that Lara handed her from the tea cart.

"Well, if you ladies will excuse me, I've finished my tea and have an important appointment in town."

The Earl rose and left the room. Amalie could see that Lara immediately relaxed when he left.

"Don't mind him," Lara said apologetically, "He has a loud bark but never bites."

"Are you sure he doesn't mind that I am here?" Amalie asked.

"Of course not. Having you here to help me pass the time gives him more time to pursue his *other interests*. His other interests have names, and all work for Madame Isabelle at the brothel," Lara said, adding a shot of rum to her tea. "Want some?"

"Oh," Amalie said with a blush on her cheeks. "No thanks."

"It's fine, really," Lara said, sipping her tea. "I prefer he seek out those women and leave me alone. As you can see, Maria, this is not a love match. He married me for my family's money and to produce an heir. No other reason. I have no delusions about my marriage."

"I'm sorry. I feel sad for you. Then again, loving someone can equally break your heart. I speak from experience," Amalie shared.

"Yes, I know, and I'm hoping that your time here will help you heal from your loss," Lara said with genuine warmth.

"It already has," Amalie said truthfully, "Just knowing that I am secure for now has already helped a great deal."

"I'm so glad! And I'm so happy you're here!" Lara sang excitedly.

Oliver took the train to the north country and planned to inquire at each stop along the route. He knew someone somewhere had to see her and point him in the right direction. Thank God for that red cape Annabelle gave to Amalie. It will help to identify her by those who may have seen her. He was heartsick that Amalie was out there somewhere, thinking he did not come for her. He came as soon as he was free, but Amalie had no way of knowing that *The Society* nearly killed Oliver and that they only released him because the Supreme Leader confirmed that he was the future Duke of Corrington.

As Amalie lay in her bed that first night, her thoughts were only of Oliver. Her heart ached, remembering that he never came to be with her. She cried into her pillow and wondered how she would manage with a child. She replayed the whole scene at Corrington House and felt deep resentment for those who lied to her and abandoned her. She always longed to know who her father was as a child, but now she wished she didn't know the truth. His denial of her was unforgivable, and she was glad that her child would not grow up in a family such as theirs.

Amalie settled into life at the Attenbury Estate and felt serene in her surroundings. Lara was a very late sleeper, so Amalie had no trouble hiding her morning sickness from her. The piano lessons were going well because Lara was an enthusiastic student. The lessons were still in the beginner stage, and Amalie enjoyed teaching when someone was as eager as Lara.

The Earl was not home very much, which seemed fine with his wife. Amalie and Lara were becoming close friends, and they enjoyed spending time together. After lessons, they would take long walks in the gardens or play the dice games Lara loved.

One morning at seven o'clock, there was a knock on Amalie's door. It was Lara, and she burst into the room with utter excitement. "Maria, get up! It's my birthday today, and I want to celebrate all day! Put on your robe. We're having breakfast on the patio. The sun is shining, and it's a beautiful fall day."

"Happy birthday," Amalie said sleepily, climbing out of bed. She slipped into her robe and followed Lara downstairs to the patio outside the west entrance. The staff had set a beautiful table adorned with flowers, fresh fruit, and fresh warm breakfast rolls.

"Will the Earl be joining us?" Amalie asked.

"No, he's off already to God-knows-what, and I would rather have breakfast with you, my friend," Lara said, pouring them both some breakfast tea.

"What else will you be doing to celebrate your birthday?" Amalie asked, trying to wake up.

"We have some guests coming for a dinner party this evening, and I was hoping you might play the piano for them. You play so beautifully, and it would be a wonderful birthday present for me."

"I would be happy to," Amalie said, fighting the sickness that visited her every morning. She took a bite of bread hoping to settle her stomach.

"Now my birthday is perfect!" Lara declared excitedly.

Amalie could no longer keep the nausea at bay and hurried to the bushes to throw up. She was embarrassed in front of her friend.

Lara rushed to her side and rubbed her back. "How far along are you?" she asked gently.

"Just a few weeks," Amalie answered honestly. "I guess I couldn't hide it much longer anyway."

"I've suspected for a while now. I have four sisters, and they all have children. I can recognize the signs," Lara said, handing Amalie the napkin she had in her hand.

Amalie straightened herself and took the napkin to wipe her lips. "I'm sorry, I didn't mean to keep it from you, it's just that...." she searched for the right words.

"There is no shame in being a pregnant widow, Maria. I'm so sorry that your loss was so recent. He must have just died when I met you, and I feel bad now that I babbled on and on while you were so deep in mourning."

"Lara, let's sit down and talk. I want to be honest with you. You have become a trusted friend, and I feel safe telling you the truth."

"Now you have me intrigued," Lara said as they sat back down at the table.

"I'm not a widow," Amalie began.

"But you said you—oh wait, I assumed that, didn't I?" Lara realized.

"Yes, and I'm sorry I didn't correct you, but I honestly thought I would never see you again and it wouldn't matter."

"What happened to your husband?" Lara asked.

"I'm going to tell you the story from the beginning, and it will take some time," Amalie said, then proceeded to tell her the complete story from that day Helene claimed her at the Abbey to the family meeting at Corrington House. Lastly, she told her what her real name was.

Lara listened intently, and when Amalie finished, Lara reached for her hand and held it. "Oh my God, this is incredible. You poor thing—what you have been through—I read books like this but have never heard a tale so heartbreaking that is real life."

"So, you see, I am with child, unmarried, and hiding from some unknown group that wants to kill me. And the man I love has abandoned me. I was utterly devastated that day we met. Yet, you have been the answer to a prayer. You have provided me with the refuge that I needed," Amalie said, feeling free to speak honestly.

"Maria—I mean Amalie, you can stay here as long as you like. I love having you here. You have offered me some refuge also from the living hell that is my marriage. It seems we have helped each other."

Amalie reached out and embraced Lara. "I am so grateful you sat down at my table that day. You have become my first real friend."

"Yes, me too," Lara said sincerely.

"I'm sorry I wasn't honest with you from the beginning, but it's been so hard for me to know who I can trust."

"That is certainly understandable," Lara said, "We should stick with Maria Bennett for now for your safety. No one else needs to know your real identity."

"Yes, I agree, that would be best," Amalie agreed.

"I'm so envious that you are with child," Lara admitted, "I so want to have a child, but not with that monster."

"Is he that bad?" Amalie asked, finally being brave enough to sip some tea.

"Well, I have plotted his demise in my head many times, but of course, I would never act on it. He is a cold-hearted, mean-spirited bastard, and I haven't spoken to my father since he made me marry him. I was only sixteen, Maria, and on my wedding night, he brutalized me in so many ways. It was the worst night of my life. I considered killing myself rather than submitting to him again, but I couldn't go through with it. I confided in my mother, and she taught me a little trick to help me get through those nights when he comes into my room. While he is doing his business, I go to faraway places in my head. I imagine I am at a ball with a handsome prince or on a beautiful beach somewhere. It gets me through it."

Amalie reached for Lara's hand and cupped it in hers. "I'm so sorry, Lara. That is horrible. No one should have to suffer like that, husband or not."

"You're right, but what choice do we have? I have my little ways of exacting revenge on him, and he has no idea about it. You see, he wants an heir, and I refuse to bring something into the world that came from that evil seed, so I make sure he will never have one. Remember, I told you that we do have power, but we must deliver it in very subtle ways."

"How do you prevent a pregnancy?" Amalie asked innocently.

"My mother has a close friend who owns an apothecary. She makes this special salve for women, and if you use it down there, the seed cannot get where it needs to go, and there will be no baby. It's worked for six years now."

"I had no idea such a thing existed," Amalie declared, touching her belly. "I wish I had known."

"You conceived your child in love, Maria. Your baby will be a blessing to you, even without a husband."

"Yes, I suppose so. I only wish that Oliver was sharing this with me, but it seems he chose his family over me," Amalie sighed.

"Do you know that for sure? Have you written to him? Something might have happened that kept him from coming to you. If I had a man who loved me like that, I would give him the benefit of the doubt and at least write to him. Then you will know for sure," Lara suggested.

"I thought about writing to him, but I never did out of fear that the letter would be intercepted by those who wish me dead. I didn't want to take that chance," Amalie confided in her friend.

"If you decide to write to him, I will make sure the letter gets delivered by private messenger. It would be someone that I trust. I promise you; it would be safe."

"I will consider it. Thank you, my friend."

"Now, we've talked so much I'm starving. Can you eat something now?"

"Yes, it has passed. I'm hungry too. My appetite since I came here has been enormous," Amalie said, taking a breakfast roll from the basket.

"Well, my dear, you are eating for two now," Lara said warmly. "Your baby wants his breakfast."

Oliver was getting more frustrated with each passing day. Every stop on the train trip resulted in no one having seen her. He asked railroad personnel, spoke to the conductors, inquired at local inns and restaurants, and no one saw her. Oliver visited schools and churches, thinking Amalie would seek employment there but always came up empty-handed. It was like he was chasing a ghost. Oliver was beginning to lose hope of ever finding her. He had one more stop at the end of the line, and if she wasn't there, he would turn around and go back to Halston Harbor and start over. It had occurred to him that he may have been following the wrong trail, but how many Maria Bennetts could there be at that inn? Oliver also realized that she may have purchased the train ticket to fool anyone who might be chasing her. She had used a decoy in the past. Oliver's deep love for her compelled him to keep searching.

Amalie sat down at the desk in her room and began a letter to Oliver. She still wasn't sure she would send it to him but wanted to write it anyway.

My dearest love,
It has been weeks now since we were together. So much has happened and there is so much I want to share with you, but you are not here with me. I need to know why you didn't come. I waited every day for over a week until I realized you were not coming. I have been heartbroken ever since.
If they are looking for me, I am not where they think I am. I never boarded the train to the north country. I met a delightful woman who has hired me to be her music teacher. I am staying at their estate. She has kindly given me refuge from the dangerous world I was living in when I was with you. I have found peace here with a very dear friend.
I need to tell you that our evening together has given me a precious gift. I am carrying your child, Oliver, and I wish you were here to share this with me. Our child will be born shortly after the Lover's Festival where you will pledge your love to another. My heart will not accept that reality. Since you didn't come to London, I must assume that duty won over love.
I understand the pressure you are under to fulfill your duty, and I know that you have struggled with your love for me. I am sorry I came along and complicated your life, but I do not regret a single moment of my time with you. I will cherish those memories and our child, who I know will be a boy. I want a little Oliver to love if I can't have his father with me. Having your son will be what keeps me going into the future.
I wish you nothing but happiness in your life, my love, and hope that when you become Duke, it will bring you all the satisfaction your heart desires.
With love always,
Amalie

Amalie sealed the letter and put it in her desk drawer. If she chooses to send it, it will be ready.

Chapter 9

Sir Thomas

Doreen, the chambermaid, cleaned Amalie's room and began to tidy the desk. She closed the ink well and gathered up the writing paper. When she put the stationery in the desk drawer, she saw the letter addressed to Captain Oliver Corrington. She slipped it into her pocket, then hurried out of the room.

Doreen located the Earl in his study and closed the door behind her.

"Sir, you asked me to keep an eye on the Duchess and her new friend, and today I found this. I thought you should see it," Doreen said eagerly.

The Earl read the name on the front and wondered out loud, "Now why would a music teacher be writing a letter to the future Duke of Corrington?"

"That's why I thought you should see it," Doreen said, "I thought it was odd."

"Thank you for bringing this to my attention. Good work, Doreen."

Doreen's face lit up as she realized she pleased the Earl. "My allegiance is to you, not her."

"Yes," the Earl said, touching her cheek, "And let's keep it that way, shall we?"

When Doreen left the study, the Earl broke the seal and read the letter. When he finished, a calculating smile crossed his lips. *Well, well, I just found a way to pay my debt to Sir Thomas. He will be most interested in this.*

Oliver reached the end of the line and had not found Amalie—not even a possible clue from anyone who may have seen her. He fought hard not to feel defeated as he headed back to Halston Harbor. His mind was in turmoil, trying to regroup and start from scratch in his search. If she didn't leave Halston Harbor by train, then how did she leave? Or did she leave at all? Was she hiding right under his nose, and he didn't see it? It tortured Oliver that Amalie was out there thinking that he wasn't looking for her, yet she was careful and covering her tracks because she believed *The Society* was still after her. That was keeping Oliver from finding her also.

Amalie anxiously hurried down to breakfast and asked, "Lara, did you mail my letter?"

"What letter? I didn't know you wrote one. What's wrong? You look terrified."

"It's gone. The letter I wrote to Oliver it's missing from my desk. Oh my God, who could have taken it?" Amalie said in a panic.

"Calm down, Maria, this is not good for your baby. I will find out what happened to it; I promise you. Perhaps Doreen thought it was outgoing mail, but she wouldn't just take it without asking you. At least, I don't think she would. Let me call her in here, and we'll figure this out."

Lara summoned Doreen, and she came promptly.

"Doreen, did you remove a letter from Maria's room?" Lara asked firmly.

"Yes, ma'am. I thought it was outgoing mail," Doreen lied.

"Why would you remove it from the desk and mail it without asking Maria or me? You have overstepped in your duties!" Lara shouted angrily, "And this is not the first time."

"I beg your pardon, ma'am, it won't happen again," Doreen said flatly.

"So, you mailed it?" Amalie asked.

"No, I gave it to the Earl to send along with his other correspondence."

Lara stepped closer to Doreen and was close enough to feel her breath. "If you ever go into someone's private things and remove anything at all, I will have you arrested. I am watching you, and you better not overstep again, or you will be relieved of your duties at once. Do you understand me?"

"Yes, ma'am," Doreen said without flinching.

"Get back to work," Lara commanded.

Doreen shuffled out of the room.

Amalie was distraught. "I hadn't decided if I was going to mail it, but the bigger problem is that anyone could open it and realize who I am. I could be in danger if that happens. I thought I was safe here—I don't know what to do now."

"Let me handle the Earl. Doreen is a simpleton, but the Earl can be so evil. That letter in his hands could be problematic."

Amalie began to cry. "Do you think I should leave?"

"No, please don't. It may never come to that. I will do everything I can to protect you and your child. Please, trust me, you are safer here than out there somewhere with no protection."

"Do you think it's possible he just mailed it along with his correspondence, as Doreen said?" Amalie asked, seeking reassurance.

"With the Earl, I never predict what he will do. But I promise you; I will find out—one way or another. Please, calm your heart. I hate to see you so upset."

"There have been two attempts on my life. I have someone else to worry about now," Amalie said, placing her hand on her stomach. "I wrote in the letter that I am with child."

"I know, and I promise you I will get to the bottom of this, my friend. I will speak with my most trusted messenger to see if the Earl mailed your letter. If he didn't mail it, then we might have a problem," Lara declared.

"Can your messenger truly be trusted?" Amalie asked.

"I trust him with my life," Lara said and then lowered her voice. "He is the man I love and have loved for years. Owen followed me here after I married and gained employment with the Earl to be near me. He serves as the Earl's secretary. He knows how evil the Earl can be. He hates him even more than I do."

"You never cease to amaze me, my dear friend. I'm so glad you have someone to love, even if it has to be in secret," Amalie said sincerely.

"Owen is Irish, and he's the most beautiful man I've ever seen. If I ever have a child, I want it to be his," Lara said dreamily.

"Please get in touch with him and see about the letter. I won't have any peace until I know for sure."

"I will see him later today. He handles the Earl's correspondence. If he mailed the letter, Owen would know."

Lara couldn't find a safe time to speak with Owen because the Earl was always near, so she slipped him a note. They often exchanged messages and knew to always burn them after reading them. After he held the note in his hand and read it, he nodded to Lara to let her know he understood what she needed.

Lara had afternoon tea with Amalie and tried to reassure her. "Owen knows what we need. He will contact me as soon as it's safe. Please don't worry about *The Society* finding you here. This is England, and those two territories haven't been part of the United Kingdom for centuries."

"They seem to be relentless once they have a target, and for some reason, their target is me," Amalie sighed.

"If he did mail the letter, then Oliver will know that you are safe and that you are with child. Did you tell him where you are?" Lara asked.

"No. Do you think I should have?"

"Yes. My dear Maria, how can he find you if you don't tell him where you are?" Lara gently chided.

"I don't think he's looking for me. I waited at the pier for over nine days. He never came like he said he would. As I wrote in the letter, I think duty won over love."

"You will never know for sure until you hear it from Oliver himself. Give him the benefit of the doubt, Maria. If I could be with Owen forever, I would move heaven and earth to do it," Lara said.

"Well, I can always send him another letter through Owen and tell him where I am. If Oliver comes for me, then I will know. If he doesn't come, then I will know that he chose his duty."

The Earl of Attenbury met with Sir Thomas in a private back room at Madame Isabelle's, where they first met. Sir Thomas is his title, as the current head of *The Society*, his real name is Winston. At Madame Isabelle's, he prefers to go by Winston. When King Henry VI formed *The Society* by Royal Decree, he appointed Sir Thomas Killinger as the group's first Supreme Leader, and he led the group until his death. Every designated leader since that time has been called Sir Thomas as a manner of honoring the first Supreme Leader of the group.

"What is it that you have for me?" Winston asked, drinking his third or fourth mug of dark ale. "I don't cancel gambling debts as a practice, so I'm fairly sure you are wasting my time."

"I think this might change your mind," The Earl said, pulling the letter out of his jacket pocket. "But, before I show it to you, I need your assurance that we have a deal."

Winston leaned closer to the Earl and said with gritted teeth, "You're lucky you're not dead yet. No one is as delinquent as you in your debts to me. I don't make assurances either."

The Earl handed him the letter. Winston looked at the addressee and said, "Where did you get this?"

"From a young woman living at my estate at the moment," the Earl said with a sheepish grin.

Winston read the letter, refolded it, and put it in his pocket. "You have done well, but not well enough. I will reduce your debt by ten thousand, but you still owe me thirty."

"Only ten thousand? For that important information? You talk too much when you're drunk, Winston. I happen to know that you have been searching for this woman for some time now. I just handed her to you. I won't let you shortchange me like this!" the Earl insisted.

Winston pounded his fist down hard on the table, making the Earl jump. "You are not in control here, you simple little man! When will you learn? If you cannot honor your debt, I can legally shoot you, and no one will care, especially that young wife of yours. Shall I do her a favor and shoot you right now, or are you going to work off the remainder of your debt?"

The Earl knew that Winston had killed several who owed him money and knew better than challenging him further. "What is it you would have me do?"

"Kill her, and I will cancel the remainder of your debt. I will let you live when I have proof that she is dead. Fail me, and your young wife will be a widow before the week is out," Winston said, leaning closer to the Earl. "And in case you're thinking of double-crossing me, I have installed our people in every noble household in the land. Trust me—I will know."

"I will take care of it," the Earl said, trembling. "Consider it done."

Lara was walking down the long hallway to her bedroom when Owen grabbed her arm and pulled her into one of the unused bedrooms. They kissed and held each other for a few precious moments, then Lara asked him, "Is the Earl gone?"

"Yes, he said he had a meeting in town, but you and I both know that he's at Madame Isabelle's."

"Were you able to find out about Maria's letter?" Lara asked in a hushed voice.

"Yes, and he never mailed it. At least, he never gave it to me to send, and I can't imagine he would mail it himself," Owen replied.

"This is not good," Lara said nervously, "He is up to something. Why on earth would he keep that letter? I'm worried about my friend. She's been through so much already."

"I wish I had better news for you, my dearest Lara, but when it comes to the Earl, there is never any good news."

Lara looked up at him and gently touched his face. "If it weren't for you, I swear, I would go mad in the place. Having Maria here has been so wonderful, and for some reason, he wants to spoil that for me. Now he knows who she is and that scares me."

"Who is she?" Owen asked.

Lara told him a shortened version of the story of Amalie and Oliver. Owen listened and then had a realization. "Lara, if he has something personal to gain from exposing her, trust me, he will do it without flinching. You say she's in danger from *The Society,* and they've already tried twice to kill her. The Earl could use that to his advantage somehow."

"Oh, Owen, what are we going to do?" Lara asked anxiously.

"Let her know to be on her guard at all times. I will see if I can somehow find out what he's up to."

"I love you, Owen," Lara said, kissing him. "Please be my eyes and ears too. I will need your help with this."

"Always, my love. Anything for you."

Then the lovers used their alone time together to share their love. These stolen moments were all they had, and they made the most of each opportunity.

Later that afternoon, Lara brought Amalie up to date on Owen's findings during their piano lesson. Amalie grew anxious knowing that the Earl knew her identity. Lara took her hand and tried to calm her.

"Listen to me; I will be with you as much as I can. Owen is watching the Earl closely. He may just be using this as some leverage against me. He's done this kind of thing before—anything to keep me in my place. He knows he can't leave me, then my father will demand the dowry back, and he cannot afford to let that happen, so he's playing games with something he can hold over me."

"I am very uneasy about this. The Earl knows who I am. Do you think he could somehow get that information to *The Society*?" Amalie asked nervously.

"My husband is many things, but I doubt even he would do something like that," Lara lied. The moment the words rolled off her tongue, she realized that he would do precisely that if he had something to gain from it. "Please don't worry but keep your eyes open and your senses keen—at least until we know what he's up to."

That evening at dinner, Lara was surprised to see different faces at the dinner table when she and Amalie entered the dining room.

"Darling," Lara said nervously, "You should have told me we were having guests for dinner. I would have asked the staff to prepare a more elegant meal."

"No need to fuss on my account," Sir Thomas said, "It was a last-minute invitation following our business meeting this afternoon. You must be the lovely lady of the house. I am Sir Thomas, my lady."

"Welcome to our home," Lara said, forcing a smile. "This is my music teacher, Maria Gilchrist." Lara was so nervous she mixed up Amalie's name.

Sir Thomas bowed to both ladies.

"You already know Owen. I invited him to join us this evening as well so the three of us could continue our business meeting after dinner," the Earl said, eyeing his wife's reaction.

"Nice to see you again, Countess," Owen said.

"Yes, I'm glad you could join us," Lara said, taking her seat at the table.

Amalie was unsure of the situation but could sense the tension in the room, so she just watched and listened. She, too, noticed that Lara mixed up her name and hoped no one else noticed.

As the staff began to serve the meal, Amalie noticed that the Earl was nervous and appeared to have beads of sweat on his forehead. Amalie wondered what his relationship was with Sir Thomas, who seemed to be the only one in the room who wasn't anxious.

"How's the hunting in those woods?" Sir Thomas asked the Earl. "I hear the wild boar are plentiful."

"I'm not much of a hunter, only small game like pheasant and duck, maybe rabbit," the Earl said stiffly.

"Well, I have my rifle in the carriage if you decide you want to do some hunting tomorrow."

"Are you staying with us, Sir Thomas?" Lara asked.

"Why yes, I thought your husband would have told you. I will be here until my business concludes with the Earl."

"He failed to mention it, but you are certainly welcome. I will have the staff prepare a room for you," Lara said tensely.

"We hate to inconvenience you, Sir Thomas," Owen interjected, "We could conclude our business this evening if you would prefer."

"Let's just see how it goes, shall we?" Sir Thomas replied, then he fixed his eyes on Amalie. "So, you are a music teacher, Miss Gilchrist? Were you educated at the Abbey?"

A cold chill ran through Amalie. "How do you know about the Abbey?"

"Your last name, dear," he replied, "Many of the orphans have that last name when there is no family name."

"There are also many families whose last name is Gilchrist. You make quite the assumption, Sir Thomas," Amalie said with confidence to hide the anxiety beneath the surface.

"I beg your pardon if I am mistaken, but I don't think I am. There is no shame in being an orphan, Miss Gilchrist. The late Mother Superior taught many of those children music to provide them with a means to earn a living."

Now Amalie was sure he knew who she was. "How do you know Mother Superior? Were you an orphan yourself, Sir Thomas?"

"No, I once lived near the Abbey as a child. I am very familiar with it—a beautiful setting, nestled there in the mountains far away from everything and everyone."

"Maria is an excellent teacher," Lara said, trying to change the subject. "I have learned much from her, and my playing has improved greatly."

"I'm sure she is," Sir Thomas said, stabbing his meat with his fork, making the Earl jump. "Perhaps you could play for us after dinner, Countess?"

"I don't think I'm good enough yet to play for guests," Lara said, "Perhaps another time after I've mastered at least one piece?"

"Of course," Sir Thomas said without looking at Lara. His eyes fixed on Amalie, and she felt utterly exposed, so she tried to take the focus of conversation in another direction.

"What is your line of business, Sir Thomas?" Amalie asked him with a return stare.

"I operate a gambling establishment in town for the upper echelon of society with high stakes and high profits. It is very reputable, I assure you."

"Of course," Amalie said sarcastically, "And the Earl is one of your, uh, investors?"

Sir Thomas pursed his lips in a contorted smile. "You could say that I guess."

Lara was fuming that the Earl was gambling again but decided not to say anything at the table. The last time he got into gambling trouble, she had to let staff go and sell most of the horses and some of her jewelry. The Earl avoided eye contact with his wife.

Everyone at the table had their own reason for suffering through the remainder of the meal, and there was minimal discussion. As the staff served dessert, Amalie made her excuses and left the table. She went to her room and locked the door behind her. Her thoughts were in turmoil, and she didn't know what to do about Sir Thomas knowing who she was. It was apparent that he knew—he did everything but come out and say it. For the first time since she arrived at the estate, she did not feel safe there. She longed for Oliver and the sanctuary she always found in his arms.

As Amalie undressed for the night, she began to feel sick to her stomach. She thought it was odd to have nausea at night but hoped it would pass. It quickly got worse, and she broke out in a sweat. Then stabbing pains erupted in her stomach, and she doubled over in agony. Her vision blurred and she couldn't focus on anything in the room. Her mouth filled with foam, and she felt like she had to vomit but couldn't. She felt paralyzed and couldn't move. Then the room spun around, and she collapsed to the floor.

After dinner, the three men went to the study for brandy and cigars while Lara decided to check on Amalie. She knocked on the door, and when Amalie didn't answer, Lara assumed she was asleep. She tried to open the door to peek in and was surprised to find it locked. At second thought, of course, Amalie would lock the door after the unsettling discussion at dinner, but that also made Lara think that Amalie would not be asleep so early. Lara knocked again, and when Amalie did not answer, she went to get another skeleton key for the door.

Within minutes, Lara returned with a key and opened the door. She immediately saw Amalie lying on the floor and rushed to her side. Amalie was ashen white, and her lips were blue. Lara knew something serious was wrong and called out for help. She patted Amalie on the cheek, trying to wake her with no success.

When no one came to help, Lara ran downstairs to the study, burst in, and breathlessly cried out, "I need help! Something has happened to Maria! Owen, please fetch the doctor now! Take my best carriage and bring him back with you. Hurry!"

Lara ran back upstairs to tend to Amalie while Owen left to get the doctor.

Back in the study, the Earl turned to Sir Thomas and said, "I told you I would take care of it. It is done."

"Well done. How did you do it?" Sir Thomas asked.

"Rat poison. They say it's tasteless. I paid a staff member to put it in her food. She'll never wake up."

"Well then, if she dies tonight, we won't need to go hunting tomorrow, and I can go back to making money instead of eliminating thieves," Sir Thomas growled. "You see, when you do not pay your debts, that is like stealing from me, and where I come from, we shoot thieves."

Lara checked to see if Amalie was breathing and could barely detect any breath. "Don't you dare leave me, my friend," Lara cried, "I can't live here without you—please stay with me—open your eyes, Maria, wake up!"

Amalie didn't move. Her skin felt clammy to the touch, and Lara was frantic and feeling helpless.

After what seemed like an eternity, the doctor finally arrived. Owen and Dr. Richards lifted Amalie onto the bed, and when they did, there was a bloodstain on the back of her nightgown.

"She's with child, doctor," Lara said quickly, "Please help her!"

"I will do everything I can. At first glance, I would guess this woman has ingested poison—would she intentionally do that?" the doctor asked.

"You mean suicide? No, never, she would not do that!" Lara cried.

"Let me do a thorough exam, but I would prefer she be in the hospital. If she's been poisoned, I will have to move her to the clinic in town."

Lara and Owen left the room but stayed just outside the door. "He poisoned her," Lara whispered to Owen with tears streaming down her face. "I can't believe he would do this."

"I can believe it," Owen said quietly. "He's a monster, but what I don't understand is why? Why would he do that to her?"

"To hurt me—he does nothing but hurt me, and this is just one more way he found to do it. He knows how much my friendship with Maria means to me. And then to learn that he's been gambling again and owes that awful man money—it is almost more than I can bear."

"If he could do that to her, my concern is that he will do that to you. I don't think you're safe here anymore," Owen said, touching her shoulders.

"I can't think about that now," Lara sobbed. "My friend may be dying, and all I can think about right now is her."

"I'm going back downstairs before the Earl gets suspicious. Chin up, my love. I am always near you."

Lara nodded as he walked away, then she turned and went back into the bedroom. The doctor confirmed that

Amalie was indeed poisoned and needed to go to the hospital immediately.

"We must move her right now. Her heartbeat is faint and her breathing shallow. I'm sorry, but it looks like she's lost the baby. I cannot save her life here," the doctor concluded.

Lara ran back down to the study and called out for Owen. She burst into the room again and tearfully asked him to help move Amalie to the carriage because the doctor said her life was hanging by a thread. Owen rushed out to help with the transport.

"Well, it would seem that we may be going hunting tomorrow, after all," Sir Thomas said bitterly.

"She won't survive the night. I assure you. I gave her enough to kill a horse," the Earl said nervously.

"You fool, did you see how little she ate? She picked at her plate all through dinner. Kill a horse, rubbish! You are an absolute imbecile!" Sir Thomas raged.

Lara accompanied Amalie and Dr. Richards to the hospital. When they arrived, hospital workers came out with a wheeled cart to move Amalie into the building. The patient was rushed into an exam room while Lara waited in the hallway. Lara fluctuated between worrying about Amalie and rage at the man who did this to her friend. Lara eventually fell asleep on a wooden bench in the hallway. A tap on the shoulder by Dr. Richards awakened her.

"She's still alive but barely," Dr. Richards said. "I'm sorry, but she did lose the baby. Is there a husband we can notify?"

"No, he's dead," Lara lied.

"That makes this loss particularly sad then. Maria is unconscious, and we've moved her to a room. We have done all we can to counter the poison but won't know if it was successful until she wakes up. I would say if she makes it through the night, she will survive," the doctor reported.

"May I see her?" Lara pleaded.

"Yes, but she is extremely pale due to the flushing of her system. We have not induced her state of unconsciousness, so a good indicator of survival would be how soon she wakes up."

Lara sat with Amalie throughout the night, holding her hand and talking to her. It worried Lara that Amalie remained still and showed no sign of waking up. The loss of the baby broke her heart for her friend. Lara was looking forward to sharing the baby with her dearest friend, and she felt the loss too.

Oliver returned to Halston Harbor. He was weary from the traveling and lack of sleep. His heart was heavy, but his determination to find Amalie was stronger than ever. Thoughts of her filled his days and haunted his nights. He checked in to *The Restful Inn* and inquired about mail delivery.

"We have a box right over there on the desk," Mrs. McCoy said as she handed him the key to his room, "And my husband takes it to the Post every morning."

"Thank you. I will need to send a letter to the Corrington Territory. How much postage will you need?"

"We pay the postage and then add the charge to your account. No need to prepay," Mrs. McCoy smiled. "Enjoy your stay with us."

"Thank you," Oliver said, "I may be here for a bit."

Oliver penned a letter to his parents with an update on his search for Amalie. He expressed his frustration in not being able to find her while at the same time feeling appreciation that she was being careful not to be seen by those who would do her harm.

Later that afternoon in Amalie's hospital room, Lara was startled awake by Owen tapping on her shoulder.

"What are you doing here?" she asked him as she scrambled to sit up in the chair.

"How is she?" he asked, looking at the pale patient in the bed.

"She lived through the night, so I am very hopeful. You look terrible, Owen. What's wrong?" Lara asked.

"I've come with bad news, Lara. This morning, the Earl went hunting with Sir Thomas and was shot in a hunting accident. He's dead."

"What? He's dead?" Lara repeated as if she didn't hear correctly.

"Yes. I would say I'm sorry for your loss, but that would be a lie. You are needed at home. The constable wants to speak with you. I came to bring you home," Owen said.

Lara was shocked, but there were no tears. "Of course, I will let Dr. Richards know I have to leave." Then she turned to Amalie and said, "I will be back, my friend. Please try and wake up. I need you. Oliver needs you. Please wake up."

When Lara and Owen arrived at the estate, they saw a wagon parked in front. There was a body under a blanket in the wagon. The constable met Lara by the wagon and held out his hand. "I'm so very sorry for your loss, Countess. I need you to identify the body. I know this will be difficult, but it is protocol."

"I understand," she said with eyes fixed on the wagon.

The constable pulled back the blanket, and Lara gasped at the horrific sight of her husband with half of his face gone. The bloody sight made her immediately ill, and she had to vomit. Lara tried to compose herself enough to speak. "Yes, that is my husband."

"I have taken a statement from Sir Thomas who told us it was a hunting accident. He said the Earl was cleaning his rifle and it went off in his face. Do you have any reason to doubt his story?" the constable inquired.

Lara shook her head. "My husband wasn't much of a hunter, but I have no reason to doubt his story."

"I understand you were at the hospital all night with a sick friend?" the constable asked.

"Yes, she lost her baby. I stayed with her," Lara said, still staring at the cart.

"Sir Thomas has returned to his residence pending further inquiry, but it seems that this is a tragic accident and nothing more," the constable said, covering the body. "I will leave you to your grief, Countess, and again, I am very sorry for your loss."

"Thank you," Lara said as she walked into the estate with Owen steadying her walk.

Once inside behind the closed door, Lara burst into tears and fell into Owen's arms. "I'm free," she sobbed, "He will never brutalize me again. Am I a horrible person that I'm glad he's dead?"

"No, my love. No one mourns when a monster dies."

Later that afternoon, Amalie woke from her deep sleep. For a moment, she thought she had a nightmare, but when her eyes focused, she realized where she was and knew it was true. Amalie could feel that she had lost her baby, and her deep sorrow brought tears that would not stop. She cried silently and alone in her hospital room, mourning the baby she made with Oliver. Now she had nothing of his to hold on to, and her heart was shattered.

Amalie's profound grief quickly turned to anger because, once again, forces beyond her control were wreaking havoc on her life. The doctor confirmed that she was poisoned. She felt powerless over her own life and that she had no voice in controlling her fate. However, unlike the women of her time, Amalie decided that she would retake control of her life and that she alone would determine her future. Anger made her stronger, and she used that to plan a fight against those robbing her of living life in peace, but mostly because they had just stolen the most precious thing in her life, and she would never accept that without fighting back.

Chapter 10

A Kiss to the Sky

"I want to go to London," Amalie said to Lara as they sat on the patio, soaking up the afternoon sun. Lara thought some sunshine might make Amalie's pale complexion look a little better.

"But you've only been home from the hospital for a few days." Lara reminded her, "You should fully recover first."

"I feel fine. I'm getting stronger each day," Amalie insisted, "I can't sit around any longer. I need to start fighting back, and I can't do that without learning everything I can about the peace treaty and *The Society*. I want to visit the National Library and search the archives for historical documents. I want to read the decrees King Henry VI handed down. I need to know my enemy better."

"I understand," Lara said, "But I'm supposed to be in an official year of mourning, and I don't want you to go alone."

"I can't sit here and wait for the next attempt on my life," Amalie declared. "Sir Thomas is still out there. I can go alone, but I will need a carriage, and I don't know how long it will take."

"I'm going with you!" Lara announced, "Damn those old bitties if they don't like it. I'm not going out to have fun, I'm accompanying a friend, and there's nothing improper about that."

"Great! I will love having your company."

"When do you want to leave?" Lara asked.

"There's no time like the present."

"Wonderful! We can stop at the inn where I met you for supper. Then we can go to the library first thing in the morning. I need to go change into my mourning clothes, and then we can leave."

Oliver was sure that Amalie never took the train and that it was a decoy for *The Society*. He began to search around London, visiting schools and churches to see if anyone hired a new music teacher. He went into cafés and pubs to see if anyone might have seen her. Oliver even visited a private detective to see if he might help him find her. The detective declined because he said, "By now, the trail is cold. It's been weeks. You don't even know for sure which name she is using. I wouldn't know where to begin."

Oliver refused to become discouraged, but it was getting harder to do with each passing day. In one of the pubs he visited, he met an older man named Howard Blankenship, a semi-retired college professor. He was intrigued with Oliver's search and offered his resources to help.

"At the university, we have students who love to solve mysteries like this. Meet me for dinner Friday evening here at the pub, and we can discuss it further. I will need some detailed information from you," Howard said.

Oliver agreed to meet Howard for dinner even though he doubted that some college students could help find Amalie, but he was willing to try anything at this point.

Amalie and Lara arrived at *The Restful Inn* just in time for supper. After they checked in, they went to the dining room to eat. Amalie still had no appetite but knew she needed to eat to regain strength. Mrs. McCoy came to the table to greet them.

"Countess, it's so lovely to see you again! I'm so sorry about the Earl—such a tragedy—my sincerest condolences. And welcome back, Miss….Bennett, was it? I see you're still working with the Countess."

"Thank you," Lara said, "Yes, Maria is still with me. And thank you for your kind words."

"What'll you ladies have tonight? Our special is stew with carrots and potatoes," Mrs. McCoy announced, "And I know you'll be wanting your favorite tea."

"That sounds fine with me. Does that sound good to you, Maria?" Lara said to Amalie.

Amalie nodded. "Yes, that's fine."

When Mrs. McCoy left for the kitchen, Lara looked around and said, "This is the same table where we met. One of the luckiest days of my life."

"It was for me too," Amalie smiled. "I don't know where I would have ended up if I hadn't met you."

Just then, Amalie felt a strange feeling sweep through her. It was as if a cool breeze passed right through her. She turned around to see what could have caused it but saw nothing out of the ordinary.

At the exact moment, Oliver had just come down the stairs and waved at Mrs. McCoy as he left for his dinner with Howard Blankenship at the pub on the next block.

"What's wrong?" Lara asked, "Are you ill?"

"No, just a strange feeling swept through me. I have been feeling it since we arrived. Maybe just a chill in the air."

"I wish you would have waited to come until you were stronger. I hope this trip won't set you back in your recovery," Lara said with genuine concern.

"I'm fine. I will go to bed early tonight and be fully rested for tomorrow."

"I know you are determined to find out who is trying to kill you, but Maria, you've suffered a profound loss, not to mention that your body is recovering from poison. I worry about you, my friend."

"I know, and I love you for it, but I cannot rest until I know who my enemy is and how I can fight them. I owe that to my child….." Amalie's voice broke, and she bit her lip to keep from crying.

Lara reached across the table and touched Amalie's hand. "I know. That's why I'm here with you. You can always lean on me."

"Thank you, my friend. I don't know what I would do without you right now," Amalie said, still fighting tears.

"You tried to comfort me when you came home from the hospital, but I'm not the one who needs comfort," Lara said warmly, "I have not suffered a loss—you have."

Oliver and Howard Blankenship shared an interesting chat over dinner at the pub. Howard explained that many of his psychology students belong to the Mystery Club on campus and that they often take on real-life mysteries and try to solve them. Howard thought that they might be interested in helping to figure out Amalie's mindset and therefore figure out where she might have gone. Oliver thought it was an appealing notion and agreed to provide him with essential information to see if the students could guide him in the right direction.

"Well, it sounds like she is very special to you," Howard said, finishing the notes on his pad. "Do you know anything about *The Society*? It intrigues me that an organization can be so secretive that even ruling parties have no information. Someone must fund them. Perhaps I should guide the students in that direction and see if we can't help you with that also."

"Yes, I would greatly appreciate that. Thank you. And yes, Amalie is very special to me. I love her, and as soon as I find her, we will be married."

"I must ask this, to be sure for the students' sake, but can you assure me that this young woman is not running from you? I don't want to facilitate a reunion that she does not want," Howard said delicately.

"Mr. Blankenship, I am Captain Oliver Corrington III, and on my word, I assure you that she is not hiding from me. As I explained, she agreed to wait for me, but then *The*

Society captured me for days, and she must think I changed my mind. I came as soon as they released me. I fear that she thinks I didn't want to come, and nothing could be further from the truth."

"I believe you. Odd though that your family, as the Corrington Territory's ruling party, has no information about *The Society*. If memory serves me correctly, King Henry VI surrendered those territories in the 1400s and forced them into self-rule. Yet, you and the Duke of Herzstein have no control over the group designated to enforce the peace treaty."

"That's correct, and we are working on changing that. My father and the other Duke have ordered their security councils to investigate."

"Well, I think the students are going to love digging into this mystery. I hope we will be able to uncover some information that will be useful in helping you find your young lady."

"I am staying at *The Restful Inn,* and you can reach me there anytime. If I am not there, please leave a message with Mrs. McCoy at the front desk."

"And you can reach me at the university. I am there on Mondays and Wednesdays."

The men shook hands, and Oliver left the pub feeling a bit more optimistic than he had in a long while. As he walked back to the inn, he realized that staying there made him feel close to Amalie. Oliver knew she stayed there while she waited for him, and being there made him feel closer to her. It seemed silly, yet when he was there, the feeling was intense.

Amalie and Lara headed out early for the National Library in central London. Mrs. McCoy accommodated them with an early breakfast before the other guests were awake. Amalie wanted to have plenty of time for researching the archives.

The National Library was home to all official government documents, and the building was an impressive feat of architecture. The government also used the building to house books, maps, and artwork of dignitaries, royalty, and famous places, such as Buckingham Palace. Amalie and Lara were in awe as they entered the building and saw the high painted ceilings in the main lobby.

Amalie asked the clerk at the information desk about the archives from the 1400s, specifically King Henry VI and the peace treaty. The clerk named Violet led them to a small room down a long stone hallway and said she would be back shortly with the official books from that era. She gave them white gloves to wear when touching the priceless documents.

"What specifically are we looking for?" Lara asked.

"Oliver told me the peace treaty had three parts. Part one dealt with forcing the territories into self-rule. Part two laid out the peace treaty and declared the Festival of Lovers every hundred years to designate the new couple to be married, and part three formed *The Society*. I am most interested in part three."

"I sure hope we find what you are looking for," Lara said, and then she felt compelled to tell Amalie about Sir Thomas. "I know Sir Thomas killed the Earl because he could not pay his gambling debts, but I also have this terrible feeling that his presence that night you were poisoned was not a coincidence."

"What makes you say that?" Amalie asked.

"I don't know. The whole evening was very strange, didn't you think so? I mean, I've never seen the Earl so nervous, and Sir Thomas seemed to know an awful lot about you. Had you ever met him before that night?"

"No, never."

"My hunch is that the Earl was trying to enrich himself with Sir Thomas to pay off his gambling debt, and somehow that brought him to our home and you," Lara said, sharing her thoughts out loud.

"Do you think Sir Thomas is connected to *The Society* in some way?" Amalie wondered.

"If he is, then that would make sense of all the unexplained behavior that night," Lara concluded.

Amalie felt a shudder in her body. "And I was sitting across the table from him. Oh God that is frightening."

The clerk returned, pushing a cart with two colossal leather-bound ledgers and a box labeled *Addendums*.

"I think this is what you are looking for," Violet said, a bit out of breath as she placed the items on the table. "This covers the years you asked about, and the index includes the 1465 Peace Treaty and the royal decrees. Take all the time you need, and please remember only to touch the pages with your gloves."

Amalie and Lara each took one of the books and began to study them. The indexes helped narrow down which sections to review. Amalie read the original Decree surrendering the two territories and forcing them into self-rule. It stated unequivocally that King Henry had no further authority and designated the Dukes of each nation to assume leadership.

Amalie read part two of the Royal Decree declaring the Peace Treaty to be in effect immediately, and she studied the section that covered the Festival of Lovers. King Henry designated that the firstborn of each territory must marry each other to uphold the peaceful union, but its wording took Amalie by surprise.

"Listen to this, Lara," Amalie said, "This is from King Henry VI—*I hereby declare that these marriages must be carried out every hundred years without fail as punishment for the bloodshed resulting from the death of two young lovers.* He did it to punish the people of those territories."

"Well, they always said ole King Henry VI was the mad king. By all accounts, the king hated being a monarch."

"And here I thought he was just an old romantic," Amalie sighed. "What I don't understand is how he could surrender his domain over the territories yet command they follow this Decree? It makes no sense to me."

"That's the thing about monarchs. They don't have to make sense, but everyone must still obey them," Lara said, "Look at my late dear departed—he was a complete fool most of the time, and yet he had the power to command and demand."

"There is nothing in this book about *The Society*," Amalie said, gently closing the book. "While you look in that one, I will examine this box of documents."

After several minutes, Lara said, "I found the part about *The Society*. Here, take a look at this."

Amalie scooted her chair closer to Lara and read with her. Within moments, they looked at each other in disbelief.

"Oh my God," Amalie cried, "Sir Thomas isn't affiliated with the group. He is the Supreme Leader!"

"And the Earl knew him and brought him into our home," Lara said in disbelief.

"Look at this," Amalie continued, "The original Supreme Leader was Sir Thomas Killinger, who King Henry VI appointed. The Decree says that once the leader is appointed, he remains in the role for life. The king also designated that all future Supreme Leaders be titled Sir Thomas to honor the group's founder."

"So, the original Sir Thomas founded *The Society,* and the king made it law?" Lara concluded.

"It would appear so," Amalie said, continuing to scan the document. "Here it says that the sole purpose of *The Society* is to enforce the Peace Treaty of 1465 between the Corrington and Herzstein Territories, and that use of force is sanctioned under the Decree. It also says that any member recruited into the group must be willing to die for the cause and that the group's inner workings are to remain secret. Any member who discusses *The Society* outside of the group shall be hanged. Membership is by invitation only."

"That's insane," Lara said, shaking her head.

Amalie kept reading, and then she found what she was looking for. "Lara, look, it says right here that the control and oversight of *The Society* **shall remain under the rule of the monarchy, and only the ruling monarch can alter the operation of the group. The monarchy will, in turn, fund the group and compensate its members.** That is why Oliver's father couldn't find any information about them. The two Dukes have no domain over the group."

"So, the mad king kept his control over the group but relinquished the territories. He must've wanted peace badly to come up with such a crazy idea," Lara determined.

"I don't think he cared about peace. According to Oliver, he cared about making himself look good, and the long war that raged between the territories made him look like a weak ruler."

"But that was four hundred years ago. Today the territories live in peace, yet this group continues its mission? That is astonishing."

"Yes, and like my mother before me, I am a threat to that peace treaty, and they want me dead," Amalie said with a shudder, touching her empty belly.

"It's hard to believe that not one monarch over the years didn't do away with this group. I mean, I can't imagine Queen Victoria would approve of this," Lara said.

"Do you know the queen?" Amalie asked.

"I've met her twice. I don't know her well because she was not a fan of my husband, so we were never invited to the palace very often."

"Do you think you could get me an audience with her?" Amalie asked.

"I'm not sure how much weight my request would carry, but I would do it for you. It's nearly impossible for a commoner to get an audience with the queen. My father tried once, and he is a very wealthy businessman. She denied him."

"After what I have learned here today, she is the only one who can stop this. Please, we have to try," Amalie pleaded.

"I will send the request. It may take days for the queen to reply."

"Thank you, my friend. Now, let's look at some of these additions in the box. It looks like these are documents about all the leaders of the group. There have been at least a dozen or more Sir Thomases, maybe more. And from what I see here, only the first one was a real Sir, knighted by the king," Amalie said, carefully laying out the pages from the box.

"Is there anything in there about the one who shot my husband? I think that might be something the queen should know. I mean, yes, he owed him a great deal of money, I'm sure, but the Earl had nothing to do with the peace treaty, so how does he justify killing him?"

"Let's use that to get our audience with the queen," Amalie said, "That might get her to agree to see us."

The women studied the papers in the box and found the leadership declaration for the current Sir Thomas. His real name is Winston Abernathy, and he was hand-selected by his predecessor. Winston was once a soldier in Her Majesty's royal army. According to the document, his commander expelled him for killing a fellow soldier unjustifiably. The leader of the group deemed him a perfect candidate for *The Society*. He was a member of the group for seven years and then was appointed leader by the outgoing Sir Thomas.

"So, he recruited Winston because he killed someone and to this day continues his killing spree," Lara said with a shudder. "I'm fairly certain the queen knows nothing about this. I can't imagine she would sanction anything like this. And to think he was a guest in my home. Now I'm certain that Sir Thomas got my husband to poison you to cancel his gambling debt. I'm so sorry, my friend. Can you ever forgive me?"

"Lara, there is nothing to forgive. You didn't do anything wrong. But I can tell you this—if your husband weren't dead already, I would end him with my own hands."

"And I would hand you the rifle."

Waves of grief and mourning swept over Amalie as they have done since she lost her baby—but she wouldn't give in to the tears that always seemed to come without any warning. Lara could see it in Amalie's face and touched her hand.

"Let's go back to the estate and work on our request to see the queen. Our bags are already in the carriage. I told Mrs. McCoy we might not stay another night," Lara said, carefully placing the papers back into the box. "Now, I want to see the queen myself. I want this Sir Thomas brought to justice for what he did to you, but I will say it's because of what he did to my husband. The Earl had a royal title, and his killing should not go unpunished—whether he deserved it or not."

"I want more than that. I will ask the queen to abolish this barbaric group once and for all. Otherwise, I will never have a day of peace as long as I live," Amalie declared.

Oliver met with Howard Blankenship again for dinner after Howard sent him a message saying his students had uncovered some information. The two men met again at the pub, and Howard laid out his notes.

"They discovered that the king retained control over this secret group of his and that the monarchy is the funding source," Howard said, reading from his notes.

"How did they manage to uncover this?" Oliver asked. "I'm impressed that they were able to find this information when my father has come up empty."

"That's because your father didn't know where to look. I sent them to the National Library to research the archives. They found it right away based on the year given."

Howard relayed all the information to Oliver from the notes his students compiled.

"I'm astonished that the crown is responsible for *The Society*," Oliver said, studying the notes. "It is in contrast to King Henry's relinquishment of the territories."

"Yes, it is, but that's not the most significant thing they learned," Howard said.

"What else did they learn?" Oliver asked.

"When the students went to the clerk at the library and asked for the archives from those years, particularly the peace treaty and *The Society,* the clerk commented that just two days prior, two women were there inquiring about the same documents. The clerk named Violet found it odd that no one had inquired about those documents for many years, but then within two days, two different parties were there asking about them."

Oliver felt a rush surge through his body. "It has to be Amalie! She is trying to find out the same thing I am—but who could that other woman be? Did they say who the women were?"

"No, sadly, they don't record who the visitors are, but when I heard this, I thought the same thing you did. Your young lady is in London, and she is trying to learn more about who is trying to kill her. I thought you would find that information useful," Howard said.

"I'm thrilled to know that Amalie is in London. For the first time in a long time, I have hope that I am on the right path."

"The students are doing a profile and are hoping to be able to predict what her movements might be. I will keep you updated on any progress they make," Howard said, handing Oliver the notepad. "You can have the notes."

"I am so grateful to you. I want to buy your dinner as my way of saying thank you," Oliver said sincerely.

"That is not necessary, I'm happy to help, and the students are thrilled to have this project. Solving a real-life mystery is a great teaching tool."

Later that night, in his room at the inn, Oliver was sipping his second glass of brandy when he looked out the window overlooking the harbor and noticed a bright full moon shining down on the water. He opened the window and sat on the windowsill gazing at that bright moon. His thoughts turned to Amalie, as they always do, and his heart longed for her. Yet, on this night, he had hope—something he was beginning to lose until he learned that Amalie was in London. *Oh, Amalie, where are you? I can feel that you are near—yet I can't reach you, hold you, or touch you. Do you feel me too? I hope you know that I have been looking for you. I have not abandoned you. Wherever you are, please wait for me. I will never stop searching for you.*

Amalie finished her chamomile tea with a shot of rum, her nightly drink hoping to find sleep, and noticed bright moonlight shining into her room through the window. She opened the doors to the balcony and stepped outside, gazing up at that bright full moon and thought of Oliver. She wondered what he was doing at that moment and if he ever thought of her. *Do you remember me, my love? Do I ever enter your thoughts the way you always enter mine? I remember our magical night together and the wonderful gift you gave me that night. Oh, Oliver, I miss you so much. Do you look at the same moon and feel the things that I feel? I will look up at this beautiful moon and blow a kiss to the sky—and hope it finds you wherever you are.*

Chapter 11
A New Alliance

Amalie and Lara were in the middle of a piano lesson when Owen hurried into the room.

"Your Grace, you have a letter from Her Majesty," he announced.

Lara smiled at him and said, "Really, no need to be so formal. Maria knows about us."

"I know, but until your official year of mourning has concluded, I prefer not to bring any scandal to your good name. There are already questions about you having a male secretary living in your estate."

"Let them question all they want," Lara said flatly, "I truly don't care. No one questioned when the Earl was beating me, and I appeared in public with obvious injuries. Everyone knew how horrible he was and yet showed very little concern for me. Now they are concerned?"

"Open the letter!" Amalie said eagerly, "I can't wait one more second."

Lara broke the seal and opened the letter. "This is fantastic! She has granted us an audience this Friday afternoon. It will be at the palace and held in her office on the second floor. I am to show the guard this letter, and he will let us in."

"Oh, thank God," Amalie sighed heavily. "She is my only hope of ending this nightmare. What did you write to convince her?"

"I wrote that Sir Thomas murdered my husband and that we have discovered he leads a group of murderers in the form of *The Society* and that they have attempted to kill you three times," Lara said, "We got her attention!"

"I wonder if she knows about the workings of the group and sanctions it. She might be upset that we are bringing this to her so publicly when the group is supposed to be ultra-secret," Amalie wondered.

"I can't imagine she would ever approve of that, but nonetheless, we must gather our thoughts and put them in writing. We need to be precise and factual in our claims, or she will dismiss us, and nothing will happen," Lara said, looking at Owen. "Will you help us compile the information?"

"Of course," he replied with a warm smile.

"Let's begin immediately," Amalie said, "I can't concentrate on anything else right now."

"I'll go fetch my notebook, and we can begin to work on it straight away," Owen said, leaving the room.

"I'm a bit nervous about appearing before the queen," Amalie admitted, "I never felt at home in the Duke's estate even though the man I love lived there. But this is the queen of England—I hope I don't get tongue-tied."

"That's why we're going to write it all out, so we won't forget what we need to say. Owen is a great writer, and he will help."

"I'm so glad you will be there with me," Amalie said, "I don't think I could do this alone."

"I will be right by your side, but I think you sell yourself short. You have more strength and courage than any woman I know. Look what you have been through and survived. You came up with the idea to go to London and read the archives. You wanted to bring this to the queen. I admire you so much. I would have left the Earl long ago if I had your strength, but my father said he would disown me. I could have set out like you did and started a whole new life—and look where you are now—a pending audience with the queen!"

"Thanks to you," Amalie said sincerely, "It does seem like a lifetime ago that my life was simple at the Abbey. So much has happened....and so much has been lost."

"Say, did you ever write another letter to Oliver?"

"No, I haven't. I'm not sure why. I think I'm afraid that even if Oliver knew where I was—he wouldn't come," Amalie confessed.

"You will never know unless you send it. Do you not want to know once and for all?" Lara asserted, "Or do you want to wonder for the rest of your life?"

"You are right. I should write Oliver a letter. I will do that this afternoon."

"Or," Lara began, "We could travel to the Corrington Territory and see him in person. Maybe we could do that after we return from London."

"But your year of mourning?"

"I'm following your example, Maria. I'm going to be stronger and not let others control my life. Most everyone already knows I'm not in mourning. I can't name one person who is sad that the Earl is dead, except maybe for Sir Thomas, who will never collect his debt."

"Are you sure we're not sisters?" Amalie smiled.

"We are sisters—sisters of the heart."

Lara reached out and pulled Amalie into a warm embrace. Amalie loved feeling close to someone that felt like family.

Owen came back into the room with his notepad, ink well, and pen. The three of them spent the remainder of the afternoon compiling a list of items to present to the queen.

Oliver decided to take a short trip home to regroup and find out if his father discovered anything about *The Society*. He told Mrs. McCoy to keep his room for him and that he would be back Friday morning. Oliver returned home to a warm welcome.

"Oh, I'm so happy to see you," Helene said, hugging her son. "It's not the same around here without you. You look well."

"Thank you, mother," Oliver said, walking into the house with his mother on his arm. "Mrs. McCoy is feeding me very well, but sleep still eludes me."

"Let's go have some tea, and when your father joins us, he can fill you in on what he knows," Helene said, holding tight to Oliver's arm. "I've missed you so much."

When they stepped inside the house, Michael and Anthony came to greet him.

"Welcome home, brother," Michael said, sounding more mature with each passing day.

Oliver hugged him and said, "Goodness, did you experience a growth spurt while I was gone?"

"Yes, I'm as tall as father now," Michael said proudly.

"And barely eighteen," Helene mused.

"Did you find Amalie?" Anthony asked eagerly. "I truly miss her."

"No, Anthony, not yet, but I have learned that she is in London and traveling with another woman. I'm certain I will find her soon," Oliver tried to encourage his little brother.

"I have mastered most of the music she left for me. I want to play it for her when she comes home," Anthony said.

Helene and Oliver looked at each other. Then Oliver said, "Keep practicing, little brother, and hopefully, one day soon, you will be able to play that music for her."

"Father is going to commission me to Captain very soon," Michael announced, "Then I can assume the duties you once had."

"I couldn't choose a more qualified soldier to replace me," Oliver said sincerely. "You will make a fine Captain."

The family gathered in the parlor while Margot served them tea.

"Welcome home, Captain," Margot said, handing him a cup. "Your father should be home at any moment. I will let him know you are here."

"Has there been any communication with the Herzsteins?" Oliver asked his mother.

"No. Your father conferred with the Duke recently regarding any progress he may have made regarding *The Society*, but there has been no discussion about marriage."

"My position has not changed. I will not marry Davina," Oliver said firmly.

"I know, son, and your father has accepted that. He may never understand it, but he has accepted it."

"I have learned a lot about *The Society* that I think he will find helpful. I have also learned that Amalie was searching for the same information."

"I wonder if she is well," Helene said sadly. "I feel so horrible about how she left here. Do you think she will ever forgive me?"

"She has a very kind heart, and she was very fond of you. I think with time, she could learn to forgive us all," Oliver said.

"Why would she need to forgive you? You knew nothing about her real identity. The deception was mine alone, and the Duke of Herzstein."

"I told her I would come for her. I shouted it from the pier, and she said she would wait for me. I allowed those thugs to capture me, and she must think I lied to her or that I changed my mind. The harbormaster told me she waited for over a week and lost hope. I can't imagine what she must think. Knowing that haunts me every moment," Oliver unburdened himself to his mother.

"Amalie will understand once she learns that you were captured and beaten. She loves you. I could see it in her eyes," Helene said, trying to comfort Oliver.

"I hope and pray you are right. I won't stop until I get the chance to explain it to her. Not finding her has tortured me, yet I feel that I am so close."

Just then, the Duke came into the room and walked over to Oliver. "Welcome home," he said, holding out his hand. "It's good to see you."

Oliver shook his hand and was a bit surprised by the warmth his father displayed. "It's good to be home, even if it's just for a day or two. I need to be back in London by Friday."

"What's happening on Friday?" the Duke asked.

"I will be meeting with Howard Blankenship, a professor from the university who has been helping me with information about *The Society*," Oliver answered.

"What have you been able to learn?" the Duke asked. "I have found nothing, and neither has the Duke of Herzstein. It's as if they are a ghost group."

"That's because they are," Oliver replied. Then he filled his father in on all the information Howard found in the national archives. Oliver also told him that Amalie had searched for the same information.

"But I don't understand," the Duke said, "The king kept control and oversight of the group but by Royal Decree forced the territories to accept this?"

"Yes."

"So, we could have rejected this command and would not have broken any law because he forced us into self-rule?"

"Yes."

The Duke walked over to the fireplace and leaned his arm on the mantle. "For all these years, we have followed this Decree and wrote it into our laws when in reality, we could have rejected it and formed our own peace treaty."

"That is correct," Oliver confirmed. "Mr. Blankenship was amazed that our forefathers accepted this without question."

"Does that mean that the marriage command the king handed down is invalid?" Helene asked hopefully.

"It would seem so," Oliver replied, "But it would take an agreement by both territories to change our laws. By the wording of the Decree, there is nothing England can do to stop us."

"This is astonishing," the Duke said. "I wonder if that is why we never received a copy of the original Decree. I mean, four hundred years ago, the people accepted a command from the king without question, but we have been free to change these laws for four centuries and have not done so. I must meet with the Duke of Herzstein to discuss this."

"I think that is long overdue," Oliver said.

"Have you made any progress on finding Amalie?" the Duke asked. "How did you learn that she was searching for the same information?"

Oliver briefed his father on what Howard Blankenship discovered from the clerk at the National Library.

"So, she is in London?" the Duke concluded.

"Yes, it would seem so. However, I have no idea who the other woman was that Amalie was with at the library."

"Interesting," the Duke said, deep in thought. "Amalie has been able to learn more about *The Society* than two Dukes have been able to learn. After two attempts on her life, that girl is fighting back, and even though I'm not too fond of her strong opinions, I must applaud her determination."

Helene and Oliver looked at each other and smiled. It was the most affection the Duke had ever displayed for Amalie.

"She has the most to lose, father," Oliver said, "If I hadn't gotten to her when I did, she would be dead. And the danger is still out there. I am so thankful she is being careful, but that also makes it nearly impossible for me to find her. She used the name Maria Bennett when she stayed at the inn. Amalie is smart, and her guard is up. I hope that will be enough to protect her until I find her."

"Shall we invite the Herzsteins for dinner tomorrow evening to discuss Oliver's findings?" Helene suggested.

"Yes," the Duke replied, "That would be good."

"I agree," Oliver said. "It's time for both territories to assume the leadership that was forced on us four hundred years ago and make it our own."

Oliver felt good to be home, yet it didn't feel the same anymore. Amalie was everywhere he looked, and when he passed the Blue Room that was once her bedroom on his way to his bedroom, he realized that it would never feel like home again unless Amalie was with him.

Oliver was pleased to see that his father's attitude toward Amalie had softened and that he had accepted his stance on marrying Davina. Oliver was no longer angry with his mother for her deception and realized that if she hadn't brought Amalie into their family, he would have never met the love of his life. Now he felt only gratitude for his mother's intentions when she brought Amalie home.

Oliver was also glad to have some time with his brothers, who he had missed while he was away. Michael had grown so much while he was gone, and Anthony had become a piano master. He enjoyed playing chess with them and still could never win against Michael. No one could. Anthony played him some of Amalie's music, and Oliver was deeply moved by how well he mastered the pieces. Hearing Anthony play always brought Oliver's thoughts back to Amalie, and he hoped that she would soon be back with him listening to Anthony play the pieces she loved.

Thursday evening, the Herzstein family came for dinner, and this time there was no pretense. It was a relief to both Oliver and Davina not to have to pretend anymore. The two Dukes were in deep discussion before dinner as Duke Oliver brought Duke Carl Gustav up to date on Oliver's findings regarding *The Society*. Carl Gustav was astonished by the information and relieved to hear that Amalie was safe in London.

"I'm so relieved that she is well," Carl Gustav said over dinner. "When I heard about the incident at the ship, I was very concerned for her. This news about *The Society* concerns me greatly. Is this Sir Thomas an actual Sir who the queen knighted, or is he simply using the name he inherited?"

"My associate in London, Howard Blankenship, says Sir Thomas inherited the title from his predecessor, and his real name is Winston Abernathy. He is not a knight. The royal army expelled him for murdering a fellow soldier. That's when *The Society* recruited him."

"So these men are nothing but a band of rogue murdering criminals sworn to uphold a peace treaty that England has no domain over?" Carl Gustav summarized.

"Yes, that seems to be the case," Duke Oliver confirmed.

"And now Amalie is the target. We must do something to stop them," Oliver said. "Do you think we should take this to the queen?"

"Do you think that would do any good?" Helene asked. "I mean, the crown has been funding this group for centuries. They must sanction the behavior if they are funding it."

"I think we must put our heads together and prepare a joint proclamation from both territories stating our strong objection to the operation of this group. And remind Her Majesty that she has no jurisdiction over our peace treaty and therefore must abolish *The Society*," Duke Oliver said.

"We need to tread lightly with the queen," Carl Gustav said, "We cannot demand anything of her, but we can ask her to work with us to resolve this."

"What about the peace treaty itself where it says that the firstborn of each house must marry every hundred years?" Davina asked. "The Festival of Lovers is supposed to be next spring."

"There is no reason we can't hold the festival but without proclaiming the marriage of Oliver and Davina," Helene replied.

"We must first stop *The Society*, then we can deal with the festival," Oliver said. "They will not stop until Amalie is dead."

"Yes, of course," Helene said quickly. "The festival is secondary."

"If old Queen Victoria could meet Amalie, she would never allow those criminals to hurt her," Anthony said. "She would love her as we do."

"Yes, she would," Helene concurred with her compassionate youngest son.

Oliver suddenly had a thought. "I wonder if that is why Amalie was searching for the archives. She knows what we know, and she might be thinking the same thing. I wonder if she wants to enlist the queen's help?"

"A commoner can't get an audience with the queen. How would she go about that?" Carl Gustav asked.

"What if she tells the queen she is your daughter, which she is," Oliver replied, "That might be enough."

"I highly doubt that," Carl Gustav said. "I've never met the queen, and we haven't been part of Britain for four hundred years. I would be surprised if she knew anything about us."

"But there was another woman at the National Library with Amalie. Maybe that woman can somehow help her. Either way, when I return to London tomorrow, I will follow up with Mr. Blankenship to see if he might know. He has been very helpful to me so far," Oliver said.

"I still want to convene our security council and see what we can do about a proclamation regarding *The Society*. Let's work together on the wording, and with both of our houses signing the document, the queen would have to consider it at least," Duke Oliver said.

"I agree," Duke Carl Gustav said.

"I'm so relieved we don't have to plan a wedding that neither of us wanted," Davina said.

"Yes, I am too," Oliver agreed, "Although there will be a wedding as soon as I can find Amalie. I will not let her slip away ever again."

"Do you think there could be a war over this?" Michael asked.

"No," both Dukes said at the same time.

"It looks like we agree on that too," Carl Gustav said.

"Our territories have lived in peace for four hundred years, and if anything, this will unite us further," Duke Oliver stated, "Our people would not go to war over an arranged marriage. We all value our peace too much for that. I would never sign a declaration of war over this."

"Nor would I," Duke Carl Gustav concurred.

"Then this means Amalie can come home," Helene said with relief.

"If she wants to, yes," Duke Carl Gustav replied, "But she was furious when she left. I pray she will forgive me, but I fear that she may not. I have failed her in so many ways."

"Amalie is a forgiving soul," Oliver said, "It may take time, but I am certain she will forgive all of us."

"I'm not sure I would," Duchess Marta chimed in. "I still haven't forgiven my husband for keeping that from me. I can only imagine how Amalie feels."

"Amalie has the heart of her mother," Duke Carl Gustav said softly, "Thankfully, Juliet lives on in our daughter."

Duchess Marta glared at her husband but knew enough not to continue the discussion.

"Perhaps we could use the festival to celebrate a new peace between our nations and celebrate four hundred years of peace with a new doctrine written by both of our houses," Duke Oliver suggested. "We can call it the Festival of Peace."

"Oh, I love that idea!" Helene gushed.

"So do I," Davina agreed.

"I must say, I like it too," Marta concurred.

"That is an excellent idea. Yes, we will release this in newsprint in both territories," Carl Gustav said, "And give the people plenty of time to get used to the idea."

"Let us drink a toast to peace," Oliver said, raising his glass, "And to the beginning of a new era where we will marry for love and leave the ghosts of the past where they belong."

The dinner turned into a celebration, with every person at the table joining in the toast. "To peace, love, and happiness for all our people," Duke Carl Gustav proclaimed as they touched their glasses together in unity.

The following day Oliver returned to *The Restful Inn* after arriving on the *Hyacinth*. He went to the dining room to eat a late breakfast after not eating before the crossing. He suffered from a bout of seasickness during the last trip and thought an empty stomach might prevent that from happening again. Mrs. McCoy came to his table to take his order.

"Bangers and eggs this morning?" she asked him but then noticed he looked a bit pale. "You alright, Captain?"

"Yes, just a bit queasy from the trip. No bangers and eggs this morning. How about just some bread with marmalade and some tea?"

"Coming right up," she said and rushed off.

His visit home uplifted Oliver, but he was reminded of his unsuccessful search for Amalie when he arrived back at the inn. The nights were the worst when he could not sleep; his thoughts kept him awake thinking of Amalie. He worried that *The Society* would find her before he did, and that fear robbed him of any rest.

"Here you go, Captain. My fresh-baked bread rolls and homemade gooseberry jam," Mrs. McCoy said, pouring his tea. "Eat up now and enjoy."

"Thank you," Oliver said, forcing a smile.

"Did ya not enjoy your visit home?" she asked, noticing his demeanor.

"Oh, yes, I did, very much so, but arriving back here reminded me of my unsuccessful mission, and that weighs heavily on me."

Mrs. McCoy sat down across from him and felt comfortable enough to ask him, "What mission are you on, Captain?"

"Like I told your husband when I first arrived here, I was supposed to meet my future wife, but forces beyond my control detained me, and I could not come in time. She waited for over a week, but she thought I was not coming and left. I have not been able to find her, and it causes me many sleepless nights."

"Oh, dear, that is sad. Well, I hope you will have success soon. Young lovers should be together. Does she have family in the area?" Mrs. McCoy asked.

"No, she has no family. I have been searching for her for months now. I even took the train to the north country because your husband told me she bought a ticket, but no one had seen her. Then I discovered another woman was with her in London, and that was very recently, so I am encouraged that I am on the right path."

"Well, I wish you well, Captain. You said your lady bought her ticket here? Did she stay here?" Mrs. McCoy asked, thinking she should know the woman if she was a guest there.

"Yes, she stayed here while she waited for me, but when I didn't arrive, she left," Oliver recalled while he ate his bread and jam.

"And my Walter told you she bought a train ticket?"

"Yes, he checked the registry, but it was a dead end. I don't think she took the train. I think she's been in London the whole time," Oliver said, taking a bite of his roll.

"What is her name? Perhaps I might know something if she stayed here."

"She used the name Maria Bennett when she was here," Oliver said.

"Wait, did you say Maria Bennett?" Mrs. McCoy said quickly.

"Yes, do you remember her?" Oliver asked hopefully.

"Yes! She was here recently."

"Yes, I just told you she stayed here while she waited for me."

"No, she was just here a week ago with the Countess!" Mrs. McCoy said, realizing she knew the woman he was searching for.

"What? With who?"

"Oh, my dear man, I know where your lady is! I've known this whole time!" Mrs. McCoy said excitedly. "That day you didn't arrive, she was sitting right over there by the window looking very sad. We were full, so I asked her if the Countess, a frequent visitor, could share her table. She agreed, and they hit it off straight away. The Countess employed her as a music teacher. She never took the train. She went with the Countess to the Attenbury estate that very day and she's been there ever since."

"But you said she was just here a week ago." Oliver's mind was racing, and his heart began beating fast.

"Yes, they came to town to visit the National Library. I fixed them both an early breakfast to give them plenty of time to get there. You were here then. How did you not run into her?" Mrs. McCoy shook her head.

"Oh my God, this is incredible! We were both here at the same time and never saw each other? I felt it—I knew she was near me, but I can't believe I didn't see her. How is that possible? I mean, we all dine right here in this room."

"No, you went to meet that man at the pub that night. She dined here with the Countess," Mrs. McCoy recalled.

Oliver's mind was scrambling to grasp this news. "You say she is still at the Countess' estate?"

"Yes—good thing too. After Sir Thomas killed the Earl in a terrible hunting accident right there on the property, the poor woman probably needed some company. It seems shady to me. I mean that Sir Thomas is a despicable character. He runs a gambling establishment and is a frequent visitor at Madame Isabelle's brothel. Rumor has it that the Earl owed him a lot of money."

"Oh my God, did you say Sir Thomas? And he was at the estate?" Oliver said, trying to process this information.

"Yes, do you know him?"

"Where is the Attenbury Estate? I must go there! Maria could be in danger!" Oliver said, reaching over his shoulder to grab his jacket and pistol.

"Two hours west of here. Just follow the road leading west past the livery stable. It will take you right to it."

"Thank you!" Oliver said as he shot up from the table and ran out the door.

Oliver's heart was pounding in his chest during the entire ride to the Attenbury Estate. Amalie was at the estate, and Sir Thomas knew she was there—that was all Oliver could think about—getting to her before he did.

When Oliver arrived at the estate, he ran to the front door and pounded on it. After a moment, a tall man answered the door.

"I'm here for Maria Bennett," Oliver said forcefully, stepping into the doorway, "I need to see her at once."

"Hold on, sir, my name is Owen, and I am the Countess' secretary. Identify yourself, or I will remove you from the premises."

"I'm sorry, my name is Captain Oliver Corrington III, and I have just learned that Amalie—I mean Maria has been staying here. She may be in danger!"

"Well, Captain, come in, sir. I've been wondering how long it would take you to show up here," Owen said, closing the door.

"Is she here? Please, I've been looking everywhere. I need to see her," Oliver said in desperation.

"No, she and the Countess have gone to London to meet with the queen. Maria is aware of the danger. We all are."

"But Sir Thomas was here already. Did he do anything to Maria?" Oliver asked frantically.

"We need to chat for a few minutes. There are things you should know," Owen said.

Owen relayed the events from the night when the Earl poisoned Amalie on Sir Thomas' orders. He also told him that she survived the attack but lost her unborn child.

Oliver was in shock. "I….I didn't know….oh my God, this is unbelievable. Please tell me she is alright."

"Yes, she seems to be fine. Maria was in the hospital for a couple of days, and while she was there, Sir Thomas shot the Earl in a staged hunting accident. The Countess is quite certain that it was because the Earl owed him a lot of money."

Oliver was still processing the loss of the baby. "I didn't know about the baby. Oh God, she went through all that, and I wasn't here with her. Our child….she lost our child. This is too much….."

Oliver felt weak in the knees as it sank in that Amalie was carrying their child and that the baby died in the attempt on Amalie's life. His heart ached to know that Amalie had to face that tragedy all alone—and that he wasn't there with her.

"Yes, I'm so sorry to be the one to tell you, but you need to know that is the reason they are seeing the queen today. Maria is fighting back against the group that is trying to kill her," Owen said.

"I knew she would," Oliver said, still in disbelief. "I have to go to her. Are they seeing the queen at the palace?"

"Yes, second floor in her office, but they may not let you in. Security is strict there."

"I won't take no for an answer. I have searched from one end of England to the other—I have been out of my mind with worry. Now I find there was another attempt on her life, and they killed our child. **Let them try and keep me out!**"

Chapter 12
The Queen

As the carriage pulled up to Buckingham Palace, Amalie was awestruck as the palace came into view. She had never seen anything so magnificent or elegant. The architecture dating back to 1705 included a French influence in its design and featured large columns that frame a balcony used by royals to greet the public. The carriage entered the courtyard through the grand archway of the East Front and revealed the palace behind it. That was the moment Amalie realized she was about to appear before the queen of England.

"Oh goodness, my stomach is full of butterflies," Amalie said to Lara. "This place is so beautiful."

"The queen only recently returned to the palace," Lara stated. "After Albert died, she retreated to Windsor Castle and withdrew from public life. She is still in mourning even after four years. They say she only wears black."

"She must have loved him very much," Amalie concluded.

"Yes, by all accounts, they were devoted to each other."

"Then, perhaps, she will have understanding for my situation," Amalie hoped out loud.

"That's what I am counting on," Lara said as the carriage pulled up to the entrance.

A member of the Queen's Guard greeted them at the door and asked for the invitation. Lara handed him the letter, and he led them up the grand staircase to the second floor.

As they climbed the staircase, the guard informed them of meeting protocol. "Speak only when spoken to. Do not approach the queen within five meters unless summoned. Sit only when she sits, or she tells you to be seated. You must initially address the queen as Your Majesty, and then it is acceptable to say Ma'am. Show respect and maintain formal decorum."

The guard led them to the official office of the queen and instructed them to wait in the hallway until called. He showed them to a bench along the wall and said the queen's secretary would come for them when the queen was ready. Then the guard returned to his post at the main entrance.

"Don't be nervous," Lara said, reaching in her pocket for the outline Owen prepared for them. "If we stick to our notes, we will be able to convey what we are asking of her."

"I am so thankful that Owen prepared that for us. I fear my mind will go blank once I'm standing before her," Amalie said nervously.

"You are stronger than you think, Amalie."

"You called me Amalie."

"It's your name, and it's beautiful. There is no need for you to be Maria Bennett any longer," Lara declared.

"Thank you, my friend. Did I ever tell you why I used the name Maria?"

Lara shook her head. Amalie told her it was from Ronan and Maria in the archive documents.

"Ah, they were the lovers who couldn't be together and caused the war—and you felt like you and Oliver were Ronan and Maria."

"Yes, because we are—only we didn't jump off a cliff."

Owen offered Oliver a carriage for his trip to London so his horse could rest and decided to accompany him. The men chatted during the two-hour ride, and Owen brought Oliver up to date on everything since Amalie arrived at the Attenbury Estate. Oliver was astonished that Amalie was at the estate the entire time he searched the country for her.

"The Countess relayed to me that Amalie was heartbroken when you didn't come to London. If I may be so bold to ask why you didn't come then but are here now?" Owen asked.

Oliver explained his capture by *The Society*. "I set sail for London the moment I was released, but I was one day too late. Amalie had already left with the Countess, but I thought she had taken the train to the north country, so I went there to search."

"She has become close friends with the Countess," Owen said, "And I think the Countess was hoping Amalie would stay on even after she had the baby. Amalie wrote you a letter that the chambermaid took from her desk before she could mail it, and that is how the Earl discovered her identity. Then in his desperation to settle his gambling debt, Sir Thomas forced him to poison Amalie."

"I wondered how he knew where to find her," Oliver said.

"The Earl saw his way out of debt, but when she survived, Sir Thomas shot and killed him—either out of anger that Amalie lived or that he knew he would never collect the large sum of money the Earl owed him," Owen explained. "Lara, I mean the Countess, kept vigil at the hospital with Amalie. By all accounts, Amalie was inconsolable when the doctor told her that her baby didn't survive."

"I still cannot believe it. It breaks my heart that Amalie had to face that without me, but I am so thankful she had the Countess to support her."

"I was initially the Earl's secretary, and after his death, the Countess asked me to stay on. I have to say honestly that the estate is a much happier place without the Earl. He was abusive to the Countess and could be quite ruthless. With one exception, most of the staff has not mourned his passing. When the Earl died, Doreen, the chambermaid who took the letter from Amalie's desk, left her employment. Doreen was unusually close to the Earl, and we all had our suspicions about that."

Oliver quickly read between the lines, and his gut told him that more than a professional relationship existed between Owen and the Countess. His tone whenever he spoke of her was tender and personal.

"You seem to be very fond of the Countess," Oliver said, stating the obvious. "She's lucky to have you."

"Yes, she is an extraordinary woman," Owen admitted openly.

"It's alright," Oliver assured him, "You're talking to a man who has walked in your boots. I knew Amalie was forbidden to me, but the heart has a mind of its own. I understand."

"Why was she forbidden to you?"

Oliver shared with Owen that the Peace Treaty of 1465 would force him to marry Lady Davina of the House of Herzstein but that the two leaders of the territories had formed a new alliance that did not include that stipulation. Now, he was free to marry Amalie without surrendering his future title.

"Does Amalie know this?" Owen asked.

"No, and I cannot wait to tell her. These past few months have been hell without her. Have you ever loved someone so much that it completely consumes your entire life?" Oliver asked.

"Yes, I have, I do," Owen replied honestly. "And I had to watch while her husband abused her and violated her in unthinkable ways. I wanted to kill him myself numerous times. He was a monster."

"That must have been terrible for you. When you told me that Sir Thomas poisoned Amalie and killed our child, I was mad with rage. I can only imagine what you must have felt."

"That is all in the past now. After a year of mourning, we will be married. I want to take Lara far away from society's prying eyes and judgments. The Earl was deep in debt, and I don't believe she will be able to keep the estate on her own."

"I wish you the best of luck for your future," Oliver said.

"And I wish the same for you," Owen replied.

After a short while, the queen's right hand, Sir William, came and called for the women. Amalie and Lara followed him into the large, elaborately decorated room used solely for the queen to hold court. There were sofas and chairs arranged in theatre style, and there, seated at the end of the long aisle, was Queen Victoria. The queen sat in an elegant high back chair flanked by three aides and two more guards. The queen was rotund and dressed in black, including a short black veil on her head. Her expression was resolute and fixed.

Amalie and Lara curtsied to the queen when they stood before her. Amalie hoped the queen wouldn't notice her trembling hands.

"Thank you for agreeing to see us, Your Majesty," Lara said. "As I stated in my letter, there are urgent matters that need your attention. Your Majesty, this is Amalie Gilchrist, and her story relates directly to mine."

The queen nodded in Amalie's direction. "You make startling accusations in your letter, Countess," the queen said. "But what troubled me more is that I do not recall ever knighting Sir Thomas. And how did he come to know the late Earl?"

"It pains me to say this, but my late husband had a gambling weakness, and he owed Sir Thomas a great deal of money. Sir Thomas owns a gambling establishment just outside of London. I discovered that the Earl was a frequent visitor there. Sir Thomas' real name is Winston Abernathy, and he is not a reputable man, not at all. I think he killed my husband and staged the hunting accident. After what we learned about Mr. Abernathy, now I am certain of it."

"In preparation for your visit, I reviewed official the report of the constable regarding the Earl's death. The constable deemed it a hunting accident, and in the report, it stated that you concurred with that conclusion," the queen stated firmly.

"But that was before we learned who Sir Thomas really is," Lara said, fumbling with Owen's notes. "He is Winston Abernathy, supreme leader of *The Society*, a murderous group of recruited thugs who operate under the umbrella of the monarchy. We felt we needed to bring this to your attention," Lara said nervously. "I cannot imagine that Your Majesty would sanction such actions."

"I most certainly would not, and I have never heard of this group you speak of," the queen indignantly. "How did you come to know this? These are serious allegations."

"May I speak, Your Majesty?" Amalie asked.

"Yes, of course."

"We learned of these things from the archives in the National Library," Amalie began nervously. "Your ancestor King Henry VI formed this group, and its original purpose was to enforce the peace treaty between the territories he surrendered in 1465. But somehow, over the generations, they have strayed from their original intent and have become the murderous group they are today. I should know. They have made three attempts on my life."

The queen studied Amalie for a moment and then said, "Go on."

"But first, I must tell you why they see me as a threat," Amalie said and then told the queen the story of her mother, the Duke of Herzstein, and how she ended up in the House of Corrington.

"It was not my intention to fall in love with Captain Corrington, but I did, and he fell in love with me. *The Society* sees me as a threat to the peace treaty if the Captain didn't marry Lady Davina, so there was an attempt on my life within my first week of arriving there. It was the Captain who saved me in the last second before the chandelier crashed down. We didn't know our enemy then, but both Dukes convened their security councils and tried to find that information. They never found it, but the Countess and I did when we searched in the archives. When King Henry VI surrendered those territories, he forced them into self-rule, yet he maintained control of *The Society*, contrary to his decree ordering the self-rule."

The queen listened intently to Amalie speak. Lara tried to hand Amalie Owen's notes, but Amalie declined. "I don't need the notes. I want to speak from my heart, with the queen's permission."

"Please proceed," the queen said.

"The second attempt on my life occurred at Halston Harbor just before I was to sail for London. With orders from Sir Thomas, a member of *The Society* pushed me off the pier into the water and tried to drown me. I thought I died, but once again, it was Captain Corrington who pulled me from the water just in time."

"And how do you know Sir Thomas ordered it?" the queen asked.

"Because when the man grabbed me, I fought him, and I fought hard. He told me that Sir Thomas warned him that he would be hanged if he failed in his mission. That's when he grabbed me and pulled us both into the water."

"I see," the queen said. "And Captain Corrington just happened to be there?"

"Yes, he was looking for me. When I found out that I was not related to the family, I was upset by the deception. I also discovered that the Duke of Herzstein is my father. I was angry and upset, so I left and wanted to set sail far away from them, but thankfully Oliver—Captain Corrington—was there in time."

"You seem to have a guardian angel, Miss Gilchrist," the queen noted flatly. Amalie wondered if she didn't believe her.

"Yes, but unfortunately, he was not there when the third attempt happened. Sir Thomas found out who I was from the Earl and showed up at the estate for dinner. The Earl had one of his servants poison my food during that meal. I nearly died. But my….." Amalie's voice broke, "My unborn child did not survive."

The queen's expression relaxed as she listened to Amalie talk about losing her baby. "I'm sorry to hear that," she said. "Where was Captain Corrington during this time?"

"I assume he went home because he never joined me in London as promised. I must conclude that his duty to the peace treaty was stronger than his feelings for me. He is an honorable man and wants to prevent a war," Amalie explained.

"But those territories have lived peacefully for hundreds of years. They are almost one nation—they are so similar. I highly doubt war would break out over affairs of the heart," the queen said, much to Amalie's surprise. "I cannot imagine, based on what you have told me, that he would abandon his child."

Amalie was fighting hard to keep her composure. "He never knew about our child," she said, tears filling her eyes. "I never had the chance to tell him….I never had the chance to….." and suddenly Amalie broke into tears.

"Your Majesty, when I first learned I was going to have a baby, joy filled my heart. Once I felt the movements and twitches, I thought my heart would burst with happiness. I would daydream about what he would look like—would he have wavy hair like his father? Would he be tall? Would he love music as his mother does? I wondered what he would become one day. Then…..when I woke up in the hospital, and the doctor told me my baby boy was gone, I was beyond heartbroken. I never got the chance to hold him—see his face—to give him a name. I have never been so devastated in my life to learn my son had died."

The queen swallowed hard as she watched Amalie sob.

"They have taken everything from me, Your Majesty. My joy, my peace, my freedom, and my unborn child. The only thing they haven't taken from me is my life, and if you do not abolish this group, that will happen—it's just a matter of time."

Lara handed Amalie a handkerchief, and she wiped the tears from her face and blew her nose.

"We discovered that the monarchy has compensated them since the group's inception based on the documents in the national archives. That is why we are here today—to ask you to be the monarch that finally puts an end to this atrocity," Amalie pleaded.

"This information is troubling, to say the least," the queen stated sternly.

"I apologize for my emotions, Your Majesty, I tried to maintain decorum, but I have not spoken about my baby since he died, and it was more than I could bear. I do apologize."

"There is no apology necessary," the queen assured her. "It is most understandable." Then she turned to her aides and said, "Sir William, bring Sir Thomas to me at once."

"Yes, Your Majesty," he said as he turned to leave the room.

"Mr. Ganthom, as my Minister of Finance, I want a full explanation of why we are still funding this group, and I want it today!"

"Yes, Your Majesty, I will get to the bottom of it, I assure you," he said as he left the room.

Queen Victoria turned back to Amalie and Lara and said, "Would you be so kind as to stay for afternoon tea? I will have Arthur take you to a room where you can freshen up and have tea. We can resume this matter later today."

"Yes, of course, Your Majesty," Lara replied. "We would be honored. Thank you."

"Thank you for your consideration, Your Majesty. I am extremely grateful," Amalie said.

The queen's butler, Arthur, escorted the ladies out of the office and down the hall to a sitting room.

Once they were alone, Lara reached out and hugged Amalie. "Oh, my dear friend, you could have talked to me about the baby."

"No, I couldn't—because saying it out loud would make it real, and I couldn't accept that it was real," Amalie confessed as more tears flooded her eyes. "It has just now sunken in."

"Well, I'm glad you could say those things to the queen. I think you moved her with your story. I don't think she believed me, but you got through to her."

"I'm not happy that she has summoned Sir Thomas. I don't think I can face him without paralyzing fear," Amalie said, trying to compose herself.

"I see that as a good sign that she wants to do something about this group. I am very optimistic right now," Lara said, hoping to encourage her friend. "Besides, there are guards all around the queen. He can't hurt you here."

"As long as Sir Thomas is free, I will never be safe," Amalie declared.

The queen's clerk returned to the sitting room within an hour and asked the ladies to rejoin the queen in her office. Amalie tried to prepare herself to come face-to-face with the man who killed her child and nearly took her life. More aides and guards surrounded the queen when Amalie and Lara re-entered the office.

There, standing off to the side, was Sir Thomas looking highly displeased to be there. He glared at Amalie as she arrived before the queen. Amalie was surprised that she didn't feel fear. A surge of anger swept through her like a tidal wave when she saw his face, and she glared right back at him.

The queen broke the silence. "I have been telling Sir Thomas about the accusations against him," she began, "Not to mention my complete displeasure that he represents himself as a knight, which he is not."

"My title comes from a higher authority," Sir Thomas snapped back.

"Silence!" the queen shouted, "There is no higher authority than the crown unless you refer to God, and He would never authorize you to kill anyone!"

"Our group is sacred and sanctioned by King Henry VI himself," Sir Thomas argued, "We have honorably carried out our duties for four hundred years. It's a pity that you do not understand our purpose."

"Oh, I understand it more than you think," the queen retorted, "Sir William, explain to Mr. Abernathy what you found in our private archives regarding this group."

Amalie and Lara stood there watching the events unfold.

"I discovered that when Henry VII took the crown, his mission was to help the country recover from the War of the Roses. He restored control of the country to the monarchy and eliminated rogue groups who had acquired too much power. That included *The Society*. King Henry VII officially abolished it in 1489 by Royal Decree," Sir William stated, reading from his notes.

"That's impossible," Sir Thomas argued, "We never saw such a decree, and the crown continues to fund our work."

"Do you argue with the royal archives written in the King's own hand?" the queen challenged.

"Yes! King Henry VII must have changed his mind because the crown never informed us of such a decree," Sir Thomas insisted.

"Such impudence!" the queen snapped at him, "You dare to stand before me and call my king predecessor a liar! King Henry VII abolished your group nearly four hundred years ago. How would you know of events that happened that long ago? Do you have archives of your own?"

"Our sacred group has never been abolished. I stand by that," Sir Thomas said defiantly.

"I demand to know on what basis you make your stand!" the queen demanded. "Simply saying it does not make it so."

"We are a sworn society that has honored King Henry VI's wishes for generations with authority passed down from leader to leader. Another monarch must have reversed King Henry VII's decree because we continue to be compensated by the monarchy. It is not the fault of our group that you do not know what falls under your realm," Sir Thomas said mockingly. "How do you explain our compensation?"

"Mr. Ganthom, would you like to respond to that question as Minister of Finance?" the queen said, seething with anger.

"Um, yes, Your Majesty," Mr. Ganthom said nervously, "Upon reviewing the finances of that era, in which accounting was less than desirable, it appears that the funding remained in place due to an oversight. It fell under the blanket of security and other groups sanctioned by the crown, which the keeper of the books never listed individually. The treasury minister paid the compensation to Sir Thomas, and no one ever questioned why Sir Thomas had been compensated for over three centuries. As I said, it was an oversight."

"It is beyond an oversight and is outright irresponsible!" the queen shouted. "That funding ends today. Prepare the order, and I will sign it. Do you understand, Mr. Ganthom?"

"Yes, Your Majesty, right away," Mr. Ganthom replied meekly.

"Now that we have corrected a long-running mistake, let's discuss the accusations at hand," the queen said, pivoting to Amalie and Lara. "The Countess of Attenbury says you killed her husband deliberately. How do you respond to that?"

"It was a hunting accident. The Earl was loading his rifle, and it went off. The constable deemed that to be accurate," Sir Thomas replied.

"Did the Earl of Attenbury owe you a gambling debt?" the queen persisted.

"Yes. A rather large sum, but why would I kill someone who owes me money? Then I would never see my money," Sir Thomas argued in his defense.

"You are lying!" Lara cried out. "You forced him to go hunting with you. He hated hunting. He would never have gone on his own."

"I don't make a habit of killing those who owe me money," Sir Thomas said flippantly, "How would I ever collect my debts?"

"No, you make a habit of killing unborn children," Amalie blurted out. "You are a murderer who belongs in prison….or at the end of a rope."

"These women are hysterical," Sir Thomas dismissed, "Women should not be allowed to speak in the queen's court. They diminish the sanctity of the proceedings."

"Silence, you ill-mannered fool!" the queen snapped, "There are serious allegations against you, and disparaging your accusers will not serve you well here."

"I beg your pardon, Your Majesty, but you are not a barrister. If you wish to accuse me of a crime, then accuse me and let me have my day in court," Sir Thomas insisted.

The queen squinted her eyes at Sir Thomas and had enough of his disrespect. "You are in no position to make demands, Mr. Abernathy. I can send you to prison on my command. I am giving you a chance to defend yourself, and so far, you have done an abysmal job. I would hold your tongue if I were you. These women accuse you of murder and attempted murder. You claimed to work under the direction of the crown. Yes, Mr. Abernathy, I can send you to a prison where no one will ever see you again. Am I making myself clear?"

"Your Majesty," Amalie broke in, "I will never be safe as long as this man remains free. He has ordered three attempts on my life, with the latest one resulting in the death of my unborn child. I refuse to spend the rest of my life looking over my shoulder and living in fear because he has a misguided notion that he has been divinely bestowed the power to kill when that was never the initial purpose of the group he represents. I am begging you to stop him and dismantle the men who follow him."

"We do not need the queen's permission to continue to follow our mission," Sir Thomas said defiantly, "I can fund the group myself. I am a wealthy man in my own right."

"Are you mad?" the queen bellowed. "You are being accused of murder. There will be no group for you to fund. It was abolished, and I will confirm that with my own decree. Your group has attempted to kill this young woman three times, resulting in the death of her unborn child. I'm also beginning to believe that the Earl's death was no accident, and yet you stand here defiant in the face of certain imprisonment. Have you lost your mind?"

Sir Thomas was growing irritated and was unable to hold still. "You have no authority over me," he repeated firmly, "Only a king can stop our mission—not some emotional woman who doesn't understand law and order."

"How dare you address the queen in that manner!" Sir William shouted. "Mind your tongue, sir, or it will be cut from your head!"

"I will never surrender my mission!" Sir Thomas roared. "I am willing to die to fulfill my purpose! I happily give my life for our cause!"

With those words, he pulled a long knife from his pocket, grabbed Amalie from behind, and held his arm around her neck with the knife to her throat. Lara screamed at the sight. Amalie froze with fear.

Oliver and Owen arrived at the palace, and the Queen's Guard met them at the main entrance. "What is your business with the queen?"

"Sir, my name is Captain Oliver Corrington, and I understand that the Countess of Attenbury is here with my fiancé. I believe they may be in danger. You see, Sir Thomas...."

"Sir Thomas is here," the guard said. "The queen summoned him. The Countess is here also with a young woman."

"Sir Thomas is here?" Oliver said frantically, "Please, you must let us see the queen. We must warn her!"

Suddenly, there was a piercing scream that echoed through the corridor. Oliver pushed the guard aside and ran up the stairs. Owen and the guard followed him.

"Which one is the queen's office?" Oliver bellowed as he ran toward the sound of the woman's scream.

"The second door on the left," the guard answered, following close behind.

Oliver put his finger to his mouth when the men reached the door to indicate hushed silence. Then he whispered, "I don't want Sir Thomas to hear us coming," as he carefully and slowly opened the door. As the door opened, he could immediately see what was happening. Sir Thomas had Amalie by the throat, Lara was standing off to the side, and the queen was standing with her guards trying to remove her to safety, but she wouldn't budge. The queen saw Oliver, Owen, and the guard tiptoeing toward them, but Sir Thomas had his back to them and didn't see them.

Oliver held his finger to his mouth again, hoping the queen wouldn't give them away. Oliver pulled his pistol from his belt and aimed it at Sir Thomas. Slowly, they made their way toward Sir Thomas, step by silent step.

The queen knew she needed to distract Sir Thomas, so she spoke to him. "I command you to release that woman! She has not harmed you in any way. If you release her now, I will let you go," she lied. "Harm her, and you die here today."

Amalie felt a rush of rage flow through her body—this man had taken her child, and she had enough—she would not allow him to victimize her one more time. *No, no, no.....not again! You will not do this to me! NO!*

Amalie suddenly pulled her arm up and thrust her elbow back as hard as she could into Sir Thomas' diaphragm, causing him to exhale violently and gasp for air. He loosened his grip on her throat, and she freed herself from his grasp. She stepped back away from him, but he recovered enough to raise the knife in the air and, while still gasping for breath, attempted to stab Amalie with the knife. Suddenly a shot rang out, and Sir Thomas fell to the floor. He was bleeding from the head and was dead.

Amalie and Lara stood frozen at the horrible sight. Then Amalie saw him—he was coming toward her—it was Oliver, and seeing his face made Amalie break down emotionally.

"Oliver!" she cried out, her lip trembling.

"Amalie!" Oliver called as he ran toward her.

Oliver swept Amalie into his arms and wrapped her in a protective embrace. Amalie buried her head into his shoulder and cried. She wrapped her arms around him to keep from collapsing to her knees.

They stood there, clinging to each other as the room fell silent. "You came," Amalie cried, "You came for me."

Oliver cupped her face in his hands. "My love, I have been looking for you for months. I never gave up. I love you so much."

"But the ship—you weren't there," Amalie sobbed, her face wet with tears. "I waited and waited."

"They captured me—*The Society*—and held me for days. I came as soon as they released me, but I was too late. You were gone. I've been searching for you ever since."

"Oh, Oliver," Amalie wept, "Our baby…..he killed our baby."

"I know, my love, I know. I'm so sorry I wasn't there with you. I will never leave your side again. Ever."

"I have missed you so much," Amalie cried into his shoulder. "I thought your duty was stronger than your love for me."

"Never, no, never. I told my father I would surrender my title to marry you. There is a new alliance between our territories, and I am free to marry you, my love. We can go home," Oliver said, stroking her hair and wiping the tears from her face.

"But the peace treaty—your father said….."

"I have his blessing, my love. And your father has given his."

"Oh, Oliver! I love you so much."

Oliver wrapped his arms around her again, and they stood there, holding each other, oblivious to others in the room who were watching the reunion in respectful silence.

The queen cleared her throat loudly and broke the spell. "Captain Corrington, I presume?"

Oliver turned his eyes to the queen but kept his arms around Amalie. "Yes, Your Majesty. I apologize for not introducing myself right away—I was distracted."

"I can see that," the queen replied. "Thank you for arriving at the right moment. I was afraid he was going to kill her. Your bravery saved her life."

"I'm sorry I had to shoot him, but I'm not sorry he's dead," Oliver said.

"Guards, please remove Mr. Abernathy from the room," the queen ordered. "And have the floor wiped clean."

The queen sat back down in her chair, trying to calm herself while two guards carried Sir Thomas from the room.

"Amalie, please come here," the queen said, signaling with her hand to come closer.

Oliver released Amalie from his embrace, and Amalie ambled toward the queen, still shaken.

Queen Victoria's face had softened, and her tone was gentle. "You were courageous to come here and bring this issue to me. I am so glad you did so I could right this horrible wrong. With Mr. Abernathy's death, I think you can feel safe now and won't have to live in fear any longer. I assure you that any remaining members of his group will be captured."

"Thank you, Your Majesty, that is a comfort to me."

The queen held out her hand to Amalie. This was strictly against protocol, but Amalie honored the queen's request and placed her hand in the queen's.

"I wanted to tell you that I had nine children," the queen continued, "I know that feeling when you carry them and have hopes for their future. I want you to know that I understand what that man took from you. I am so very sorry for your loss."

"You humble me with your compassion. From the bottom of my heart, I thank you."

The queen released Amalie's hand. "Now, go and live your life with the man you love. I miss my Albert every day. Savor each moment you have together."

"Yes, Your Majesty. I shall."

Amalie and the queen looked at each other, and to Amalie's surprise, the queen formed a slight smile.

"You remind me of myself when I was a young queen. There were attempts on my life as well. One particular event left me quite shaken when a man with a pistol fired at my open carriage from close range, nearly hitting me. I, too, refused to live in fear and fought back against those who would end my reign. As you can see, they were not successful either."

"I'm so very thankful for that, Your Majesty," Amalie said sincerely.

"I am happy to be the monarch that finally put an end to this travesty. I owe you my thanks for bringing it to me," the queen said, signaling with her hand for Amalie to step back.

Amalie returned to Oliver and put her arm around his waist. Oliver put his protective arm around her shoulders.

"Your Majesty, please allow me to introduce my secretary, Owen McBride. He brought Captain Corrington here," Lara said, still shaken from the events.

Owen bowed to the queen. "Your Majesty."

"I must leave you now," the queen said wearily. "This has been a trying afternoon, but I feel we have done some good today."

Sir William escorted the queen out the door behind her desk, leading to her private chambers. The session with the queen was over, and so was Amalie's long nightmare.

Chapter 13
The Homecoming

The Queen's Guard escorted them from the palace to the waiting carriages at the front gate. Amalie stood there for a moment gazing at the palace, trying to process everything that had just happened. Lara stood beside her and put her arm around Amalie.

Amalie turned to Lara and said, "We did it, my friend. We fought back and won."

"You did it, Amalie," Lara corrected, "You moved her in a way that I couldn't. Thank God Sir Thomas is dead. Say, where did you learn to do that when you hit him in the gut? That was impressive."

"I was wondering the same thing," Oliver added. "How did you come up with that?"

"We used to do mission work in the poorest slums around the Abbey. After one of the sisters was attacked, Father Sebastian's brother came in and taught us how to defend ourselves. It came in handy today."

"Most certainly," Lara agreed. "We have two carriages here, so why don't you and Oliver take that one, and Owen and I will follow you in this one. We can get caught up on everything back home. I'm sure you and Oliver have much to discuss."

Oliver put his arm around Amalie and said, "Yes, we do. I will never let this woman out of my sight ever again."

Then Oliver turned to Owen. "Thank you, sir, for your assistance." The men shook hands.

"You're welcome," Owen replied. "We'll meet you back at the estate."

As the carriage rolled away from the palace, Oliver turned to Amalie, who was in his arms, said, "First things first," and put his lips on hers. He kissed her passionately, releasing months of longing. Amalie pulled him closer, allowing herself to feel things again. She had safeguarded herself for so long living in fear that she had pushed her emotions to the back of her mind to function and survive. It was hard to let go of, but once Oliver kissed her, she set her feelings free, and she kissed him back enthusiastically.

"I love you so deeply," Oliver whispered in between kisses, "I long to hold you and touch you and lay in your arms."

"I love you too," she sighed, feeling stirrings deep inside her body. "I have missed you so much. I thought I might never see you again, and it was more than I could bear."

"I promise you, my love, we will never be apart again. I want us to marry as soon as possible," Oliver whispered, kissing her again.

"Oh, Oliver, I'm so happy right now. It's over. The long nightmare is over. Are you sure your father approves of this? And when did my father give his blessing?"

"I went home for a brief visit to bring my father up to date on Mr. Blankenship's findings."

"Who's Mr. Blankenship?"

Oliver filled her in on Professor Blankenship finding the same documents at the National Library that she did. Then he told her that Mrs. McCoy finally sent him in the right direction. "Did you know that just over a week ago, we were both at the inn at the same time and never ran into each other?"

Amalie sat up. "Yes! I felt it. I had the strangest feeling one day, but when I looked around, I didn't see anything."

"Me too. I could almost sense that you were near me. Our connection to each other is deeper than we ever imagined. That feeling drove me to keep looking for you."

"How long were you home?" Amalie asked, touching his face with a gentle caress. It was as if she needed to make sure he was real.

"Just a couple of days. We met with the Herzsteins, and both Dukes agreed on forming a new alliance of peace between the territories without the marriage provision. There will be a festival in the spring, but they will call it *The Festival of Peace*. Both of our fathers agreed. Your father is worried that you will never forgive him. As is my mother."

Amalie was silent for a moment, then said, "I felt betrayed by both, for different reasons. How could my father deny me when I was standing in front of him looking like my mother?"

"He regrets it a great deal, but it was for your safety. He and your mother were threatened by *The Society* too, and he didn't want to expose your identity and put you in harm's way. Then after the chandelier came down, he realized they knew who you were. When they came for dinner, the first thing he did was ask about you. He was very concerned."

"I suppose that with time I could forgive him. I want to know my father. I want to learn more about my mother too," Amalie said, then looked at Oliver and smiled. "It will be a bit awkward having a half-sister that was supposed to be your wife, and I'm sure that Duchess Marta is not thrilled to have me in their family. I must remind her of her husband's first love."

"The Duchess is still angry at your father for not telling her about you, but she is not angry with you," Oliver clarified.

"I would be angry too if you kept something like that from me."

"Do you think you can forgive my mother? She is heartsick about what happened. She truly wanted to honor her friendship with your mother by bringing you to our home. We should be grateful that she did; otherwise, I would have never met the love of my life," Oliver said, kissing her hand.

"When you say it like that, how could I not forgive her?" Amalie smiled, "She brought me to you, and I cannot imagine my life without you. I was utterly heartbroken when I learned that our baby had died. I had the feeling from the beginning that it was a boy, and the doctor told me that the baby I lost was a boy. I wanted a little Oliver to love and cherish if I couldn't have his father."

Oliver kissed her forehead. "You have me now, my love. We will make another little Oliver or little Amalie as soon as possible. I would be thrilled with either one."

"I meant what I said that night we loved each other. If that night were all we would ever have, I would die happy having that beautiful memory to cherish. It was magical, and I am so happy to know that there will be many more nights like that one. My heart is overflowing right now."

"I love you," Oliver whispered as he kissed her again.

"I love you more," Amalie said breathlessly. "And I will love you more each day for the rest of my life."

At the Attenbury Estate that evening, Oliver and Amalie joined Lara and Owen for dinner. Lara seemed a bit melancholy and said what everyone was thinking. "I suppose this means you will be going home with Oliver?"

"Yes, I will be leaving, but I promise you we will visit and see each other as often as possible," Amalie assured her, "You are my dearest friend and have helped me through so much. We will forever be sisters of the heart. Please come to our wedding. I can't get married without you there."

"Can Owen come too?" Lara asked.

"That goes without saying," Oliver replied. "We would love to have you both there."

"Of course, we will come! I am so happy for both of you," Lara gushed. "It gives me something to look forward to after you leave. This house won't be the same without you here."

"What will you do with this estate now that the Earl is gone?" Amalie asked. "You've never really been happy here."

Lara looked at Owen. "I will go wherever Owen takes me. I never wanted to be a Countess. That was my father's dream, not mine. Owen and I want to live a normal life, have a little house somewhere and fill it with children. I would be the happiest woman in the world living like that. I have a meeting with the Earl's lawyer in two weeks. He will advise me about the estate and what, if anything, happens to my title."

"My father owns a textile factory that he built with a loan from Queen Victoria's initiative to restore industry in our country," Owen shared. "The plant is very successful, and he has been after me for years to manage it for him. I had to decline because I couldn't leave Lara here alone with that monster, but now I may take him up on his offer—but only if she comes with me."

"That sounds wonderful," Amalie said, "Where is the factory?"

"North of London," Lara replied. "I would love to go there with Owen, but I must meet with the lawyer first before we can decide anything. Because the Earl didn't have any children, thank God, his title will more than likely be declared defunct, which frees me to do as I please. I highly doubt the crown would continue to pay for the estate without the Earl. Besides, the queen was not fond of my husband, so she has no reason to allow me to stay here."

"There are too many unpleasant memories here," Owen said somberly. "I would like to leave here and never look back."

"That might be for the best," Amalie said. "I know Lara was never happy here."

"You are always welcome to visit Corrington House," Oliver said, "We have plenty of room, and you can stay as long as you like. Please plan a long visit for the wedding."

"Yes!" Amalie agreed, "I would love to have Lara there to help me prepare for the wedding."

"When you have set a date, you must let me know as soon as possible. We will come, I promise," Lara said. "What about the deceptions that drove you from there? Have you made peace with that?"

"I have already forgiven Helene. Her heart was in the right place, but her methods were all wrong. But as Oliver said, if she hadn't brought me into their home, I would have never met my future husband. As for my father, that may take some time, but I am willing to work toward a closer relationship with him. I hope we will be close one day, but he is a stranger to me. I need to get to know him."

"I know he is very hopeful for a relationship with you," Oliver said.

Lara lifted her wine glass and proposed a toast. "Here's to new beginnings—for all of us."

They clanked their glasses together with a renewed hope for a happier, brighter future.

Oliver and Amalie retreated to her bedroom at bedtime and locked the door behind them. Amalie kicked off her shoes and pulled the pin from her hair, letting it fall to her shoulders. Oliver threw his jacket over the chair and removed his belt with the pistol holder.

As they began to undress, Amalie took his hand and said, "I need to tell you something. I'm afraid you will be disappointed because I know what you were hoping would happen tonight, but it has only been two weeks since I lost the baby, and the doctor said I must refrain from intercourse until I heal. I'm sorry, my love."

Oliver was moved by what she was saying, and it also saddened him to realize what Amalie went through when she lost their child.

"My darling, you never have to apologize to me for something like that," he said, gently caressing her cheek. "I truly understand, and I would not take any pleasure in doing anything that might hurt you. We have the rest of our lives to make love. Besides, two people in love can be intimate without having sex. Holding you, feeling your skin on mine, laying with you—those things can bring pleasure too."

"I'm so glad you understand because I want to be with you so badly, but I know I can't yet. You are nearly impossible to resist," Amalie blushed, "I want to be that close to you, but I don't want to make it any harder for you to refrain."

"Oh, my sweet Amalie," he whispered as he gently kissed her lips. "The most important thing is that we're together. I want to hold you in my arms and fall asleep with the woman I love beside me. These past months have been torture without you. Just holding you close will feel like heaven to me."

Amalie was moved to tears by Oliver's loving words. "I can't even begin to tell you how much I missed you. I cried almost every night. I blew a kiss to the sky and sent it over the moon hoping it would reach you somehow. My only comfort was our child—and then they took that away from me too. And now you're here with me being so gentle and loving—it's a dream come true."

"I want to make all your dreams come true, my love," he whispered and held her close. "I will dedicate my life to making you happy. I live for you—and only you."

The lovers shared a warm kiss and then finished undressing. They climbed into bed together naked and snuggled under the featherbedding holding each other close. Oliver and Amalie savored the togetherness as they drifted off into a contented sleep.

The return trip on the *Hyacinth* to Halston Harbor was smooth sailing most of the way. Oliver and Amalie commissioned a carriage to take them to the Corrington

Territory and home. The family had no advance notice that they were coming, and Oliver and Amalie looked forward to surprising them by arriving together.

"The goodbye this morning was hard," Amalie sighed. "Lara became such a dear friend, and I don't know how I would have survived the last few months without her. She was the answer to my prayer. I'm going to miss her."

"You will see her again very soon, sweetheart," Oliver assured her. "They will come to the wedding, and I want to get married as soon as possible."

"Me too," Amalie said with a smile. "Do you think that I should ask my father to give me away?"

"That is up to you, although it is tradition for the father of the bride to give her away."

"Well, if you are a believer in tradition, you will have to ask him for my hand," Amalie suggested gently.

"I will go through the motion of asking him, but there is only one answer I will accept. I think he knows that. Nothing will ever keep us apart again, my love," Oliver said as he kissed her forehead.

Amalie snuggled close to Oliver and laid her head on his shoulder. Then she looked out the carriage window and sat up. "Oliver, it's snowing!"

"Well, so it is. I thought it felt bitter cold this morning. That always reminds me that Christmas is coming. When we were kids, I used to play in the snow with Michael. Anthony was still too little, and the nanny was afraid he would catch a cold. We would slide down the hill on the east side of the estate on a wooden sled and did that repeatedly until we couldn't feel our toes," Oliver recalled warmly.

"That sounds lovely. I want our children to have those memories too," Amalie said dreamily.

"I just had an idea," Oliver said. "Why don't we get married on Christmas Eve? I can't think of a better present than to gain a wife."

"Oh, that sounds wonderful. Do you think we can be ready in time?"

"That depends on the kind of wedding you want—if you want a simple ceremony or a lavish wedding. I will give you whatever your heart desires, my love," Oliver said warmly.

"I'm not a lavish wedding kind of gal. Simple is good enough for me."

"Then we will be married Christmas Eve at the house," Oliver said with a smile.

"I would like Father Sebastian to officiate. It would mean the world to me for him to marry us."

"Whatever your heart desires, my love. After everything we have been through, you deserve to have the wedding of your dreams."

Oliver grabbed the blanket from the opposite bench and covered them both. They snuggled together in anticipation of their arrival at Corrington House.

There was measurable snow covering the ground when the carriage pulled up to Corrington House. It was still snowing as the sun hid behind a dark, grey sky. Oliver and Amalie hurried into the house, and the first thing they encountered was the sound of piano music waffling through the halls.

"It's Anthony playing!" Amalie said excitedly. She grabbed Oliver's hand, and they followed the sound of the music.

In the doorway, they stopped as Anthony finished his piece. "That was lovely," Amalie said.

The boy turned around and called out when he saw them. "Amalie!" he cried as he ran toward her. He threw his arms around her, and she pulled him into a warm embrace. "I'm so glad you're home! I have missed you."

"I've missed you too," Amalie said, holding him for a moment longer. "I see you've been practicing. You've mastered that piece."

"It's from the music you left for me."

"Yes, I recognized it. Say, did you grow while I was gone? I swear you are taller," Amalie said, touching the top of his head.

"Mother says so. I had to get all my winter pants altered. They were all too short for me."

"Hey, little brother," Oliver broke in, "What about me?"

Anthony quickly hugged his brother but went back to talking to Amalie.

"I see where I rank in this family," Oliver teased.

"Are you home for good now?" Anthony asked with large pleading eyes.

Amalie touched his cheek. "Yes, I'm home for good now."

"I'm so glad you will be here for Christmas! I made a gift for you, and I was hoping to be able to give it to you," the boy said enthusiastically.

"I look forward to seeing it," she smiled at him.

"Oliver! Amalie!" came the shriek from the doorway. Helene had come running when staff told her that Oliver was home. Helene faced Amalie. "I'm so thankful you are safe. I have prayed every day for you. Welcome home."

Amalie looked at Helene, who had an apprehensive look on her face. Amalie pulled Helene into a hug and said, "I'm happy to be home with you."

Helene began to cry with relief as they hugged each other. "Does that mean you have forgiven me? I am truly sorry for the deception, but it was the only way I could bring you into our family."

"I know that now. Let's not dwell on that any longer. Oliver and I have wonderful news to share."

Helene looked at her oldest son. "Is it what I hope it is?"

"Yes, mother, we are going to be married, hopefully on Christmas Eve," Oliver replied, hugging his mother.

"Oh my! This is a happy day!" Helene squealed. "I am so happy for you both. There is so much to do—to plan—will we have enough time before Christmas Eve?"

"We can talk about the wedding at dinner tonight. Where's father?" Oliver asked.

"He's still in Brighton at the office with Michael. They will be home soon."

"I want to talk to him about Amalie's audience with the queen," Oliver said.

"*The* queen, as in Victoria?" Helene asked to make sure she heard it correctly.

"Yes, my darling fiancé met with Queen Victoria, Sir Thomas is dead, and *The Society* is no more. Amalie did that all on her own, with a little help from a Countess."

"Good heavens, it looks like you both have a lot to share with us," Helene said, taking Amalie's hand. "Are you sure you're alright, dear? You look a little pale. Have you lost weight?"

"I'm fine. I will tell you all about it when we have a chance to chat, just you and me. Right now, I sure would love some hot tea," Amalie said, smiling at Helene.

"Of course! I'll get Margot on it right away! Lord, it's good to have you both home!" Helene said as she left the room calling out for Margot.

"Yes, it is good to have you both home," Anthony concurred. "I missed you both, especially my brother."

Oliver tousled his little brother's hair and smiled at him. "Chess rematch after dinner?"

"Yes! I still can't beat Michael, but I think I can beat you now!"

Amalie felt happy to be back in Corrington House, especially since she once felt like she had to run away from it. At this moment, it felt like home—and not someplace where she felt out of place, but rather where her heart was—especially with Oliver by her side.

Oliver and Amalie went to their separate rooms to dress for dinner. As Oliver left her at the door of the Blue Room, he kissed her forehead and whispered, "This is going to be hard to sleep separately from you until the wedding, but my parents are very old-fashioned and would never allow us to sleep together."

"I know, and I understand. Besides, think of all that anticipation building up for both of us. It will make our wedding night just that much more passionate," Amalie said, kissing his cheek.

"I may have to dig a secret tunnel from my room to yours," Oliver whispered, "I don't know if I can wait that long to hold you again like last night."

"I know, my darling, but we have to wait anyway, so this might be a good thing. I had a hard time last night not touching you the way I wanted to," Amalie confessed.

"Me too," he admitted. "It would be impossible for me not to make love to you if we slept together again."

"On that note, I will bid you farewell until dinner, my sweet Oliver."

"And I will go outside and roll in the snow to put out this fire in my body," Oliver teased,

Amalie smiled at him as she started to close the door. Oliver made a pouty face followed by a sly smile and a wink as the door closed in his face.

When Amalie and Oliver came down for dinner, everyone was seated in the dining room. Oliver held her hand as they walked in, then pulled out the chair for her. Oliver sat next to her.

The Duke spoke first. "Let me be the first to say how pleased I am that you are both home and that Amalie is safe. Your mother told me that she met with the queen?"

Oliver filled him in on everything since he was home last and about Amalie's time with Lara. He shared the details of the encounter with the queen and Sir Thomas' demise. Oliver never mentioned the baby they lost. He wanted Amalie to share that when she was ready.

"Well, it would seem we owe a debt of gratitude to the Countess," Helene said as the staff served dinner.

"I am impressed at the initiative you took in looking for the documents at the National Library and then seeking an audience with the queen," the Duke went on, "That took courage, and I applaud your determination. I'm so glad the queen was able to stop that madness once and for all, but I must say I am proud of my son also for showing up there when he did. It sounds like he once again was there precisely when you needed him. I've never seen him so determined as he was to find you."

Amalie smiled at Oliver. "Yes, I am grateful too."

Oliver reached over and put his hand on Amalie's. "I think she managed Sir Thomas just fine without me. Amalie punched him so hard in the gut that she knocked the wind out of him. That is how she got free from the knife. I shot him when he tried to stab her."

"Alright, Amalie!" Anthony cheered.

"Goodness, that sounds horrible," Helene shuddered. "When I think of how close to death you came, and not just once, Amalie—I cannot imagine how you have come through this without being affected by it."

"Oh, it has affected me—there is no doubt about that. I will carry the trauma with me for the rest of my life, especially about...." Amalie stopped herself from mentioning the baby.

"Let's talk about happier things," Oliver came to her rescue, "We want to get married on Christmas Eve."

"Yes! A wedding is a much happier topic," Helene said after she noticed how Amalie's demeanor changed as she remembered her ordeal.

"You can wear my wedding dress," Miss Annabelle said out of the blue. "I would love to see someone wear it again. I think it would fit you."

"That's very kind of you," Amalie said politely but wondered what kind of old, faded dress she might have.

"It is a beautiful dress," Helene added. "I wore it on my wedding day too. Let's look at it after dinner. I think you would like it, Amalie."

"I'd love to see it," Amalie said, smiling at Miss Annabelle. "Thank you for offering it to me."

"Well, while you ladies go fuss over a dress after dinner, Anthony and I have a rematch chess game waiting for us," Oliver said with a wink at Anthony.

"I'll play the winner," Michael said but then added proudly, "I'm still the reigning champion in this house. Not even father can beat me."

"Well, everyone has their special way in which they shine. Yours is chess, Michael, and Anthony's is music," Helene said diplomatically. "And Oliver's is perseverance. If he weren't so stubborn and steadfast about what he wanted, we would have never seen Amalie again. I never thought in my wildest dreams I would ever say this because as a child, you drove me crazy with your stubbornness, but now I am thankful for it because it brought Amalie home to us."

"Thank you, Helene," Amalie said sincerely, "I am also very thankful Oliver never gave up on finding me. I didn't make it easy for him."

"Did you tell Amalie about the new alliance with the Herzstein Territory?" the Duke asked Oliver.

"Yes, I did. Has it been ratified yet?" Oliver asked his father.

"Yes, and we have been running newsprint about it weekly so that the people will get used to the idea. Comments in my office have been overwhelmingly positive. Everyone loves the idea of a Festival of Peace," the Duke replied.

"The day after both Dukes signed the new alliance, Lady Davina announced her engagement to the printer she's in love with," Helene shared. "It looks like everyone will have a happy ending, and I think it's all because of Amalie. We have her to thank for this." Then she turned to Amalie and said, "Do you realize how much you have changed all of our lives for the better?"

"You humble me, but I cannot take credit for the changes. They were long overdue, and I think they would have happened even without me," Amalie said.

"No, sweetheart, you are too modest. None of this would have happened without you. You were the catalyst that made it all happen," Oliver insisted. "My God, you refused to accept what was happening to you, and you found a way to change it. None of us here thought of going to the queen. That was you. And *The Society* is now defunct because of you. And because we fell in love with each other, our fathers saw the need for the new alliance of peace. That would have never happened if it weren't for you. My mother is right. You changed our lives—especially mine."

Amalie's cheeks flushed. "Thank you, everyone. I'm very grateful for your kind words. There was a time when I felt that I had to leave here—that I would never belong here. But now, I feel at home, and it is a feeling I've never really had before. Yes, the Abbey was home to me, but it was never a real home with a family like this. I want you all to know how much that means to me."

Helene's eyes filled with tears. "You are truly the daughter I never had…and now, on Christmas Eve, you will become my daughter by marrying my oldest son. I couldn't be happier! Your mother would be so proud."

"Thank you," Amalie said, fighting tears of her own.

"If you're finished with your dinner," Annabelle said, gulping the last of her wine, "Let's go and try on my dress. It would make me so happy to see you wear it."

Helene, Amalie, and Annabelle went to Annabelle's bedroom on the main floor. Her room used to be on the second floor, but it became too difficult for her to climb the stairs, so they converted the old cloakroom into her bedroom. Annabelle dug through her cluttered wardrobe and pulled out a large box. Helene helped her move it to the bed. When Helene opened the box and carefully folded the paper aside, Amalie gasped when she saw the dress. It was breathtakingly beautiful. Helene lifted the dress carefully out of the box to reveal an ivory-colored silk dress covered in delicate lace and trimmed in pearls.

"Oh, Annabelle, it's beautiful," Amalie declared. "I've never seen anything like it."

"It was made in France for my wedding," Annabelle said proudly. "My daughter wore it when she married the Duke, and now you will wear it. I'm glad you came along. With three grandsons, I never thought anyone would wear it again."

Amalie tried the dress on, and when she turned around to see herself in the full-length mirror, she became emotional. "I feel like a princess in this dress. It would be an honor for me to wear it."

"I think we can have the seamstress take it in just a bit for you, so it doesn't look so loose, but otherwise, you are a picture of perfection in that dress," Helene said.

"I want you to know that I would have never offered my dress to that horrid Davina," Annabelle shared. "But for you, yes, and for Oliver. He was always my favorite, but don't tell the other boys."

"Your secret is safe with me," Amalie smiled, "He's my favorite too."

The following day, the Duke of Herzstein arrived unannounced in the early afternoon. He came alone and asked to see Amalie. Margot had him wait in the sitting room while she went for Amalie. The Duke paced back and forth with nerves and wondered what he would say when his daughter came into the room. Carl Gustav had nothing prepared but felt compelled to come when he got word that Amalie was safe and with Oliver at Corrington House.

"You asked to see me," Amalie said as she entered the room.

"Yes, please sit with me. I got word from Duke Oliver that you were home safe. I wanted to come and see you in person," he began nervously.

Amalie sat down on the green velvet sofa, and Carl Gustav sat beside her.

"I'm glad you did. I think Oliver wants to speak with you," she said, noticing that her father seemed tense.

"I came to see you. I can speak with Oliver later," he fumbled ahead. "I owe you an apology for the way I treated you after you arrived here."

Carl Gustav looked into Amalie's eyes and just spoke from his heart. "That moment I saw you—you were the image of your mother. I couldn't believe you were standing in front of me. I will forever regret not acknowledging you at that moment, but it truly was for your safety—yet that is no excuse. I am asking you to forgive me for failing you as a father."

"I can forgive you, of course," she said sadly, "But I will never be able to forget it. All my life, I wondered about my father. I knew my mother died in childbirth, but I never knew anything about my father, only to learn that he is a Duke and denied me when he finally saw me. I cannot tell you how much that hurt me when I realized you knew who I was and said nothing. I know you thought you were protecting me but what you did was reject me all over again. The first time was when you let me grow up in an orphanage and let twenty-one years go by without ever visiting me. And then again that day I arrived here. That is going to be very hard to overcome."

Carl Gustav nodded in agreement. "I understand. I truly do."

"Why did you never come for me in all those years? Why did you never try to do anything about *The Society* if you knew they wanted to hurt me? I was able to find out who they were and how to stop them. I often wonder why you never did that. You went on and lived your life and never tried to make me a part of it. We can never get those years back. I wish I didn't feel this way, but I do." Amalie said, allowing herself to say it out loud finally.

"You have every right to feel the way you do," he acknowledged. "I hate to admit it, but after a few years went by, I felt so low about myself—that I was not worthy of being your father—that I convinced myself you were better off without me. I was a coward as your father, and I am ashamed of that. You deserved better from me."

"Yes, I did."

"When your mother was carrying you, we used to daydream about what you would be like," Carl Gustav remembered. Suddenly Amalie could relate to what he was saying. She felt the same way about her child.

"She wanted a boy, and I wanted a girl," he went on. "When you were born, it was the happiest moment of my life—until moments later when she began to bleed and then died. Then it became the worst moment of my life. I was lost in my grief and not thinking clearly. I left you there because it was safer for you, but also because I couldn't bear the thought of losing you too after losing your mother."

Amalie's anger softened as she listened to him speak.

"Then my father made me marry Marta, who is a cousin of Olga von Gosselburg, who is a cousin of the queen. He insisted on 'royal bloodlines,' so he never accepted Juliet. That is why we ran away. After her death, there was no reason not to claim my title. I crawled back to my father and have hated myself ever since. I should have stayed away when I was free. I should have claimed you from the Abbey and made a life for us, but I didn't, and that is a regret I will take to my grave."

Hearing her father speak from the heart moved Amalie deeply, but she didn't know what to say to him. Part of her wanted to comfort him, and the other felt he deserved his torment.

"I have forgiven you," she reiterated, "But I think we will need some time to establish a relationship. I am willing to try if you are."

"Of course," he said with hope in his voice. "I am willing to do whatever you need of me. I have discussed this with my family. They understand that this is what I must do."

"What about the people? Will you acknowledge me publicly? I am your daughter. You and my mother were married," Amalie said delicately.

"I already have," he said, pulling some paper from his jacket. "I wrote an editorial in newsprint and published it throughout Herzstein. I printed it in conjunction with our new declaration of peace between our territories. I brought a copy for you to read."

Amalie took the paper from him and unfolded it. Amalie read it out loud just as Oliver came into the room. He sat down opposite them on the red velvet sofa.

"To the people of Herzstein: I cannot celebrate our newfound peace treaty without sharing with you how it came to be. Twenty-two years ago, I married the love of my life. Her name was Juliet, and she was a commoner. Sadly, I lost her when she gave birth to our daughter, Amalie. I returned home a broken man without my daughter. My father, Duke Bernard of Herzstein, never recognized my marriage to Juliet and treated it as if it never existed. Regretfully, I allowed him to do that, so you never learned who she was or how beautiful our daughter is. I married Duchess Marta and had two more daughters and lived the life my father chose for me."

Amalie looked at her father, then kept reading.

"Recently, Amalie came back into my life. She was staying with the Corrington family in our neighboring territory. I did not acknowledge her when she arrived, and for that, I humbly apologize to her and all of you because if you knew her, you would love her the way I do. Because of Amalie, our two territories have entered a new alliance for peace without the outdated marriage requirements. Amalie taught us all that love is the only reason people should marry—not because of some ancient condition handed down by a king who surrendered his rule over our territories. Both of my grown daughters will marry the men they love—not someone a king chose for them four hundred years ago. As we go forth and celebrate our ongoing peace with our neighbor, let us also celebrate the love we feel for one another. That is the best way to honor lovers like Ronan and Maria—by being happy with the people you love. In humble gratitude, Duke Carl Gustav of Herzstein."

Amalie was speechless and very moved. "You published this all over the territory?"

"Yes, and across the Corrington Territory as well."

"I don't know what to say. It's beautiful and very heartfelt," Amalie said sincerely.

"I meant every word, "Carl Gustav emphasized.

"How does your family feel about this?" Amalie asked.

"Marta has adjusted to the fact that I have three daughters, and Davina is thrilled to be engaged to the man she loves. That seems to be all she cares about these days. Little Anneliese is excited to get to know her older sister. I hope you can find some time to spend with her," Carl Gustav said, "She doesn't have a close relationship with Davina, so I am hoping she will have that with you."

"I would like that very much," Amalie said sincerely. "I will gladly set aside some time for us to spend together. Perhaps she could be part of our wedding?"

"Yes, on that topic," Oliver said. "When I heard you were here, I came down because there is something I want to ask you."

"Please, go ahead," Carl Gustav said.

"I want to ask for your blessing to marry Amalie, but after hearing what she just read, I think I know your feelings on the matter," Oliver stated.

"Yes, of course. I wholeheartedly give my blessing. I want my daughter to be happy, and I am confident you will not disappoint me—or her."

"Thank you, sir," Oliver said, reaching out to shake his hand.

"There is something I want to ask you too," Amalie said. "Would you give me away at the wedding on Christmas Eve?"

His daughter's request moved Carl Gustav. "It would be my honor."

"Thank you," Amalie said, "And thank you for this editorial. May I keep this?"

"Of course. Before I leave you, I want you to know that I think your mother would be so proud of the woman you have become. You are like her in many ways and have the same qualities that made me fall in love with her. I am proud of you as well. I am honored to call you my daughter."

"Thank you," Amalie said, deeply emotional.

"My father wanted to speak with you before you leave," Oliver said to Carl Gustav. "May I take you to his study?"

"Yes," the Duke said, rising from the sofa. "Amalie, thank you for letting me say what I needed to say. It was long overdue, and I hope you will soften your heart to me. We have lost a lot of time, but we still have the future. I very much want to be part of yours."

Amalie stood to face him. "I want you to be a part of it too. I think that my mother would want that too."

Carl Gustav took her hand and kissed it. "Thank you for your grace. I hope to be worthy of it."

Oliver and the Duke left the room, and Amalie sat back down on the sofa. She clutched the editorial where her father publicly declared his love for her and acknowledged her as his daughter. An indescribable feeling moved through her and came out in a single tear that trickled down her cheek. *My father loves me.*

Chapter 14

The Wedding

There was a light dusting of snow on Christmas Eve as the wedding guests began to arrive. Lara and Owen, who had arrived three days earlier, were busy helping the bride and groom get ready for the ceremony.

Helene had the staff set up the sitting room with rows of chairs, each decorated with a white satin bow on the back. The household staff had beautifully decorated the room for Christmas with pine garland draping the fireplace and red candles on the mantel. The staff decorated the Christmas tree in the corner with red ribbons, glass ornaments, and candles in clip-on holders on the branches. A porcelain angel with feathered wings crowned the top of the tree.

Amalie asked Anthony to play the piano as she walked down the aisle. He chose The Wedding March by Mendelssohn. Amalie had left him the music from *A Midsummer Night's Dream,* and Anthony loved the song.

Amalie, Helene, Lara, and Miss Annabelle were all in the Blue Room helping Amalie dress for the ceremony. When Lara saw Amalie in the wedding dress, she gasped. "Oh, my lord, you look beautiful," she gushed, "Like an angel."

"That was my wedding dress," Annabelle said proudly.

"Well, it's positively gorgeous. You must have been a beautiful bride too," Lara said, smiling at Annabelle.

"Amalie will be the third one in our family to wear it," Helene said, fastening the delicate buttons down the back. "Who knows? Perhaps one day her daughter will wear it too."

"Yes, who knows?" Lara smiled at Amalie.

"Are you nervous, dear?" Annabelle asked Amalie.

"No, surprisingly, I'm not. I'm just happy. I can't remember ever being this happy," Amalie said, looking at herself in the mirror.

"You should see Oliver. He was so nervous at breakfast that he spilled his tea and put marmalade on his eggs. He might be all thumbs on his wedding night," Annabelle chuckled.

"Oh, I'm sure by this evening he will be just fine," Lara said with a wink to Amalie.

"I've never seen my son so happy," Helene said. "He cherishes you, Amalie, and as his mother, I could not ask for a better wife for him. He loves you deeply, and you love him. You two are fortunate to have found each other."

"Yes, I agree," Amalie said, "I feel truly blessed."

"Alright, enough with the love talk. You're making me cry," Annabelle said as she turned to leave the room. "I have something I must do before the ceremony starts."

After Annabelle left, Helene said, "She is going to her room to drink her beloved brandy before the wedding, you know, to calm her nerves. She's not fooling anyone. I swear, she's more nervous than the bride."

Oliver dressed in his room and decided to wear his full military suit, with his rank sash across his chest. Owen was there for moral support but also to seek his counsel.

"I'm going to marry Lara, there's no doubt about that, but she is used to living like a Countess, and she is marrying a working man. Not sure what I should do," he shared with Oliver.

"She doesn't seem to need the kind of life she's been living. At least that's the impression I got from her. Are you worried about money?" Oliver said as he tied his necktie.

"No, not just that. I'm more worried about the scrutiny from others because Lara is a widow and has been married before. I don't know how my family will feel about that," Owen shared freely.

"Oh, I see. Well, if it were me, and I loved Lara the way you do, I wouldn't give them a choice in the matter. That is how I handled my father about Amalie, and that is why we are having a wedding today."

"But to make a living for us, I need to work for my father. If he has any objections, that could be difficult," Owen said pensively.

"My advice—don't worry about problems that haven't happened yet. Take Lara home to meet your family, and they will see how happy you are together. Then take it from there."

"You are right," Owen said with relief, "I am getting ahead of myself. My father has softened a bit in old age. I'm pretty sure Lara can charm him just like she charmed me."

"If there ever is a problem, just come back here, and you can work for me. Amalie would love to have Lara close by, and I will need a good clerk when my father retires. You are always welcome here."

"Thank you, Oliver, that is very reassuring."

It was finally time for the ceremony to begin. Gerald escorted everyone to their seats, and Margot lit the candles on the fireplace. Anthony took his place at the piano to wait for the signal from Amalie. Oliver joined his father at the fireplace and shook his hand. The Herzstein family, along with Davina's fiancé, sat in the front row on the bride's side of the aisle. Carl Gustav was waiting at the bottom of the stairs for Amalie to come down, along with his youngest daughter, who will serve as flower girl. Helene, Annabelle, and Michael sat in the front row of the groom's side. Owen and Lara were seated directly behind Helene, and next to them were Julian Cartwright and his parents. A handful of friends and military personnel completed the guest list. Father Sebastian took his place at the fireplace and waited for the bridal party.

Amalie came down the staircase, and her father became emotional at the sight of his daughter in her wedding dress. "Your mother would be so proud of you. You look just as beautiful as she did on our wedding day."

"Thank you," she said, swallowing hard. Then she looked down at Anneliese holding the basket of rose petals in a pretty yellow dress. "You look beautiful, little sister. I'm so happy you are sharing this day with me."

Anneliese's face lit up. "You look beautiful, Amalie," she said. "Like a princess."

Amalie kissed her sister's cheek, then she put her arm through her father's and cued Anthony to start the music.

"That's your cue, little one," Amalie said softly.

The guests rose as Duke Carl Gustav walked his daughter down the aisle, following Anneliese dropping rose petals as she walked. Oliver became emotional when he saw Amalie in her wedding dress walking toward him. His lip trembled, and he fought to keep from tearing up. Amalie and Oliver smiled at each other, savoring the moment that they thought would never happen. But on this day, Christmas Eve, they were about to be married, and their happiness shined through.

When Duke Carl Gustav reached the fireplace, Father Sebastian said, "Who gives this woman to wed this man?"

Carl Gustav said, "Her late mother Juliet and I do."

Amalie looked at her father, and he had tears in his eyes, which made her cry. Suddenly she reached out and hugged him and whispered, "Thank you, father."

Carl Gustav held her in a loving embrace and then let go to place her hand in Oliver's.

Amalie and Oliver spoke their vows to each other, then knelt on the prayer stand to receive the marriage blessing. After another piano solo by Anthony, Father Sebastian pronounced them man and wife. Oliver kissed his bride, and the room broke out in cheers and applause.

Oliver held her close and whispered, "You are my wife—I love you now—I will love you tomorrow, and I will love you for the rest of my life."

"Oh, Oliver, I love you more than life itself. You are my husband, and my life is now your life."

The reception got underway in the ballroom, where a quintette played music while guests dined and mingled. Oliver and Amalie tried to greet each guest and walked hand in hand through the room. When they got to Julian, Amalie reached out and hugged him.

"I'm so glad you could come," she said. "I will never forget how you helped me. You will always be a dear friend."

Oliver shook his hand. "You know, at one time, I thought you were my competition, but it turns out you were helping Amalie, and I will be forever grateful to you for that."

"You're a lucky man, Oliver. You got a good one," Julian said, smiling at Amalie. "You know, I had to listen to my mother scold me the entire drive here because I let Amalie slip through my fingers. Truth be told, I never had a chance. She was always yours, Captain."

"I wish you the same happiness one day," Amalie said to Julian, who was the only one who knew what she meant.

"Thank you. You will be the first to know!" Julian said. "Be happy, you two. Life is short, don't waste a moment of it."

Lara and Owen came through the crowd with champagne glasses in their hand. "Captain and Mrs. Corrington," Lara said beaming, "Your fathers want to make a toast. They were looking for you."

Amalie smiled. "I like hearing Mrs. Corrington. It has a nice ring to it, doesn't it?"

Oliver and Amalie made their way to the head of the table where both Dukes were standing. Gerald rang a bell, and the crowd became silent. Carl Gustav spoke first.

"As the father of the bride, I would like to express my joy for Amalie and Oliver. I wish them many happy years and lots of children. Oliver, cherish her. She is exceptional. A toast to the bride and groom!"

Amalie smiled at her father. Oliver and Amalie joined in the toast by locking arms and sipping champagne.

Then Duke Oliver spoke. "I would like to add that we are delighted to have Amalie join our family. Her late mother was a dear friend of my wife, so we already felt like she was part of our clan. Today she married my oldest son and the heir to my title. I am happy and proud to welcome her officially as the newest Corrington. Welcome to the family, Amalie. Please enjoy the celebration everyone!"

Amalie was deeply touched by her father-in-law's words, especially considering that he was not fond of her when she first arrived. To show him that she harbored no resentment, she stepped up onto her tiptoes and kissed him on the cheek. Her husband's face was beaming with delight.

"Amalie," Carl Gustav said, "Do you still have your mother's journal? Helene told me you have it. If you don't mind, I would love to read it. Helene told me she would give me the missing pages so I can read what she wrote when we found out we were expecting you."

"Of course," Amalie said, handing her glass to Oliver. "Let me run up and get it for you. I'll be right back."

Amalie rushed up the stairs to her room with new energy in her step. What a happy day they all celebrated together, something that, at one point, she never thought would happen. She was excited for the future for the first time in a long time and was looking forward to a happy event—her wedding night with Oliver.

Amalie entered her room and went straight to her wardrobe to get the journal when a shadow caught her eye in the corner of the room. The appearance of a woman startled her.

"What are you doing here?" Amalie said quickly, "Do I know you? You shouldn't be in here."

The woman was young, about the same age as Amalie, but had a strange expression on her face. The woman fixed her gaze on Amalie, and she started taking slow steps toward her.

"I came with the Countess. I'm Clara, one of her many servants—and this is precisely where I need to be."

"I'm sorry, you are mistaken. Lara's room is down the hall," Amalie said with her intuition telling her this was not a friendly visit. "Please leave my room."

"You should have died that day," Clara said in a monotone voice as if she was in a trance. "I poisoned your food. But you survived."

An ice-cold chill ran through Amalie. Then she remembered that it was Clara who served her dinner that night.

"It was you. You poisoned me," Amalie realized, and then a surge of anger swept through her like a hurricane through the tropics. "You killed my child!"

"And you killed my father!" Clara shouted back.

"I've never killed anyone," Amalie argued, "You're insane!"

"They're all gone. All of them, every single one," Clara chanted, stepping ever closer to Amalie, "The queen had them rounded up and put in prison. But you and your new husband killed my father. You shot him in cold blood."

"Sir Thomas was your father? He was a murderer! He deserved to die. And his band of thugs deserves to rot in prison! I will not apologize for defending myself," Amalie shouted.

"I don't want an apology from you, silly woman. I am here to finish what my father couldn't," Clara declared as she pulled a pistol from her skirt pocket and pointed it at Amalie. "Today—your wedding day—is the day you will finally die!"

In the ballroom, Oliver chatted with Lara and Owen when the explosive sound of a gunshot echoed through the halls. There were screams from some guests as they were startled by the piercing sound. Oliver immediately dropped his glass and ran toward the sound, with both Dukes following behind him. He ran up the steps taking them two at a time, hurrying to Amalie's room. He burst open the door and saw a dreadful sight.

Standing over the body of a woman bleeding from the chest was Amalie holding a pistol in her hand. Amalie was frozen and unaware that others had come into her room.

Oliver rushed to her side. "Darling, what happened? Who is this? Are you alright?"

"Is she….dead?" Amalie asked, still holding the pistol. Oliver carefully removed it from her clenched hands.

Duke Oliver knelt over the woman, and he could see she was still breathing. "She's alive," he said.

"I want to die," Clara said faintly, "Let me die. I failed you, papa. I'm sorry."

"That is Sir Thomas' daughter. She is the one who poisoned me at Lara's. She came here to finish the job for her father," Amalie said, "I don't know what came over me. I just lunged at her and fought her for the pistol. The next thing I remember is hearing the shot."

Oliver put his arm around her. "Are you sure you're alright?"

"Yes," Amalie assured him, "She said that all *The Society's* members were rounded up and put in prison. She blamed us for her father's death and came to avenge him by finishing what he couldn't."

Just then, Lara and Owen came running in. "Oh my God," Lara cried out, "That's Clara. What happened?"

Oliver told them both what had occurred.

"I knew something was up with her," Lara said, going over to Amalie and touching her shoulder. "I'm so sorry. Did she hurt you?"

Amalie shook her head.

"Clara helped me pack for our trip here. Then she kept asking questions about the wedding and you and Oliver. Then she practically insisted she come with me and offered to serve as my chambermaid during my stay here. I'm so sorry I let her talk me into it. Oh God, she is the one who poisoned you. I can't believe I didn't make the connection. I'm so sorry, my friend."

"Should we summon the physician? Or take her to the hospital?" Carl Gustav asked.

"No," Duke Oliver said, closing her eyes with his hand, "She's gone. I will summon the constable and have her taken away."

"Come on, sweetheart, let's get you out of this room. You don't need to see this any longer," Oliver said, gently leading his wife out of the room.

Oliver took her to his room, but before they entered, he asked his father to make their excuses to the guests. He ushered Amalie inside as the others returned to the ballroom.

Oliver sat Amalie down on the loveseat by the window and sat beside her. He put his arm around her and said, "It's truly over now, sweetheart. She was the last one."

"I know," she said, taking his hand. "I refused to die on my wedding day. They took our child from us, but I was not about to let them take one more thing from us. I have a future that I am looking forward to sharing with you. I will fight for that with everything I have. After everything we've been through—all the unimaginable challenges we faced—we deserve our happiness. I won't let anyone take that from us."

"You are the strongest woman I know," Oliver admired his new wife, "You amaze me. I love that about you—that you fight for what you want. My father didn't like how forceful you were at first, but now he admires it. I think you are an extraordinary woman. And I am the lucky man who can call you my wife."

Amalie caressed his cheek. "I am the lucky woman who can say Captain Corrington is my husband. I am proud to be your wife. That is why I fought through all of this—to have our happy ending. I am looking forward to our wedding night. I am looking forward to having children. I want to grow old with you and sit by the fire reminiscing about all our happy days together. Oh, darling, the best is yet to be."

"Yes, my love, the best is yet to be," Oliver said as he tenderly kissed his new wife.

"Are the guests still here?" Amalie asked.

"Yes, I think so."

"Then let's go join our wedding celebration. I want to continue sharing our joy with those we love. Let's not let them take this from us too."

"Are you sure?" Oliver asked protectively.

"My love, I have never been more certain of anything in my entire life."

Oliver took Amalie's hand in his as they returned to the reception. As they entered, hand in hand, the guests, most of whom were still there, broke out in applause. Mr. and Mrs. Oliver Corrington III stood before their family and friends and raised their hands together to show their undying unity and their victory over those who sought to destroy their love and deny them the happiness they were celebrating on this day.

For Amalie, it was a defining moment. She had found her voice, and she stood up for herself. She fought for the man she loved and forced history to adapt to the times. She had looked her enemy in the eye and defeated him.

Amalie held up her hand with Oliver's in celebration of the day they both thought would never come, but also in victory over her enemies and those who underestimated her. The best revenge is happiness and success, and Amalie was triumphant in both.

~ ~ ~